Designs
for Nora

AN OAKDALE NOVEL

ENDORSEMENTS

Richardson weaves emotional upheavals with heartwarming victories into a truly satisfying ending.
—**Betty Thomason Owens**, author of the Homefound Suspense series

When life doesn't go as designed, Nora forges her way through tragedy for the second time. Along the way, she uncovers family mysteries and discovers hidden strengths within herself, while clinging to friends who've become like family in her beloved town of Oakdale. In Designs for Nora, author Karen Richardson delivers this novel with an exciting and tender tale of love, loyalty, and new beginnings.
—**Janet Morris Grimes**, author of *Solomon's Porch*, a 2022 ACFW Carol Award Finalist.

Designs
for Nora

KAREN H. RICHARDSON

AN OAKDALE NOVEL

ELK LAKE PUBLISHING INC.

PUBLISHING THE POSITIVE
Plymouth, Massachusetts

A Christian Company
ElkLakePublishingInc.com

COPYRIGHT NOTICE

PUBLISHED BY: Elk Lake Publishing, Inc., 35 Dogwood Drive, Plymouth, MA 02360, 2025

Library Cataloging Data
Names: Richardson, Karen H. (Karen H. Richardson)
Title: Designs for Nora—An Oakdale Novel, Karen Richardson
336p. 23cm × 15cm (9in × 6 in.)
ISBN-13: 9798891344136 (paperback) 9798891344143 (trade paperback) 9798891344150 (e-book)
Key Words: Christian contemporary romance widow second chance; Christian dating fiction widow teen child new love; Inspirational contemporary romance second chance; Christian love and relationships fiction widow; Clean Christian fiction love faith friends trust; Christian women's fiction widow new love test; Contemporary Christian fiction widow second chance
Library of Congress Control Number: 2025940762 Fiction

DEDICATION

To those who have loved and lost, risked and been hurt, been humbled by life, or felt like they were totally alone. My prayer is that this story brings you encouragement and hope.

Have I not commanded you? Be strong and courageous. Do not be afraid; do not be discouraged, for the Lord your God will be with you wherever you go.—Joshua 1:9 (NIV).

ACKNOWLEDGMENTS

Thank you to members of the Fern Creek Fire and EMS who explained how fires are fought in historic buildings and the different kinds of fire trucks that would respond. More importantly, thank you for what you do every day in real life. You are true heroes.

Thank you, Ann Hensley, for your encouragement, advising on medical scenes, and your amazing ability to find continuity issues.

None of the words you'll read in this story would have been written if it weren't for the complete support of my husband, Jay. Thank you for encouraging me to follow my passion for writing. I love you.

Even youths grow tired and weary, and young men stumble and fall; but those who hope in the Lord will renew their strength. They will soar on wings like eagles; they will run and not grow weary; they will walk and not be faint.
—Isaiah 40:30–31 (NIV)

CHAPTER ONE

Nora St. Claire's cheeks were tight from dried tears. She hadn't cried so hard since Seth was killed. She rolled over against the assault from a single ray of sun that broke through the blinds. Her head throbbed and her heart ached.

Why, Lord? Why did you take my little sister? Her phone vibrated against the brass lamp on the bedside table that hadn't moved since the 1990s. The walls still boasted of her high school successes—President of the Art Club, Beta Club, Honor Roll. Her eyes slid from past accomplishments to her cell phone.

Jim was calling. She declined it. He meant well. But nothing in her wanted to talk to him or anyone else. She covered her eyes with the crook of her elbow. *I just want to sleep. Escape from this reality.* She lay in silence and searched her heart for any reason to get out of bed.

The rhythmic beat of her heart helped her relax. A timid knock at the partially opened door broke the silence.

"Aunt Nora? Can I come in?"

Nora sat up, rubbed her aching, swollen eyes, and extended her arms toward her fifteen-year-old niece, who was now practically an orphan. "Of course."

Eve sat on the edge of the twin bed and looked directly at her aunt. "What do …" Tears flooded the girl's eyes. She leaned onto Nora's shoulder. They both cried fresh tears of grief. Nora encircled Eve with a secure embrace.

After the tears slowed, Eve pulled a tissue from the box. "What do we do now?"

Nora reached up and tucked a loose strand of brown hair behind Eve's ear. How many times had they been mistaken for mother and daughter? "First, we'll have some breakfast. Smells like your grandma is frying bacon."

Eve wiped her eyes. "Aunt Nora, you know what I mean. Besides, I'm not hungry."

Nora knew exactly what she meant, but she wasn't ready to address it yet. "I'm not hungry, either. Today, we need to make some calls and begin to plan your mom's funeral. I think Mom called the pastor from your church. I heard your Uncle Phillip downstairs already." She spoke soft, careful words. "It's going to feel like a million questions, with many decisions to make. Please speak up if it feels like too much or you need a break."

Eve nodded. "Okay." She stopped at the door and looked back as Nora stood and stretched. "Aunt Nora."

Nora looked at her niece.

"Aunt Nora, you're not going to leave, are you?" Eve might have been on the cusp of womanhood, but the words sounded childlike.

Nora stepped quickly toward the doorway and embraced Eve. "No way. I'm not going to leave. We'll get everything figured out. I promise."

Eve pulled away, looked down, and twisted the tissue in her hands. "But what about … about …" The tears pooled in her eyes again. "What about after the funeral? Who will I live with?"

Nora lifted Eve's chin as her mother called up from the dining room. "Girls, come and eat."

"Your mother made sure you'd be taken care of. Uncle Phillip will go over everything with us and answer any questions. It will all work out. Let's go eat." Nora headed for the stairs. She knew the answers Liz outlined in her will. The more complicated question would be whether Eve's dad showed up.

Phillip Samuels's six-foot, four-inch stature slumped on the couch with his head bowed in his hands. He was Nora and Elizabeth's older brother, the eldest of the Samuels children. Since their dad had passed, Phillip was supposed to be the strong, responsible one in times like these. Their mother, Vivian Samuels, sat next to him with her own tear-drenched handkerchief. Nora came around the corner from the stairs. "Phil, you okay?"

He looked up with the same, red-rimmed eyes that looked at him. "I don't know, Sis." He reached and grasped her hand. "Just can't believe she's gone."

Nora sank onto the couch with her mother and brother. "I know. I can't get the sound of the hospital machine alarm out of my head."

Phillip took a deep breath as if to regain his strength. He gestured to the file on the table. "I went by the office and got her will and list of accounts. And I called the police for the report on the accident. How's Eve?"

"She's sad and confused. I gave her ibuprofen last night, like the ER doctor recommended, for soreness she might have. Before she comes down, any word from Curt?"

"What does he have to do with any of this?" Nora's mother sat up with a grimace. "He walked out years ago and only seems to drop in at his convenience or his need for something."

Phillip patted his mother's knee. "We all feel the same way. We'll protect Eve from Curt." He opened the file. "This may help. Liz's will appoints guardianship of Eve to Nora and includes instructions for her life insurance to be put in a trust to provide for Eve through college. Liz had everything that happened with Curt well documented. I talked to our firm's managing partner this morning. He will represent the family in probate court." He rubbed the back of his neck. "And if we have any guardianship arguments from Curt."

Nora flipped through the file. "Mom's right. Curt could get squirrelly and try to fight me for Eve." Her voice cracked. "I never thought I'd ever have to do it, though." The tears streamed while her brother held her hand.

Mom stood up. "Come on, we need to eat. Curt doesn't have a leg to stand on. If he wants to contest Liz's wishes, we'll give him a fight that will scare him from here to kingdom come."

Phillip stood and shook his head. "Feisty words for an eighty-something old lady."

Nora joined him in the dining room. "If Curt gets sober and shows up in court, this could get messy."

"With his record of DUIs and on-and-off employment, I highly doubt any judge will overturn the wishes of the mother."

"What judge?" Eve's voice quivered. "Do we have to go to court because of the wreck?"

Nora locked eyes with Eve, who had finally come down to eat. "No, sweetie." She took a deep breath. Now was the time to start to explain what Liz had arranged. "Your mom was always so organized and responsible. Years ago, when

4

you were a toddler, she wrote down how you would be cared for should something ever happen to her."

Phillip added, "I work with clients all the time who put a plan together just in case. Judy and I have a will and instructions for our kids."

Nora clenched her jaw. "But nothing is going to happen to Uncle Phillip or Aunt Judy for a long, long time." Phillip nodded and sat back while Nora continued. "Your mom had a will, life insurance, and instructions on how we should make sure you're cared for. She left enough money to ensure you get through college. But since you are still under twenty-one, I'll be your guardian, and Uncle Phillip will help with the money. We'll work together."

Eve looked at them. "My dad won't show up and make me live with him?"

Nora gave Eve a side hug. "No, sweetie. I'll be honest, he may try. But your mom made sure her instructions were detailed." Eve's brows scrunched.

"Where will I live ..." Before she could finish her question, the doorbell rang.

Phillip stood to answer it. "That'll be the pastor."

CHAPTER TWO

The quick rhythmic thump of his footsteps on the treadmill echoed in Jim Preston's ears. Another mile might subdue his confusion. As executive director of the Oakdale Community Theater, which didn't have a production in the summer, his work schedule was light, but his heart was heavy. An emotion that seven months ago, he would never have expected. Their mutual friend—and Jim's best volunteer, Maggie Nelson—had asked Nora to help with set design for the February production. Over the months of preproduction, working side-by-side with Nora, his locked heart had been unlocked. Their romance still felt new as they both guarded their hearts. But he wanted Nora to know he would be there for her. Thoughts of her and their time together rolled around his mind. He kept running but got nowhere close to knowing what to do.

"Running a marathon? I've never seen you run this long," Jen teased.

Jim slowed the treadmill to a stop, grabbed his towel, and wiped his face. His Oakdale Community Theater T-shirt, dark with sweat, clung to his six-foot-three frame. "I couldn't focus on work, so I thought I'd work out."

"It's a great way to get your blood pumping and to get refocused. But be careful not to overdo it." Jen Stephens was the assistant manager of a local gym and close friends with Maggie and Nora.

Jim stepped off the treadmill and began to wipe it down. "You're right. Have you ... have you heard from Nora today?"

Jen shook her head. "No, we texted briefly last night. I can't believe her sister's gone. Nora grieved for Seth for years and had finally started to rebuild her life." She put her hand over her mouth. "Oh, I'm sorry. I didn't mean to ..."

Jim nodded. "No need. She and I have talked a lot about her late husband and what she's been through in the last six years. Losing her sister is bound to reopen some of those wounds."

Jen nodded. "In college, Nora was always put together. Nothing rattled her. Or at least it never showed. When Maggie and I ran into her last October she was the same 'got-it-all-together girl.'" Jen's hands went up in air quotes. "It was a big step for her to start dating." She poked Jim's arm. "You know that, don't you? She's come out of her shell."

"She's brought me out of my shell as well. I haven't dated anyone in a long time." His red face began to relax. "I don't want to smother her." He shuffled his running shoes. But ... but ... I miss her."

"Hang in there. You'll figure it out. If I hear from her, I'll encourage her to at least return your text."

"Thanks."

"I need to go take care of a few things. If I hear anything about the funeral arrangements, I'll let you know. In the meantime, don't abuse my treadmills too much."

Jim cracked a smile. "I'm done for today."

After his workout and shower, Jim's thoughts turned back to work. He turned the corner to the gym lobby where Maggie was signing in. "Maggie, how are you?"

Maggie smiled at her friend and boss. "Oh no, I'm busted for not being at my volunteer job."

Jim shook his head. "Please, if we got the volunteer hours from all of our volunteers that we get from you, the to-do list would be nonexistent."

Maggie picked up her gym bag. "Jen finally talked me into a beginner yoga class. And, lucky me, tonight, she's teaching."

"Have you talked to Nora?"

"I talked to her this morning. Sounds like a pretty rough night, but they're starting to figure out the funeral arrangements and how to navigate everything with Eve."

Jim tilted his head. "With Eve?"

"Yeah, Liz named Nora as her guardian. Eve will be moving up here at some point. Probably in time to start school." Maggie shook her head. "A lot of changes for both of them."

Jim hadn't thought about Nora's niece. "Yes."

"I've got to run to class."

Jim resettled his gym bag strap on his shoulder. "Of course. I'll see you at the theater tomorrow."

"I'll be there."

As Jim got in his car, Maggie's comments about Eve coming to live with Nora echoed through his mind. "A lot of changes for both of them."

For all three of us.

Wanted you to know I'm thinking about you and praying for you. Nora read Jim's text over and over. He was caring and kind. She wanted to answer him. She had loved and lost Seth. Now her sister, Liz. Barely hanging onto her emotions, could she risk letting down the protective walls of her heart? *Please, Lord, no more loss.*

Her phone buzzed. "Hello." Her voice was tired and small.

"How's it going?" Maggie knew how to ask the question without Nora feeling like she was obligated to give a long answer.

Nora, Jen, and Maggie had lost touch after college, but reconnected last fall after running into each other at a fundraiser Maggie was coordinating.

"It's okay." Nora's voice quivered as the tears threatened again.

"I'm not convinced."

Maggie's tender, heartfelt words found the weak part of Nora's emotional wall. The tears broke through. "Oh, no ..." Nora slipped from the couch to the floor and let the sobs loose.

Maggie stayed on the line and quietly reassured Nora. "Let the tears come. It's all right to cry as long and as hard as you need to."

Nora sniffed and grabbed the last tissue from the box on the coffee table. "Mags, it's an ugly cry."

Maggie chuckled. "Nora, you're always so put together. Glad you're as real as the rest of us."

Nora sniffed again and took a deep breath. "How am I going to get through this? Liz was my best friend." Tears rolled down her face. "She and I went through so much together—her divorce, me losing Seth. We've always been there for each other." Maggie was silent as Nora shared what was in her heart. "She was only a year behind me in school. We had crushes on the same guys in high school. When Dad died, we took care of Mom together ... Oh, Maggie, what am I going to do?" The sobs overtook the last of her words.

"Nora, I can't tell you what to do. But I promise that Jen and I are here to help any way we can. Even if it's just sitting and crying for a while."

Now, Nora was silent. Since Seth died, she had politely accepted encouragement from the ladies at church, but they'd never become her close friends. That was real friendship. Her voice was weak. "Maggie, thank you. I feel like my life is about to get messy again. Eve will be moving in with me. We're going to close her mom's house, and there's all the estate stuff. I know Phillip will be there too, but you remember how it was as a teenage girl."

"Whatever you need, let us know. And you know Jim will help too."

Jim. What was all this going to mean to their budding relationship? "Jim's probably mad at me. He's called and texted and I haven't responded."

Maggie jumped in. "Jim is not mad at you. He cares and is trying to be there for you without smothering you."

"I just feel like ..." Nora wiped her nose again. "I don't know ... I care about him, but ... it's a new relationship. I'm reliving the hurt that comes with losing someone I love. I don't want to lose him, but I don't know how to let him in and still protect my heart."

Maggie, the consummate big sister type, spoke soothing words. "I understand protecting your heart. Jim understands that too. Remember, he hasn't dated anyone in a long time, either. Consider accepting him as another someone special who's in your corner right now, ready to walk through this difficult time to encourage and support you. Don't try to figure out everything right now. One change at a time."

"You're right." Nora sighed. "I'll text him."

"Let us know when you have the funeral arrangements. We'll be there."

"Oh, yeah, we met with the funeral director and Liz's pastor this morning. The service will be Thursday morning at ten at the Simpson Christian Church."

"Do you want me to make reservations for lunch somewhere for the family afterwards?"

"The pastor said we could use the fellowship hall. Would you ..." Asking for help was difficult. "Would you mind picking up lunch if I call and order it? After the service and burial, we'll go back to the church."

"Don't even call and order it. Jen and I will take care of everything. Let me know how many you think will be there."

Tears returned to Nora's eyes and escaped down her face. Her voice cracked. "Thank you, Maggie."

After Maggie hung up, Nora pulled up Jim's texts. Her heart settled as she read them. She pictured him typing the words. His words to her heart. She typed a response.

CHAPTER THREE

Jim stood at the theater's reception counter with Sara Biddle, an intern and receptionist at the hundred-year-old theater who also managed ticket sales, social media, and light bookkeeping for the theater while attending college. Adjacent to her desk was a tall counter-height station where tickets were sold.

Built in the early 1900s, the building was a centerpiece in the historic district of Oakdale. His phone buzzed, and Nora's photo flashed on the screen. Jim snatched his phone off the counter when he saw Sara smile at Nora's picture. "I need to check this message."

"Of course. Please let Nora know we're all praying for her."

Jim ducked into the long, narrow conference room to check the text message.

> Jim, thank you for reaching out. I'm sorry I didn't respond. So much is happening. And it's hard to deal with. Hearing from you helps. The funeral is on Thursday. Maggie has the details. I'll probably be here through the weekend. Take care.

He took a deep breath and read her message again. Something about it felt distant. Nora was in a crisis. They had had long conversations about her grief after losing Seth and how important her family had been to her. *Close family.* Not something Jim was accustomed to. His entire family lived in Oakdale. When was the last time he'd seen them?

Sara tapped on the door. "Excuse me, Jim. Dr. Cosby is on the phone."

Dr. Cosby was the chairman of the theater department at the University of Oakdale. Jim and Dr. Cosby had developed an internship program for upperclassmen. The program and support of the university had saved the theater from being demolished last year. "Thanks, Sara. I'll take it in my office. Do we have anything going on Thursday?"

Curt Butler rubbed his hand over the three-day beard. He sat up from the 1970s-style couch where he had passed out the night before. His blurry vision and throbbing head were reminders of another drunken night. The newspaper crinkled under him as he rolled over and sat up. He remembered the article. He swiped the wrinkles out of the page with the article about the car wreck and the death of his ex-wife, Liz. Their early years were so fun. But she held a job, and he didn't. A buddy from his last job invited him out for a beer. One turned into two, then three, and on it went. Before he knew it, his so-called buddy had Curt hooked up with a dealer. "Easy money, man. Just take care of a few deliveries." That offer started Curt's journey into drugs and dealing. Eve came along, and for a few months Curt held a job and played the doting father. The sleepless nights frustrated Curt. One day, he couldn't take it anymore. He got in his car and left. Didn't tell Liz where he was going and didn't take his phone. A month later, late at night, he returned home drunk and broke. By then, the locks had been changed. Liz was done cleaning up his messes.

Liz, gone. She didn't deserve that. He looked up the obituary to find the time and location of the funeral. His phone rang. No name, but he answered. "Hello."

"Curt, it's time, man. You owe it, and it's time to pay up. Can't carry you anymore."

Curt ran his hand through his unbrushed, shoulder-length hair. *I owe everyone.* He clenched his teeth and shook his head. "Look, I don't have it. But I'm working on getting you caught up. I've got a job this weekend. Just give me a few more days."

The rough voice continued, "I'll give you until Monday night. That's it."

"Monday." Curt hung up. He had no prospect of a job. Every legit job he started, his dealer would find him and make a scene. Curt would make another run to Florida. The money was good, but he had stacked up arrests in Kentucky, Tennessee, and Georgia. He was running out of routes to southern pickup points. And he was running out of money.

His eyes looked back at the newspaper. The obituary ... Survived by her sister, Nora St. Claire, her daughter, Eve Denise Butler ... *Maybe it's time for Dad to go home to care for his daughter. And collect her mother's life insurance.*

CHAPTER FOUR

Nora's heart was as heavy as the summer humidity. She had taken care to pin her hair back in a knot that felt as tight as her stomach. Her steps were slow. She held her mother's hand. *How does a mother bury a child, no matter the age?* Nora had taken this path of sadness twice to bury her own stillborn babies. Eve slipped her hand into Nora's other hand. In silence, they followed the pastor to the top of the hill where Liz would be laid to rest next to their father. Phillip, Judy, and their son followed. There was a smattering of Liz's friends and coworkers, as well as her mother's friends from church. In the back were Jen, her husband, Mark, Maggie, her husband, Dan, and Jim. Today, her coworkers and friends were there to stand with her during a dark hour.

The pastor's message at the funeral reflected everything that Nora, Eve, Phillip, and their mother had shared about Liz and the way she lived her life. It was all for God's glory. In Liz's files with her life insurance papers, they had found a list of her favorite Bible verses and a handwritten note about what she'd like at her funeral.

They gathered under the funeral canopy. The pastor read a psalm and said a prayer. That was it. There wasn't anything left to say about a life well-lived but cut short. Nora put her arm around Eve as they passed by the coffin one last time. The pastor pulled roses from the floral arrangement and handed one to each of the family members. In a hushed tone, he offered, "If you need anything, please call me."

Nora's voice caught in her throat. "Thank you."

Phillip shook hands with the pastor. And that was that. It was done. Liz was gone, and the funeral was over. Emotion overtook Nora, and she stepped away from the group. *Just breathe.*

A hand grazed the back of her arm. "You okay?"

Nora turned to find compassion in Jim's eyes. Jen and Maggie joined them. Nora wiped her tears and looked at her friends. She reached for each of them. "I don't know if I can handle this." The tears fell. "What am I going to do without her?"

Each hug from Jim and her friends brought a hint of the answer.

"I don't think so!" Phillip's angry words broke through the solemn moment. Nora turned to see her brother standing with Curt.

"Oh no, what is *he* doing here?" Nora left her friends and headed straight for Phillip and Eve.

Phillip pulled Curt away from Liz's grave site. His mother nudged Eve to stay with her. Phillip towered over Curt's five-foot-ten-inch chubby frame. "What are you doing here, Curt?"

Curt stood back. His attempt to dress up included slicking his hair back and wearing a tie that was too short. "Hands off, man. I came to pay my respects and check on my daughter. I'm sure she's upset and needs her dad now."

Red crept up Phillip's face, and the vein at his temple pulsed. "Are you nuts? She barely knows you. She's got all the family she needs."

Curt looked at the ground and then into Phillip's eyes. "Look, I know I haven't been much of a dad. But I've changed my ways and was on my way up to see Liz and Eve when I saw the news. I want to be a part of my little girl's life."

Phillip shook his head. "I cannot believe you showed up. Given you reek of whiskey, I doubt you've changed much." He looked around and then back at Curt. "By the way, she's not a little girl anymore. She's a teenager."

"A teenager." Curt looked over the group to the young lady, recognizing her as a much older version of the child he had left behind. "I'd like to take her on a little trip. You know, so we can get to know each other again." Curt shifted. "I am her father and only living parent."

Phillip's patience ran out on that idea. "I don't think so."

Nora joined Phillip and Curt. Her voice was calm. "Curt, whatever drama you brought can wait."

Phillip didn't take his eyes off Curt. He lowered his tone. "Curt here thinks he can show up and take Eve on a little trip to get to know her. Says as her only living parent, he's ready to step in and play 'dad' now."

Nora's friends, including Jim, stepped up behind Phillip and Nora as a silent wall of support.

Curt looked at the seven of them. "I didn't mean to stir everyone up. I just wanted to see my daughter. May I do that?"

Phillip looked at Nora. Nora rolled her eyes and sent Phillip a small nod. Phillip glanced over at Eve. "Tell you what, Curt, you and I will walk over so you can pay your respects. But that's it. Don't mention trips or anything. She's got a lot weighing on her right now. You've been gone for years. We'll talk this weekend about next steps for her." Nora's eyes widened. Phillip nodded an assurance to her and looked back at Curt. "Liz had everything well-planned."

Curt started to protest but backed down, accepting the chance to speak with Eve. He fidgeted with his tie as he and Phillip approached Eve and her grandmother. Phillip nodded at his mother to bring Eve away from the group.

Phillip gently took Eve's elbow. "Eve, someone has come to pay his respects." Eve looked at Curt with a question in her eyes.

"Hello. Thank you for coming." It was obvious she didn't recognize Curt.

"Eve, it's been too long. I'm sorry about that." Curt reached for her hand.

Phillip cleared his throat to remind Curt what they agreed to. His mother wasn't quite as discreet. "Curt Butler, what on earth are you doing here!"

Eve's eyes widened and she pulled her hand back. "Curt Butler. You're my dad?"

"I am, baby girl. And I am so sorry about your mom."

The color left Eve's face and her knees began to give way. Phillip caught her. "Okay, Curt. Time to go."

"But I'm her dad—I should be here." Curt raised his voice.

Nora led Eve to their car to sit down.

Phillip leaned close to Curt. "You need to leave now. Liz made arrangements for Eve, should something happen to her, and her arrangements do *not* include you."

Curt looked over at Eve and Nora, and back to Phillip. "Well, we'll see about that."

CHAPTER FIVE

"Are you sure you're ready to do this?" Nora looked at her niece in the passenger seat. They pulled into the driveway of Liz and Eve's single-story home with boxes, tape, and markers. It had been two days since the funeral with no word from Curt but a lot of questions from Eve. Nora, Phillip, and her grandmother assured her repeatedly that she did not have to go anywhere with Curt. Liz had taken all the legal steps to ensure Eve's guardianship. That didn't mean Curt couldn't try to fight it.

Eve carried a lost look in her eye. "Yes, Aunt Nora. I need to get my things, and you said we will need to get the house on the market."

"Soon, but not immediately. We don't want you to feel rushed. This is your home. You have a lot of great memories here."

Eve drew a breath and sighed before answering, "I do."

Nora patted Eve's knee. "Let's focus on the things you want to take first. Then, if we feel like it, we'll start packing the rest."

Eve smiled. "I know, take it one step at a time. No rushing. And let myself feel whatever emotions I feel."

Nora chuckled. "So, you have been reading those grief booklets the pastor gave us."

The sound of the key sliding into the door lock broke Nora's heart again. She missed her sister and was trying to be strong for Eve. Phillip and Nora had answered all of Eve's questions and showed her the legal documents Liz had drawn up to ensure Eve's future, both financially and by appointing Nora as her legal guardian. Among the three of them, there were bouts of tears and stories of Liz. She had been fun-loving, creative, and always responsible.

Nora looked over her shoulder at Eve. She noticed Eve's jaw was clenched. *She's trying hard to be brave.* This was the first time Eve had been home since the wreck. Phillip and Judy had come over to pack a small suitcase for her the day after. Almost a week ago. Time kept moving forward even when it felt like they were living in slow motion. They walked into the living room right off the entry. The house was cool and dark, with all the shades drawn. Maybe she wasn't as strong as she believed. The silence was deafening. Nora needed a minute to gather herself as Eve wandered around and picked up small, framed photos of herself and her mom.

A soft sob broke into Nora's musing. Eve handed Nora a candle from the end table. "This was her favorite. Can I take it with me?"

"Sure. You take anything you want. Uncle Phillip is bringing his neighbor's truck if you want to take your bedroom furniture." Nora's phone buzzed. It was Jim.

Eve noticed his name. "Please, Aunt Nora, take his call. You've ignored at least two other ones from him this morning."

Nora stepped out to the small backyard and pressed the green "Answer" icon.

"Hi. How are you ladies doing this afternoon?" Jim's sweet tone gave Nora a brief respite from the sadness within.

She raised her face to feel the warmth of the sun washing over it. "We're hanging in there. We just got to Liz's to pack some of Eve's stuff to move to my house."

After an awkward pause, Jim asked, "Do you need help with moving anything?"

"No, Phillip said he would help, and I'm not sure how much Eve will feel like packing this round."

Another awkward silence. "Nora, I know you've got a lot on you. I don't want to push in. But I want you to know that I'm here for you."

His words were gentle. Since the funeral, their conversations had been short but meaningful. Nora kept remembering Maggie's suggestion to accept him as another person who cared for her and wanted to offer support. But that was hard. They had been dating for six months, and she cared for him as more than a friend. Her life was about to change in a big way.

"Thank you. Those words mean everything. We need to take this slow and make sure Eve is okay."

"Not a problem. Maggie and Jen said they were doing some shopping for Eve and might need my help when you all get here tomorrow."

Nora smiled at the surprise her friends were up to. "Yes, they said they wanted to help make Eve's room special. They called and asked for her favorite colors."

Phillip poked his head out of the sliding glass doors and waved. Nora nodded and held up her hand. "Jim, Phillip just got here. Can we talk later?"

"Of course. Call me when you have time."

Nora joined Phillip and Judy in the living room. The silence was broken by a small sob. The three looked at each other and headed down the hall to find Eve crying in her bedroom. Two of the bureau drawers were open and empty. The clothes were askew in a small square box. Nora scuffled through the empty boxes and embraced Eve.

"This is hard." Eve wiped her face with the sleeve of her Simpson High School shirt. "Now I'm going to have to change schools. What about my friends?"

"Sweetie, I know it's an adjustment. Oakdale is only thirty miles away. We'll make plans to spend time here so you can see your friends. Uncle Phillip and Aunt Judy said you could spend weekends with them sometimes. And during breaks, you can invite your friends to my house."

Eve slumped on her bed like a much younger child. "It's not going to be the same."

"No. It's not. And there is nothing we can say to make it all good." Nora's voice cracked. "I wish like crazy I could." Nora drew her niece in for a hug. She looked around the room. Maggie and Jen would have new bedding and curtains for Eve's room at her house. "Would you like to take some of your posters?"

"They won't mess up your guest room?"

"It's going to be your room. You can take whatever will help you feel comfortable there." Nora was careful not to use the word home. This was Eve's home. It would be a long time before she felt otherwise.

The sun beamed in Curt's face, aggravating his headache. After the funeral episode, he'd started drinking and hadn't stopped. Two days lost.

"Yeah, Willy. It's going to take a little more time." Curt had the call on speaker while he drove to Liz's house.

"Butler, you're running out of time."

"Look, I'm about to come into some money. My ex died and had life insurance. I've just got to get with my daughter and the lawyers."

"You don't got a kid." the gruff voice on the phone spewed.

"Yeah, I do. And I talked to her at the funeral about a trip to Florida. Didn't you say you needed another run? This one will look like a daughter-daddy trip."

"You want another run? Really?"

Curt took a deep breath and shook his head. Do another run, give Willy his take, show he's a great dad, and come back to secure the life insurance.

His voice spewed defeat. "Yes. One more run, you keep your cut, that'll make us even."

"Be here tomorrow morning at eight o'clock for the package." The phone screen went blank as Curt turned onto Liz's street. He'd never been invited, but he knew where she lived. Nice neighborhood. Probably get a good price for the house. He pulled up and cut the engine. When he got out of the car, he rubbed his chin. *Should have shaved.*

Curt was about to knock on the door when Phillip opened it, carrying a large trash bag. He immediately stepped outside, pulling the door closed behind him.

"What are you doing here?"

"I came to see Eve." Curt kept his words measured.

Phillip brushed past him. "Get away from the door. You're not going in there."

Curt grabbed Phillip's arm, but his oversized ex-brother-in-law dropped the trash and twisted loose. "Listen to me. You are not going to see Eve."

Curt leaned close to Phillip's face. "Yes, I am. I'd like to take my daughter to Florida for the week ..." Behind Phil, the door opened again.

"A trip?" Nora had another bag of trash, and Eve was right behind her.

Eve looked at Curt. "Uncle Phillip, what's going on?"

Nora set the bag down to put her arm around Eve. Before Phillip could answer, Curt stepped toward Eve.

"I'd like to take you to Florida. You're on summer break. Let's go to the beach. Have some fun ... get to know each other. I'm your dad, Evie."

Nora stepped in front of Eve. "She's not going anywhere with you. She has no idea who you are."

"She knows I'm her dad. We just need to spend some time together."

Phillip moved toward Curt. "You need to leave now. You can't show up after a ten-year absence and decide to be father of the year."

Curt straightened his back and fisted his hands. "And you can't keep my daughter from me when I'm her only living parent."

Phillip crossed his arms to his chest. "Yes, we can. And I'm pretty sure a judge will agree."

"Judge? What are you talking about?"

"Ten years ago, you abandoned Eve and Liz. Just left. Called a few times from jail trying to get bail money out of Liz. There're several other things I won't mention in front of Eve, but you see where I'm going."

Curt leaned close to Phillip. "I've changed. I'm clean and I have a job. You don't know anything about me. You want to talk to a judge. Name the day and time. I'll be there."

Phillip crossed his arms. "Yeah, you smell like you're clean."

Curt turned to Eve, softened his tone. "Sweet Eve. Your aunt and uncle can't keep us from getting to know each other. Don't worry, we'll get it worked out, and we'll take that trip."

Curt pointed at Nora and Phillip. "This is not the last of this. I will see my daughter when and where I want." Anger and frustration gripped Curt's chest. He got in his car and left.

Uncle Phillip took all the trash to the can. Eve was quiet as she and Aunt Nora walked back inside and to her room. She began to take her posters off the wall. Her thoughts dug into her memories for any scene she could remember of Curt. Her dad. But no memories surfaced. *Who is this man? My dad? Aunt Nora and Uncle Phillip seem adamant that I'm not going anywhere with him.* She rolled them up and put a rubber band around her posters.

Across the room, Aunt Nora pulled clothes from hangers and packed them. Eve couldn't stand the silence. "Aunt Nora, I ... I ... I am a little curious about Curt."

Nora turned to look at her. Eve sat on the bed. "Please don't be mad. I don't have any memories of him, and I'm wondering about ... about my dad." She lowered her head.

Nora sat next to Eve and held her hand. "I'm not mad at all. There's a lot of history with Curt. Not anything good, though."

"There had to be some good, or Mom would have never married him."

Nora grinned. "You're right, I guess." She turned and sat with her legs crisscrossed on the bed. "There were a few good years early in their marriage when they were young and in love. Your mom was twenty-four, and Curt was twenty-nine. He was good to your mom. But he always struggled to hold a job. Your mom was very patient with his job hopping. Between jobs, he would get pretty low. He'd drink and go out and stay out all night. Liz tried to get him to stop. He'd come home loud and angry." Nora paused and twisted her ponytail between her fingers. "There were a couple of times that Liz called your Uncle Phillip to come help her."

Eve tilted her head. "Help her with what?"

Nora's words were careful. "Your dad's a big man, or at least he was bigger than your mom. When he was angry, it scared your mom. Phillip came and helped get your dad settled down and in bed." She shifted her legs. "In those first three years of your life, the time between jobs would get longer and longer. Your dad got in deep with some bad people. Then one night, he just left. No note. Nothing." She looked deep into Eve's eyes. "You were only three or four." Nora took a deep breath while her words settled.

Eve's voice was timid. "But he says he's doing better now."

CHAPTER SIX

The scene with Curt played over and over in Eve's mind along with her aunt's words. Was she going to have to go on a trip with this man she didn't know? She was a little curious about him. Maybe he had changed. Aunt Nora, Uncle Phillip, and Aunt Judy worked alongside Eve all afternoon at her home, carefully packing items for storage. It was too soon to sell or throw much away. Aunt Nora and Eve worked in silence in Eve's room, each in their own thoughts and parts of the room.

Everyone met in the disheveled living room and took a break. The late afternoon sun reached through the sliding glass doors. Eve sat in an overstuffed chair. She pulled the throw she and her mother had crocheted together around her. Everyone was so quiet. What weren't they telling her? Aunt Nora and Uncle Phillip sat across from her.

Aunt Nora broke the heavy silence. "Eve, you okay? Did I say something to upset you?"

Aunt Judy came in from the kitchen with a bowl wrapped in newspaper. "Phillip, could you bring me more boxes?" She stopped and looked at the others. "What's going on?"

Aunt Nora glanced at her sister-in-law. "Curt showed up demanding to take Eve on a trip. Eve has some questions about him."

"Is he nuts?" Aunt Judy sat next to Uncle Phillip, who patted her knee.

Aunt Nora leaned forward and spoke in a quiet voice. "Eve, honey, he's not taking you anywhere." She hesitated. "What other questions do you have?"

Eve sank further into the chair. *Who is this man?* Her tears pushed through her last ounce of bravery. "I just ... who is he ... I ... don't know ..." The sobs overtook her words and washed over the myriad of emotions she didn't know how to express. "I know you want to protect me. Like my mom ..." More tears fell freely.

Aunt Nora handed her a tissue. "Yes, but we know this is all very confusing for you as well."

In a small voice, Eve asked, "I don't want to go on a trip with him ... but now I wonder ... who is he? He's my dad, but I don't know him. It's kinda strange. Hard to understand."

Aunt Nora patted her arm. "I'm sure it is."

"Tell me about him. Uncle Phillip, you said some things in the yard about him being in jail."

Phillip took a deep breath, gave Nora a shrug. He leaned in with his elbows on his knees, his fingers intertwined. "He left when you were four years old." His words were careful and gentle.

"Alcohol and drugs can make people do some very mean things. There were a couple of times after they separated, he'd call and threaten your mom. She always called me or the police. I came over to make sure you were both safe. And then Curt disappeared. The first time I'd seen him in close to ten years was at your mom's funeral."

Eve sat up in the chair. "Aunt Nora said he wasn't always like that."

Phillip smiled. "Before they were married, he had a job and seemed to be a pretty steady guy. After they got married, he had a run-in with one of his bosses and lost his job. From then on, he was in and out of work. Couldn't seem to hold a job. After you were born, he had a job he really liked but, somehow, got himself fired again. Your dad ... Curt ... got involved with some rough guys, continued to drink too much, and was involved with drugs. Your mom did all she could to get him help. One night, he left. Didn't take his phone, only a couple of duffle bags of clothes. Months later, he showed up. By then, your mom had changed the locks and filed for divorce."

Eve stared at the floor and listened. She twisted the damp tissue between her fingers as tight as her stomach felt. "I don't want to go on a trip with him. He can't make me, can he?"

"No, he abandoned you. Your mother made sure that Nora will be your guardian, and we will all love and support you forever."

Eve looked at the three adults she knew and had happy memories with. She trusted and loved them. "Okay. But ... but what if I wanted to just talk to him?"

Uncle Phillip looked at Aunt Nora then took Eve's hand. "I imagine you are a little curious about Curt. If you want to talk to him, we can call him. But I think it's best if someone is with you when you do."

Eve nodded. "I might like to do that." The thoughts of her dad both scared her and piqued her curiosity. She sat on the edge of the chair. "What about the judge you mentioned?"

Uncle Phillip took a deep breath. "If, and that's a big if, we need to go to court, we will all be there with you, and a colleague from my firm will represent us before the judge.

But, at this point, the only way we'll need a judge is if Curt calls an attorney and presses for visitation."

"Do you think he'll do that?" Eve's stomach flipped again.

"I doubt it."

The silence lingered until Aunt Nora asked, "Do you feel like doing any more packing this afternoon?"

Curt's appearance in her front yard stirred Eve's motivation to get her stuff packed and move to Aunt Nora's. "Yeah, let's do some more in my room." But before getting out of the chair, Eve rubbed her hand along the cushion. When Eve was little, she and her mom had snuggled in this chair and read books. "Aunt Nora. Do you have room for me to take this chair?"

Nora nodded. "Sure. We'll find the perfect spot for it."

A few hours later, everyone met in the living room again. Nora's car was packed, and the truck Phillip had borrowed had a few pieces of furniture, including the overstuffed chair.

Aunt Nora looked around at the unkempt living room. Furniture had been moved to make room for moving boxes. The shelves were half-empty, and the area rugs were rolled up and bound with rope. "We got more done than I expected." The three stood in silence. Their sadness was palpable. Eve plopped down on the couch. She sniffed back the returning tears.

Uncle Phillip's words caught in his throat. "Yeah." He shuffled his feet. "This just isn't fair."

"No, nothing fair about this." Aunt Nora sighed.

"We need to get on the road. Jim, Dan, Maggie, and Jen are meeting at my place to help unload. We'll plan to come back next weekend and work some more."

Nora looked around again. "Liz hosted so many of our family gatherings here. So much laughter and fun." Her voice echoed oddly off the bare spots in the room.

Uncle Phillip gave Aunt Nora a side hug. "I know. A lot of fun memories."

Before tears broke through, Aunt Nora gathered her purse and phone. "Eve, are you ready?"

Eve sprang from the couch. "I think so. When are we coming back?"

A smile of understanding curled Aunt Nora's lips. "We'll be back Friday evening. Mom's making dinner, and then we'll come back over."

Eve nodded. "Okay."

"I'll see you all in about an hour." Uncle Phillip gave his niece a hug. "We love you."

"Thanks, Uncle Phillip. I love you too."

Eve and Aunt Nora got into her small SUV that was packed to the roof. Eve stared out the window at the only home she had known. "Bye, house." The tears came fast.

Aunt Nora's warm hand wrapped around Eve's. The tears flowed freely during the thirty-minute drive. There were no words.

CHAPTER SEVEN

Nora and Eve walked into her Cape Cod-style home. It was red brick with a front porch big enough for two chairs and a small table between them. Jen met them at the door. Maggie and Dan trailed behind Jim. Nora made sure Eve remembered Maggie's husband, Dan, and Jim. Introducing Jim as her friend felt odd, but she wasn't sure how to handle a boyfriend with Eve yet.

Jim stuck out his hand to shake Eve's. "Good to meet you officially. We didn't get the chance at the funeral."

Eve sighed with a polite smile. "It's good to meet you."

Maggie clapped her hands. "Okay, where do we want to start—a tour of Eve's space and then unload?"

A wave of relief came over Nora. Her very organized friend helped move things along. "What have you all been up to? A tour of what?"

"Nora, I know you're the designer ..." Jen spoke up. "But we did a little refresh of your guest room to make it more ... cool for Eve. It needed a tiny coolness makeover."

"A what?" Nora started for the stairs and noticed Phillip was backing the truck into the driveway.

Jen waved them to follow her upstairs. "You'll see. That's why we asked about Eve's favorite colors." Dan and Jim headed out to begin unloading the car and truck.

At the top of the stairs, they gathered in the hall while Jen threw open the door to what had been Nora's guest room, now refreshed to include a royal blue painted accent wall, new shelves, and a desk in front of a window that invited the afternoon sun in. On the desk was a lamp that changed color from a soft yellow to a light blue. Eve's favorite colors. The bed was made with a new comforter with water-colored wildflowers. Hanging from the ceiling in an empty corner was a Chinese lantern-style lamp.

Nora shook her head in disbelief. Eve slowly walked in and around the room. She ran her hand along the top of the shelves and opened the desk drawer. "Oh ... you did all this for me?" Her voice cracked.

Maggie and Jen walked over and gave her a hug. Maggie smiled at Nora. "I hope you don't mind. All you had in here was the bed and chest. We wanted Eve to feel comfortable here immediately."

Nora put her hand over her heart at the sight of her two close friends caring for her niece. "Of course not. This looks great. I'm impressed you did an accent wall."

Jen laughed at Nora's teasing remark. "We may have done some Googling on the latest shades of blue."

"You did a great job. And Eve, that corner over there looks like a great spot for your chair. Unless you'd rather put it in the den."

"No, I think that'd be a great spot." Eve looked at Jen and Maggie. "Thank you so much. I can't believe you did all this for me."

"Yoohoo, Phillip's moving service is here," Phillip called from downstairs.

Nora hustled to the top of the steps. "Everything comes up here."

Jen sat on the edge of the bed in front of Eve. "Eve, Maggie and I hope you'll think of us as bonus aunts. We wanted to do something special for you."

Eve looked at Nora. Nora smiled. "I know. Left on their own, you never know what these two are going to be up to."

All four burst out in laughter. Nora gestured toward the door. "We should head downstairs to help carry your boxes up."

The evening was spent moving boxes upstairs and unpacking Eve's clothing. The overstuffed chair with the muted flowers was placed in the corner next to the bookshelves. Its color perfectly complemented the bedding. Eve released a sigh when she laid the crocheted throw, complete with a few ragged holes, across the overstuffed chair from home.

Throughout the afternoon, whenever Nora and Jim locked eyes, he would smile and give a quick wink. It warmed her heart.

The gang of friends flattened the empty boxes and said their goodbyes with promises to visit soon. Phillip hugged his little sister. "Call me if you need anything. Don't worry about Mom, we'll check on her."

"Thanks. You take care as well."

"Thank you, Jim." Eve stepped to the doorway and waved to everyone before she bounded back upstairs.

Jim was the last one to leave. When he paused at the door, his hand grazed Nora's. "You girls sleep well."

Nora squeezed Jim's hand as if to reassure him they would figure things out. "Thank you. I appreciate everything."

"Glad to help." He leaned in and gave her a gentle kiss on her forehead.

"We'll hopefully sleep in tomorrow." So many details were churning in her head.

As if he had read her thoughts, Jim stepped a little closer. "Nora." His voice was soft. "Losing your sister is huge. Please take your time, take care of Eve and yourself. Everything will work out." He gave her a tender, understanding kiss. "Sweet dreams. I'll call you tomorrow."

Nora sighed. *Jim understands.*

CHAPTER EIGHT

Nora woke earlier than she had hoped. After she tossed and adjusted her pillows, she gave up trying to sleep and got out of bed. The house was quiet. She made a cup of coffee and went out to the patio with her Bible. She read and meditated on God's Word as she prayed for the day ahead. She took a deep, refreshing breath. The warmth of the sun washed over her like the peace that came from reading the Bible. Another deep breath. *Lord, thank you that I feel your presence. I feel your warmth in the sunshine. Be with me today, as you are every day.* After several minutes, and with a renewed peace in her soul, she headed inside to start her day.

Eve was still asleep. Nora took the opportunity to call Tony Stanton, her boss, about her schedule for the next few months. She wanted to spend time with Eve before the coming school year started.

"Hi Tony, it's Nora." Tony owned Stanton Designs, a boutique interior design firm. After Seth's death, Nora worked part-time for Stanton Designs while attending design classes. Once she completed her degree, she was offered a full-time designer position.

"Nora, good to hear from you. How are you holding up?" The firm had a family-like spirit. When she called to tell Tony about Liz's accident and death, he had offered her all the time off she needed.

"We're doing okay. Yesterday, we moved Eve here. It was emotional, but overall, we did well."

"I'm sure."

Nora stood at the island in her small kitchen with her notes. There were so many details to tie up along with finding out about the school Eve would attend. She didn't want him to think she was taking advantage of his generous offer for time off. "Tony, I need to ask ..." She shifted her weight to the other side. "I need another week to get things sorted out. I know I don't have that much vaca—"

Tony interrupted her. "Nora, I'm not counting this toward your vacation days. Your sister's death was a tragedy."

Nora was thankful to be on the phone and not in person, so he couldn't see the pooling tears. Her voice was soft. "Thank you, Tony. I appreciate everything you have done." She sniffed the tears back. "Let Phoebe know if she has questions about my clients, to call me."

"Fair enough. Take care. We'll talk soon."

Nora pressed the red button on the call, sat on the stool at the counter, and let the tears go—another *ugly cry.*

Eve padded downstairs. At the bottom of the steps, she heard sobs. Crying. Aunt Nora? They had cried a lot over the last week, but she'd never heard Nora cry that hard. *Was this too much for me to be living here? Will I be a constant reminder of my mother?*

Eve took light steps into the den. Her voice was tentative. "Aunt Nora, are you okay?"

Nora started. "Oh, Eve. I'm sorry." She wiped her face with her sleeve.

Eve walked over and sat in the chair across from the one steady person she had left. "You don't have to apologize. All I want to do is cry."

Nora sighed and tugged a tissue from the box on the coffee table. "I guess we're both going to be sad sacks for a while. I miss my sister."

Eve nodded. "I miss my mother." The sadness lingered between the two. A couple of sniffs broke the silence as Eve snagged a tissue.

Nora took a deep breath. "We know these moments will come. Remember it's okay to stop and cry. But let's add something."

"What?"

"Let's finish the sad moment with something we loved about your mom. Like, I remember how good a cook she was."

They both smiled and nodded. Eve added, "I remember the Sunday brunches we had after church when the whole family would pile into our house."

"Yes! Speaking of brunch, are you hungry? I can fix something, or we can go out."

"Let's go out. But ..." Eve hesitated. The sound of hearing Nora sob so hard made her wonder.

"But what?" Nora sat next to Eve.

"Is it ... I mean ... is this going to be too much for you to have me here twenty-four-seven? Will it make you sad to see me every day?"

Nora wrapped her arms around Eve in a warm, encouraging hug. "No, I'm thankful to have you. You are the one other person on earth who was as close to your mom as I was. I'm glad you're here, and we are going to be there for each other through this grief."

Eve sighed and leaned into Nora. "Thank you. I feel the same way. I miss her so much."

CHAPTER NINE

Jim's morning routine had run amok. His distracted thoughts stole his normal timeliness. *Focus on work today. Things will work out with Nora and Eve. What do I know about teenage girls? I barely know how to date.* The thought of her gentle manner and sweet eyes brought tenderness to his heart. *Focus.* The summer was in full bloom and the fall production needed his full attention.

"Good morning, Sara." Jim hustled through the theater's lobby.

Sara walked around the desk and handed Jim a message. "There was another message from that man, James Preston. Is that a family member?"

An innocent question with a complicated answer.

"Then, this morning on the machine was a call from a Maribel Preston."

Jim barely looked at Sara. "I'll call them back."

Sara's head tilted. "Is everything okay? Who are these people? Family?"

"I can't go into this with you right now. I will return the calls this morning." He headed to his office.

Jim considered who to call first. One would fuss at him about his career choices and the other his relationships.

At least his mom would back off after his first rebuff. He dialed her cell. She answered on the second ring.

"James! So good to hear from you."

"Hello, Mother. How are you?" Jim measured his words.

"Sweetheart, I'd love for you to come to lunch on Saturday. Your brothers will be here. It's been months since we were last together."

Jim instinctively looked at the calendar. Saturday was June thirtieth, his father's birthday. "Should I bring a gift? It's his birthday." He didn't say his father's name.

"Oh no. Your father doesn't want any fuss. Just his family home for a meal together. And you can bring someone if you'd like ..."

Here we go. "I'll have to let you know. Why did he call me earlier?"

There was silence from his mother. Jim waited. "Mother, why was Dad calling?"

"I ... I don't know exactly."

Jim shook his head. His mother, Maribel Preston, was a Bible-believing Baptist. Had their family in church every Sunday growing up. She didn't believe in telling lies, but he knew she'd just told a whopper.

"Okay, Mom. I'll return his call. No need for you to get involved with whatever he's stirring up."

"Oh, James, you and your dad are so much alike, both too stubborn to listen to the other. Call him on his cell. He should be on his way home from the club. He met some men for breakfast."

"Will do. I love you, Mom."

"I love you, Son. See you Saturday."

Mom hung up before Jim could remind her that he hadn't committed to coming over. *Feisty old lady.*

Jim took a few minutes to refresh his coffee and say a short prayer for peace before he called his father back. Maybe his mother was right, maybe they were too much alike.

"Hello, James Preston here."

"Hello, Father." Jim said as he sat back down in his office chair. "I'm returning your call."

"Yes, took a few days."

"There's a lot going on right now. I had a funeral to attend in Simpson, and we're wrapping up our summer program here at the theater."

"Sorry about the funeral. Listen, your mother would really like you to come to lunch on Saturday."

Mother would like me to come. What about you? It's your seventy-fifth birthday.

"Yes, I returned her call. She extended the invitation. I need to check on a few things before I commit."

"Well ... I know you're busy. I thought it would be nice to have you boys around for a meal." The silence lingered. "How ... how are things going with your theater?"

Is he interested in the theater? When Jim rejected his dad's push to get his degree in business and ended up as a college English professor, his dad didn't talk to him for a month. Then when he walked away from the tenure track to run the theater, his dad threatened to write him out of his will. *Now he's asking about the theater. Something is up.*

Jim smiled. "It's going well. Our partnership with the University of Oakdale has led to a robust internship program. We've added additional patrons who underwrite productions. And we are now on the historic registry, so it will take an act of Congress to take our building."

"Yes, I read about your battle with Planning and Zoning last year. That couldn't have been easy."

Jim relaxed. "It was a challenge. I'm thankful for everyone who rallied for the theater's survival." Then Jim couldn't resist. "Father, what's up? You've never cared about the theater or my job."

"I'm trying to connect with you, Son. Your mother has been on me to make sure I'm not harboring any anger with you boys. I'm just trying ..."

So, this was coming from his mother, not his father caring about his life's passion. Jim sat forward on the edge of his chair. "Dad, I get it. Mom nagged you to call me. You called, we talked. We're good. I'll let you know if I can make it on Saturday."

"James, settle down. Your mother's right, you and I walk on eggshells around each other, and it needs to stop. Clearly, you've made some kind of life for yourself running that little theater."

"See, Dad, there you go, belittling my existence."

"What do you mean? I said you were making a life for yourself."

"No, you said that I'm 'making *some kind* of life for myself running *that little theater*.'" Jim felt the heat crawl up his face. His mother would not be pleased with the direction of this call.

"You know, Son, for someone who believes what he is doing is right, you're very defensive. I'm going to hang up now. Guess we may or may not see you on my birthday."

The phone went silent.

CHAPTER TEN

The week flew by. Nora and Eve got into a rhythm of sleeping in, having a late breakfast and then going out and doing something around Oakdale. Nora's goal was for Eve to feel comfortable with the city and her friends. Maggie had them over for Thursday dinner, giving Eve the opportunity to meet her two kids. Both were younger than Eve. Emma would begin fourth grade in the fall—and Danny the sixth grade. By the end of dinner, it was clear Emma wanted to be like the cool, older girl, Eve. Eve didn't seem to mind, asking Emma about her friends and favorite things to do. Eve was also staying connected with her friends in Simpson.

After dinner, the kids headed to the basement to play a game, and Dan excused himself to the den. Nora and Maggie sat at the kitchen table over a cup of tea and Maggie's shortbread.

"How's it going?" Maggie asked as she served each of them a piece.

Nora grinned. "It's going well. I've taken Eve around to see the gym where Jen works—I think she wants to take a yoga class. And we've been by the theater to see Jim. Sara had her baby there. Eve hasn't talked about her friends back home much. But I know she's texting with them."

Maggie smiled. "Friends become more important in middle and high school. I'm learning that with Danny going into sixth grade. Dan and I attended a parents' night last spring, and the counselor discussed navigating the social scene with our kids. You know, making sure they're running with a friend who won't tempt them into making bad choices."

Nora sighed. "And I'm taking Eve away from all of hers."

Maggie reached across the table and squeezed her friend's hand. "But you'll introduce her to new friends at church, and she'll make friends at high school."

"I know, but she's lost so much and is having to start over. I'd hate for her to feel like she's lost her friends too. Especially if, as you say, they are an important part of her life." Nora looked at Maggie. "The truth is, I have no idea how to raise a teenager."

"You love her, protect her, and guide her into womanhood. None of us gets an instruction manual. I thought Eve was going to spend a few weekends in Simpson with Phillip and Judy, so she could see friends."

"She is. That will help keep her connected while we get her settled here. And ... this is going to sound horrible...but it'll give me a little break." Nora looked across the table at Maggie. "I want to get this right. I'm so worried about not making a mistake that sometimes, I feel like I'm walking on eggshells."

Maggie laughed with a cackle. "Are you nuts? You are going to make mistakes. It will be fine. I promise. Just like Jen and I told Eve, we will be there for you too."

Nora appreciated Maggie's encouragement. "One other thing that I'm trying to figure out. Eve's curious about her dad, Curt. I've answered all her questions. Phillip and I told her about his past. But she's wondering if he's really changed this time."

"What do you think? Has he changed?"

"Who knows? He reeked of whiskey when we last saw him. One thing I do know is that young girls need a strong male influence to help them figure out relationships when they're older."

"You're right. But knowing who her dad is, Eve's going to need to see for herself."

Nora took a final sip of her tea. "We'll figure it out. Now I know why you keep such a long prayer list. This guardian stuff is hard." She finished her dessert. "This was really good. Will you give me the recipe?"

"Glad to. And yes, parenting will keep you on your knees in prayer. It's by God's grace that any of us survive it."

Nora knocked on the half-open door. "May I come in?"

Eve was curled up in her chair, reading with the worn, but comfortable throw over her. "Sure."

"We'll head for Simpson whenever we get up in the morning. No rush. Anything you want to do while we're there? We'll be staying until next Tuesday or Wednesday. Maybe see some of your friends?"

Eve's face lit up. "Can I?"

Nora smiled and nodded. "Of course. I wondered why you hadn't brought it up."

Eve sat back in the chair. "I don't know. You've done so much for me. I don't want you to feel like I don't like it here. But ... but I miss my friends."

"Do they have anything going on this weekend that you'd like to do?"

"Maddie is having a swimming party on Saturday. Could I go?"

"Sure, that sounds like fun. Don't forget to pack your swimsuit. I'll find you a towel to take along. Mom's fixing dinner tomorrow night, so Saturday will work out fine."

Before Nora left Eve's room, Eve had her phone out and fingers flying across the screen, texting her friends. Nora cherished the smile on Eve's face she hadn't seen all week. As Nora left Eve's room, her phone buzzed. It was Curt.

What now? Curt wasn't going to steal this small moment of normalcy with Eve's excitement over seeing her friends.

She sent the call to voicemail and headed for a bath.

Later, Nora settled into bed and reached to put her phone on the charger. When she hit the voicemail button, she immediately regretted it. Curt had been drinking. His slurred angry words practically drooled through the phone.

"You uppity, so-called Christian. You can't keep my daughter away from me ..."

Nora heard the ice cubes clink into the side of a glass. His message went on. *"I'm coming for Eve, and there's nothing you can do. You and that fancy attorney brother of yours. You ain't nothin'."*

Nora's protective instinct peaked to attention. *I don't think so, Curt.* She saved the message and shook her head. Behind the anger was a man full of regrets. She knew that. Perhaps he needed her prayers more than her judgment.

CHAPTER ELEVEN

The next voicemail was in the morning and sounded like a much more sober and polite Curt.

"Nora, please call me back. I'd like to see Eve next time you're in Simpson."

"Who's that?"

Nora whipped around to see that Eve had walked into the kitchen while she played Curt's voicemail with her phone on speaker. "Uh, that was Curt. Seems he'd like to see you this weekend." She stayed her personal feelings.

Eve got a glass of orange juice. Nora watched the young girl's expression.

"I think I'd like to see him." Eve sat on a swivel stool at the island.

Nora's heart sank, but she knew that Eve would be curious until she had a chance to talk to her dad. "Let me talk to your Uncle Phillip about how we can do this." She reached across and touched Eve's arm. "Sweetie, I'm not trying to keep you from him, but I am trying to protect you. You have questions and need to be able to ask them of your dad. We'll sort something out."

Eve nodded. "Okay. I understand."

They finished breakfast, and while Eve went to get ready to leave, Nora called Phillip.

"Curt wants to see Eve, and Eve wants to meet him. How can we make this work?"

Phillip sighed hard. "Are you kidding me?"

"We would love for him to disappear again. But he's not, and Eve is going to keep asking questions."

"Have you called him back?"

"No."

"Okay, let me call him and figure out a time and place they can meet that's very public."

"Fair enough. Thank you. But not Saturday afternoon. Eve's got plans with her friends."

"Got it. See you tonight."

Phillip stared out his office window. *I guess it's normal for a child who lost their mother to want to know their father. Ugh, why did he have to show up again?* He picked up his phone and called Curt. After multiple rings, he answered. Curt sounded half asleep.

"Curt. It's Phillip."

Curt cleared his throat, and his voice perked up. "Yeah, Phillip."

"I heard you called Nora about seeing Eve."

"She's my daughter. I have the right to see her."

Phillip rolled his eyes. "Whatever, Curt. I'm calling because Eve wants to talk to you."

"She does? That's great. When can I pick her up?"

"Slow down a little. There are going to be some guidelines around this."

"Like what? She's my dau—"

Phillip didn't let him finish. "Slow down. You can stop playing the 'she's my daughter' card. Nobody's denying it. But Nora and I have reservations about this whole 'I've changed' thing you've got going."

Curt raised his voice. "Honestly, Phil, I know my past ain't great. But I've gotten it together."

"Here's how this is going to work. There's a restaurant near Liz's that I will bring Eve to meet you for lunch on Sunday. I'll be at a coffee shop within sight of the restaurant."

"Seriously, Phillip? You'll be across the street watching?"

Phillip interrupted him again. "Just stop. This is the only way we will let this happen. I'll text you the restaurant."

Curt dropped his phone on the sofa and rubbed his hands together as he paced around his living room. *This is good. I'll have an hour or so at lunch with Eve to convince her to go to Florida with me. Every teenager wants to hang out at the beach for a week. But even if she wants to go, Nora and Phillip will try to block her.* At the thought of Nora and Phillip, his fury rose. He snatched the whiskey pint from the mantel, unscrewed the top and took a long swig. Curt's frustration escalated—owing Willy and running out of time boiled over. He hurled the empty bottle at the wall and watched as the shattered pieces scattered across the wooden floor. Much like his life.

CHAPTER TWELVE

The house smelled of sweet honeydew melon from the candles Liz loved. Nora stood alone in the middle of the living room with her eyes closed. For a brief second, she pictured Liz buzzing into the room with sweet and salty snacks for one of their movie nights. Nora smiled at the brief memory. When she opened her eyes to the reality before her, an odd sense of peace washed over her. *One step at a time.*

Nora lugged a pile of flattened boxes into the dining room. The silence was as weighty as her grief. The fireplace mantel had a myriad of framed family photos. She picked up one with Liz and Eve. Both were shown in full laughter. They had a sweet relationship. Liz had the unique ability to parent while still knowing when it was time to be goofy. A smile crawled across her lips at the next picture of herself and Liz on Nora's thirtieth birthday—pointy hats and all. Nora sat on the couch, staring at the photo. She could hear them giggling while Seth teased them about hamming it up for the camera. Great memories. But Liz was gone. And so was Seth. Nora slumped on her side with a thick moan. *Why Lord? Why did you take both of them?*

The pain and loss hurt deep in her soul. When the tears slowed, she got up to find a tissue. Crying that hard left her eyes red, puffy, and still wet. The tissue box was empty. Nora stepped into the kitchen for a new box. Turning the corner from the kitchen, she startled. Jim stood in the living room.

"Nora, are you okay?"

Nora wiped her eyes. "Jim." She wadded the tissue. "I must look a mess. Nobody was here and I ..."

He walked over and took her in his arms. "You look beautiful to me. The door was open. Hope it's okay that I came in."

She leaned into his warm strong embrace. Another wave of peace. When Jim let go, she glanced in the mirror and adjusted her ponytail. "I've been away too long. You probably don't remember what I look like."

Jim looked at the floor and then back at Nora. "I hope you're not mad at me for coming. Thought I'd surprise you. Your mom told me where you were." He tried to catch her eye. "Wanted to see you, offer some help. Or I can take you to lunch and head back."

Nora looked around and started to cry again. "I don't know where to start."

Jim pulled her back to his broad chest. "Go ahead and cry it out. You've had quite a couple of weeks." Nora nodded into his shoulder. He had been so understanding since Liz's death and Eve's moving in. His nightly calls always ended with a prayer. Several mornings, Nora awoke to a text from Jim with an encouraging message.

Nora pulled away and went to splash water on her face. Jim found the boxes in the dining room and started putting them together. "Did Phillip find a storage unit?"

"Yes, but we've decided to store everything here for now. Put all the boxes in the garage. Then once we sell, we'll store them until we've had some time and can go through the boxes. It's too soon for Eve, or any of us for that matter, to make decisions on what to keep."

Nora carefully wrapped the china from the dark cherry wood hutch that had been her grandmother's. Jim followed her lead and continued to tape boxes together. Once they were packed and labeled, he carried them to the garage. The two worked in silence for close to an hour, Nora lost in her thoughts. Every now and then, she looked over at Jim. Her need for quiet didn't seem to bother him.

With the hutch empty and the boxes moved, Nora reached for Jim's hand. "Thank you for being here with me."

"Didn't seem like you wanted to talk."

Nora shook her head. "No, I don't know what else to say about all this. I do not know ..."

The front door banged open as Phillip and Eve came in with more bubble wrap and boxes. "I've got more ... oh, hi, Jim. Great, more muscle to help." He set the supplies down and shook Jim's hand.

"Sis, Curt followed us home. We need to go talk with him."

Nora followed Phillip outside. The two walked to Curt's car as he got out. Nora put her hands on her hips. "What's up, Curt? You had your lunch with Eve."

"I was talking to Eve about her school and leaving. I don't think she wants to stay with you. I think she'd rather stay here. You know I've got a place and could make an extra room and could take care ..."

Nora raised her hand. "Stop it, Curt. We're not doing this. Liz made her wishes clear. Eve is going to live with me."

"Now wait one minute. I love my daughter."

"I'm not questioning your love. Just your commitment to parenting."

Curt looked around and rubbed the back of his neck. "This has nothing to do with the trust Liz set up."

Nora smiled. "Didn't say it was. We're talking about what's best for Eve, aren't we?"

Curt nodded too quickly. "Yeah, yeah, it's about Eve." He looked at the small red-brick house for which Liz had worked overtime to save the down payment. "So, you're selling her house."

More money talk. "Yes."

"What are you going to ask for it? Maybe ... maybe I'll buy it. You know, so when Eve is here, she can be in her home."

Phillip couldn't stand it any longer. "Now, wait a minute. We've gone from a simple two-hour meal to her staying with you. I don't think so."

Nora stayed calm. "Curt, you'll have to talk with the realtor."

"What if I bought it from you? You know ... maybe a rent-to-own kind of deal."

Nora grinned. *Not in a million years.*

Phillip stepped in. "I don't think that's in Eve's best interest. That's what we're talking about here—right, Curt? We need to sell the house and put the proceeds in Eve's trust."

"Yeah, the trust." Curt's voice trailed off. "I was just thinking ... ya know, you wouldn't have to be a normal landlord. I'd take care of all the maintenance and stuff." He kept pushing.

Phillip raised his hands. "Curt, no. We are not keeping the house."

"Okay, sorry, trying to think of a way to keep the house Eve grew up in."

Nora shook her head in disbelief. "I'm sure you were only thinking of Eve." She looked back at the house. "We need to get back inside."

"Yeah, I'm going to head out." Curt turned to get in his car and then turned back to Nora and Phillip. His face reddened. "You know this isn't over. I will call an attorney, and we will go to court if I have to."

Nora shrugged. "Do what you think is best."

Curt walked toward his car.

"Don't you want to tell Eve goodbye?" Phillip shook his head.

"Oh ... oh yeah." Curt turned and hustled to the front porch and opened the door. "Eve, I'm leaving, sweetie."

Real devoted dad in this storm your daughter's navigating.

Eve barely came to the door. "Bye." No hug.

Curt passed Nora and Phillip without a word.

Phillip and Nora stood in the driveway and watched Curt drive away in his 1980s Buick, with its taillight attached with red duct tape.

"What was that all about?" Phillip questioned. "Surprisingly, I didn't smell any alcohol on his breath. Not that I got that close."

Nora threw her hands up. "I have no idea. I don't get this sudden interest in being a parent." She redid her ponytail. "All he was focused on was the house and things that had to do with money."

Phillip nodded. "Eve didn't say much on the way back. Maybe she's ready to talk now." They walked inside the house. Jim and Eve were chatting and packing Liz's collection of Precious Moments figurines.

Her answer was simple. "He wants me to stay here in Simpson and live with him." She scrunched her nose.

Nora put her hands on her hips and shook her head. "That man told us you said you didn't want to stay with me."

Eve looked down. "Well, I don't want to leave. But ..." She looked back up at Nora. "I know it's the only way."

Nora gave her a hug. "It'll be a change. Some of it fun, and other parts will be an adjustment. Lots of feelings to be felt. Promise me that we'll talk about how you're feeling, happy or sad, frustrated, whatever you're feeling, and what you want. Like ... like with your dad. He wants to see you again."

"Yeah, I know. It was pretty awkward." Eve shrugged her shoulders. "I didn't know what to say. He said he's going to be away for a few days. Asked me if I wanted to go with him."

Phillip and Jim both stopped in the middle of moving the couch to make space to carry boxes through to the garage.

Eve quickly finished. "I don't want to go with him."

Nora and Phillip sighed in unison.

The four of them worked the rest of the afternoon. There was laughter and a few tears. Eve discovered Liz's high school yearbook on the top bookshelf, which prompted stories from Phillip and Nora about Liz's high school antics. By the end of the day, every room was packed except Liz's bedroom. The door remained closed as if there was a brick wall that no one wanted to climb over. That would acknowledge that Liz was gone forever. Never to sleep in her bed—or to wear her clothes. That blue jean jacket she wore long after denim jackets were out of style would no longer be worn.

Jim and Phillip took a load of boxes to the garage. Eve and Nora simultaneously plopped down on the overstuffed couch. Jim walked in with Phillip on his heels.

"Get a load of these two. You'd think they'd done some work today."

Phillip sat on the floor next to the fireplace. "I'm sure I'll be busy when you move the rest of this furniture. Guess it's all you, Jim."

Jim was about to protest when Nora's phone buzzed with a text.

Nora touched her stomach. "Great. Looks like Mom has dinner ready. What do you say we call it a day?"

Eve lingered as Jim, Nora, and Phillip were headed out the front door. Nora turned back. The sadness in Eve's eyes brought a hitch in Nora's throat. Eve turned and darted into Nora's arms. "How am I going to leave this place? It's ... it's home."

When Jim walked back in, Nora waved to him, mouthing that she would meet him at her mom's.

Eve pulled away and wiped her nose on her sleeve. "We haven't touched Mom's room. I don't ... I don't think I can."

Nora handed Eve a tissue, and her stomach sank. *Lord, give me wisdom.* "I feel the same way. I haven't wanted to go in there yet, either." She picked up her purse. "Why don't we wait until we come back next week. Or some other time. There's no rush."

"Are we leaving tomorrow?"

"I was thinking either tomorrow or Wednesday. Why?"

"I'd like to see my friends again before we go. Is that all right?"

"Sure. Do you want to get a group to go to lunch tomorrow? My treat. I can drive you all and drop you off, then pick you up when you're done."

"Aunt Nora, that'd be great. Thank you."

Nora wiggled her fingers at Eve. "You better get your fingers going and text your friends." She smiled, watching her niece go after it. "Wait a minute, I didn't just volunteer to buy lunch for the entire sophomore class, did I? You were thinking of three or four friends, right?"

Eve nodded and buried her face in the screen.

After dinner, Nora's mother stood to clear the dessert bowls. "You five have blessed me so much tonight. Thank you, Jim, for helping pack Liz's ... Liz's house. I wish I had the energy to be there with all of you. I couldn't bring myself to come over."

No one said a word. They sat in mutual silent grief. Judy stood and gathered the remaining dishes. Nora reached for her mother's hand. "Mom, it's okay. We're all hurting."

Mother set the bowls down, drew a tissue from her sleeve, and wiped her eyes. "I'm going to bed. Good night. I love you. Jim, please be careful going home."

"I will. Thank you for dinner."

Nora walked him to his Jeep to say goodnight. Jim promised to call when he got home or if he got tired on the way. It was only thirty miles, but it was dark, like the night of Liz's accident. *Will the echo of the hospital call ever fade?*

As promised, Jim called when he got home. "I'm home safe and sound. Everyone there in bed?"

"Yes, Eve went to bed a few minutes ago. Mom was practically asleep when I came back in from saying goodbye to you." She yawned. "And I'm about ready."

His voice was soft. "I hope you sleep well."

"Thank you. And thank you for coming over to help."

"Of course, glad to. But admittedly, I do have selfish motives."

"You do?" Nora teased. "Am I about to learn that you have a packing fetish?"

Jim chuckled. "No, my only fetish is for a fledgling community theater." He paused. "I've missed you. But that's not to put pressure, I just wanted to tell you that." He laughed. "I am so bad at this. Have I told you how long it's been since I've dated anyone?"

Now, Nora laughed out loud. It felt good to smile at his warm, awkward words. "You're funny. Thank you. I've missed our time together as well. I'm not sure how all this will work with Eve living with me. We'll figure it out." She yawned again. "I'm sorry, I must be more tired than I thought. Thanks again for your help. Can we talk tomorrow?"

"Sure. Sweet dreams."

Nora fell asleep not long after they hung up. When she awoke, the clock read 3:12 a.m. The house was quiet. She adjusted her covers and pillow, but sleep eluded her. She padded down the hall to the bathroom. Eve's door was open. Nora peeked in to check on her but found only crumpled covers. The bed was empty. Was she downstairs getting a drink of water? No sign of Eve in either the kitchen or living room, Nora's mind reeled. Panic thrashed through her. She raced upstairs and grabbed her cell.

Phillip answered on the third ring.

"Eve's gone."

CHAPTER THIRTEEN

Phillip arrived within twenty minutes of Nora's call. She and her mother were talking and pacing. They'd tried Eve's phone and there was no answer. *Where could she be? Why did she take off? How am I ever going to be responsible for her?*

"How was she when you went to bed? Was she upset? Did you all argue?" Phillip fired questions in quick succession.

Nora rubbed her temples. "She seemed fine. Maybe a little tired."

Mother wrung her hands and stared out of the front window. "This town isn't that big. This hour of the night, nothing's open."

Nora agreed. "How could she have gotten anywhere? She didn't take either of our cars."

"Wait a minute." Phillip dashed through the kitchen and out the back door. Nora looked at her mother, who wore a look of befuddlement. Phillip raced back in.

"She took my old bike. I had cleaned it up for her last week when she wanted to go for a ride."

Nora pressed her palm to her forehead. "Great. Well, now we know how she got to wherever she is." She tried Eve's number again. No answer.

Mother shook her head. "Can't you track each other with your phones now? Didn't you turn something on in mine, so you'd know where I was if we ever had a problem?"

Phillip perked up. "You're right. Nora did you connect the Find My app like I told you to?"

Nora bit her bottom lip. "Yes, I did. Why didn't I think of looking there?"

Within seconds, Nora opened the app to find Eve's location. The red dot was the one place they hadn't considered. Liz's house.

"Oh my goodness. She's gone home. Eve rode your bike three miles in the middle of the night."

Phillip grabbed his keys, and the three hurried out to the SUV.

The single-story house was dark except for the glow from one window on the front right corner. Liz's room. Nora, Phillip, and their mother all rushed out of the car and to the front door. Nora couldn't unlock it fast enough.

Her mother wisely stopped her. "Wait, you don't want to go running in and scaring the girl. Open the door and yell 'hello' so Eve knows it's you."

"Good idea." Nora slowly opened the door. "Eve? Honey, are you here? It's us ... Eve?"

They walked down the hall as Eve came out of her mother's room with a taped, packed box, her earbuds in, singing. When her niece saw Nora and the family, she started, screamed, and dropped the box. That startled the others, and they all screamed. Eve pulled her earbuds out.

"What are you all doing? You scared me to death!"

"What are you doing? It's almost four o'clock in the morning. We were worried about you." Nora's face grew warm, unsure if she was mad or relieved.

Mother moved close to Eve. "Are you okay, sweetie?" She pushed a loose strand of hair behind her ear.

"Yeah, Grandma. I'm sorry I worried you all." Eve looked down at her feet. "I couldn't sleep. Thinking about Mom, and all. I wanted to feel close to her." She waved her hand back at the bedroom. "This was the best I could do."

Everyone sighed and nodded. Being close to Liz's things was the best way to be close to her.

"So, I rode Uncle Phillip's bike over ... I sat in Mom's closet. Her clothes still smell like her. Made me feel like she was close." She hugged her grandmother, who sniffed back a tear. "I'm sorry, Grandma. I just want my mom back."

Her grandmother drew her close. "I know. I want my baby back. I was supposed to be next."

Nora spoke up. "Okay, let's not go there, Mom. Please, I can't think of losing any one of you."

"You're right. I'm sorry." Mom put her arm around Eve's waist.

Eve crossed her arms in front of her and studied the floor.

Nora recognized the denim jacket Eve wore. "Isn't that your mom's old blue jean jacket?"

"Yeah. I think it's the same one she had on in the photo." Eve shrugged and lifted the buttoned front of the jacket to her nose. "It was in the back of her closet, so I put it on."

"You look exactly like your mother in it." Nora crossed the doorway to Liz's room. "You've gotten a good start. But you didn't have to ..."

Eve interrupted. "Yes, I needed to. My counselor has been talking to me about the process of grieving and letting go. You know, the part that comes after all the funeral stuff is over. I didn't know what that would be until I got here tonight. I came to be close to Mom's things. But after I had a long cry, this feeling came over me, an assurance that boxing up her stuff wasn't forgetting her."

Nora shook her head, marveling at the teenager's wisdom. "You're right. Your mother will always be close in our hearts and memories." Nora's tone softened. "But you scared us. Please don't do that again. What you did was dangerous, riding a bike three miles late at night."

Eve nodded. "I know. I'm sorry."

"Are you ready to leave? Let's go get some rest and come back in the morning."

Eve looked around. "Yes ... I'm ready."

The last box was packed. Eve had chosen a few of her mother's personal items to keep. They took her clothing to the women's shelter. The rest was put in storage to go through at another time.

Nora looked at the time on her phone. "Oh, you've got to get cleaned up for lunch with your friends. Are you okay with me wrapping things up here after I drop you off?" Nora continued to be hyper-sensitive to Eve's feelings.

"Yes, but ... but can we stop by before we leave town?"

Nora smiled at her niece. Was it her imagination, or had Eve matured in the last several weeks? She had been outside the hospital door when her mother coded. She held up well with the funeral director and had the will and financial business explained to her. Now she had packed all her mother's worldly belongings. Experiences no teen should have to go through, Eve had done so with grace.

"Sure." Nora's phone buzzed. It was Curt. She declined the call. But not before Eve saw the caller's name.

"What does he want?"

You.

"Willy. I'm in." Curt had a bad feeling about this Florida run. There had been too many arrests and close calls over the years. *My luck is going to give out.* "But this is it, Willy. I pay you what I owe you out of my cut, and I don't want to ever hear from you again."

"Seriously, Butler? If I had a dollar every time I've heard that from you. Can you leave tonight?"

"Yeah." *Rent's late and the landlord's going to throw me out tomorrow anyway.*

"Meet me in an hour, usual place. I'll bring the stuff and enough cash for you to travel."

Curt ended the call without a 'goodbye.' His stomach gnawed. This run had to be the last. *It's enough cash to get everyone off my back. Then I can get a job, and Eve could come to stay with me.* For the first time, Curt's next thought wasn't about Eve's inheritance; it was about Liz. *I can't believe how beautiful our daughter is. You did such a great job. Guess you really didn't need me.* A lifetime of regrets flashed through Curt's mind.

He packed a couple of duffel bags, knowing he probably wouldn't have a place to come back to. He snagged the four remaining beers in the refrigerator and a bottle of whiskey, and he left. *One last run, I hope.*

CHAPTER FOURTEEN

Mr. and Mrs. James Preston Jr. lived in a rural area between Oakdale and Simpson. They owned five acres of rolling fields where they had built a sprawling home with beautiful gardens. Each spring, the cherry blossom trees along their long driveway bloomed in magnificent shades of pink. As Jim turned into the driveway, he took a deep breath. He drove up to the house and parked in the curl of the circular driveway behind his brothers' cars. He awkwardly opened the front door he hadn't darkened in close to six months. "Hello? Anyone home?"

"Jim! You came!" His mother, a stout seventy-year-old woman, came rushing through the front hall and pulled him into a big hug. "I'm so glad you're here. All my boys are home. Makes my heart happy."

The warmth of his mother's hug superseded a gnawing in his stomach that anticipated seeing his father. "Of course, Mom. Good to be here."

She tucked her arm through the bend of his elbow. "Come on into the kitchen. Your brothers are watching me cook, and your dad is out lighting the grill."

The kitchen was bright with white cabinets and wallpaper with a green ivy design on the wall next to the breakfast table. His brother Paul was perched on the counter, and John was leaning against the refrigerator next to the double sink. Opposite the counter was a gas stove and a double oven.

Paul jumped down as their mother turned the corner into the kitchen. "Big Jim! How ya doin', man?"

When Paul hugged Jim, John stepped over with a hug as well. "Good to see you."

As the eldest, no matter what was going on with his father, Jim should stay in touch with his younger brothers. He smiled and returned the hugs. "It has been too long. What are you both up to?"

The three grown men took up the better part of the middle of the kitchen. Jim's mother scooched around them a couple of times while the guys chattered about their lives. His mother gave up her dance. "While you all catch up, can you take the tray of burgers out to your dad?" She handed Jim the tray, and Paul the utensils. "We're eating outside on the patio."

Jim went down two steps out of the back door to the deck with the grill. His dad turned as Jim approached with the tray of burgers and hot dogs. "James. Good to see you."

A warmer greeting than he expected. "Dad. Happy birthday."

"Thank you."

"How'd you get stuck grilling? John, Paul, get over here and help me with the monster grill."

"Really, Jim, you can't handle it?" Paul ribbed.

John stepped up. "You losers step aside. I got this."

Paul and Jim looked at each other. They laughed as they sat at the umbrella table with their dad. Jim shook his head. "Nothing's changed. We could always get him to do our chores."

"He's the baby." Paul took a sip of his iced tea.

"Paul, how's your practice doing? Have the new medical insurance regulations impacted your billing?"

Paul turned to his father. "They haven't seemed to. Our physician leadership team met last week and reviewed last quarter's billings. Everything's on track."

"That's great." He turned to his youngest son. "John, how are things at the firm?"

John flipped a burger and answered over his shoulder. "Going well. I signed a new client last week."

There was a weighty pause in the conversation. Jim fiddled with a twig that had landed on the table. *Dad's making the rounds. How's the medical practice? How's the firm? Can't wait to hear what he asks me, the eldest, and the biggest disappointment.*

"Jim, what's the latest from the theater? How's your partnership with the university?" Dad looked across the table at Jim.

Jim smiled and looked up. "It's going well. We meet regularly to review the progress of the internship program, and they continue to help fund us."

Paul joined the conversation. "How'd you get connected with them?"

Okay, I'm glad to talk about this. Jim nodded. "Last year, the dean of the Arts and Humanities department heard we needed help with our case for historic designation. He spoke highly of our productions and the students we include in productions. That opened our conversations for more structured internships and an opportunity to apply for grant funding." Jim's words quickened as if he was afraid someone would change the subject.

Dad interjected. "How's that work—the grant money. Do you have to request it every year?"

He's asking about details. What is up? "There are administrative deadlines for requesting the funds and then reporting what we use them for and how the results of the program feed into our strategic plan."

Dad nodded. "Interesting."

Mother came bursting through the back door, carrying a steaming pot of baked beans. "Okay boys, my part of lunch is ready. John, are the burgers and dogs ready?"

"Pulling them off the grill now."

Jim took this as his cue to help carry out the rest of lunch.

The five sat at the rectangular umbrella table. Dad took hold of Mother's hand. "Guys, thanks for joining us today." He paused and looked across the sprawling backyard. "I appreciate you taking time to celebrate your old man." His voice cracked at the word old.

Jim's brow furrowed and he looked at his mother. She patted her husband's hand. "Let's say grace."

"Yes, bow your heads."

After praying, everyone was focused on adding condiments to their burgers and hot dogs. Jim's thoughts replayed the conversation about the theater over and over. *Why was Dad so interested in the theater?*

Jim's ever-cheerful mother broke the silence. "Let's have the scoop, boys. When am I going to meet potential wives and mothers for my future grandchildren?"

Paul, John, and Jim looked at each other, then at their mother and shrugged in unison. The family enjoyed a relaxed laugh. She took a sip of tea. "Paul, aren't there any cute nurses around the hospital?"

Paul's eyes widened. "Why am I on the hot seat? Jim's older. Shouldn't he be getting on with marriage and babies?"

Jim tilted his head at his brother. "Really? You're only a couple of years behind me. John, you're the hotshot lawyer. Any cute paralegals?"

John looked at both his brothers. "Seriously? I'm the youngest, it's on you both before me. Besides, I'm busy building our law practice."

Mother waved a white napkin. "Time out."

The brothers laughed. Their father sat at the head of the table with a grin as he watched the interaction.

"Change of subject. I'm going to be redoing the living room and sunroom." Mom took another bite of her dressed burger, then took one of the last two deviled eggs off the tray before passing it to Jim.

Dad shook his head. "She's hiring a designer to come in and ..." He waved his hand in a circle. "... and do whatever they do to change the room and charge us a bunch of money."

"I'm so excited. The design firm is the same one that did the mayor's house last year. Stanton Designs."

Jim coughed and almost choked on the bite of a hot dog. "Stanton Designs?"

"Yes, do you know it?"

"I've heard of it."

CHAPTER FIFTEEN

Phillip and Judy invited Eve to stay with them for the weekend so she could spend time with her Simpson friends. Nora was thankful for the time alone. Most of the time she kept her emotions in check for Eve. Some days that meant crying in the shower where Eve couldn't hear her. On other days, when her emotions were less raw, she worked on Liz's estate. Today was not one of those days. The oppressive heat of July felt like the slog of emotions plaguing Nora. She loaded the soap in the dishwasher and closed it as her phone on the counter buzzed. Her work number displayed on the screen.

"I'm glad I caught you." Phoebe Hays was a senior designer and had mentored Nora over the last year.

"Sure, what's up?"

"I know you're taking some time off with your niece, and I don't want to be insensitive, but a new client has scheduled a meeting and requested you specifically."

Nora felt a flurry of both flattery and energy. It was pleasant to discuss something other than estate closing rules and navigating teenage emotions.

"Don't worry about it, Phoebe. I miss working, and you all have been more than generous with the time I've needed with Eve. Who's the client?"

"Her name is Maribel Preston. She's good friends with the mayor's wife. Evidently, they were at the same party at the country club when Mrs. Watson gave you such a glowing recommendation that Mrs. Preston wants you to redo a living room and sunroom."

Preston. Jim immediately popped into her head. She'd not met his family. He never really talked about them. Was this a relative?

"Okay, I'm sure I can work something out with Eve. When does she want to meet?"

Phoebe hesitated. "That's the kicker. She wants to meet today. Something about getting it done by the fall, so she can have her house ready for Thanksgiving."

"Today ... I'm running Eve to my brother's this afternoon. That'll take a couple of hours with travel, and I need to stop by Mom's to check on her." Nora looked at her watch, almost eleven. "Was there a time that worked for her?"

"She said she's available between one and three. Tony's in today and can be here for introductions at two. Can you make that work? It'll take an hour at most."

Nora did a quick time check. "That should work. As long as Eve and I are on the road by three-thirty, I can be back here for my hair appointment this evening."

Eve. What would she do with Eve while she was in the meeting? She hadn't left her home alone yet. It was only an hour. But they needed to leave for Simpson right after her meeting.

"Phoebe, would it be all right if Eve came with me? She could sit at my desk and wait." Nora drew a breath. "I ... I haven't left her alone yet. I know she's old enough, but ..."

"Say no more. I'd love to meet her. Bring her along, and if she doesn't want to sit and wait, I'll show her around."

"You don't have to babysit ..."

"Really, it's fine, Nora. Bring Eve. The meeting's only an hour. It'll be fine."

"Thanks. I'll ... we'll be there at one-thirty in case Mrs. Preston arrives early."

After the call, Nora went upstairs. Eve came out of her room as Nora hit the top landing. "Good morning."

"Morning." Eve went into the bathroom and shut the door.

Nora finished pulling her hair into a tight knot and adjusted her collar on a mid-weight sweater when Eve poked her head in. "What time are we leaving for hom ... Simpson?"

"Well, a little change in our plans ..."

When Eve opened her mouth to protest, Nora raised her hand. "Hang on. We're still going, but I need to go by the office first. There's a new client who has specifically asked to work with me."

Eve's brows wrinkled. "You haven't worked since I moved here. I forgot you have a job."

Nora smiled, remembering what her counselor had told her. Teenagers lived in their own world. "Yes, I do. And they have been very kind to give me time off. But with this request, I need to go in. So, what I thought we'd do is get your weekend bag together, go have lunch, and then go to the office."

Eve looked at the floor. "Or I could stay here."

Leave her alone. Something was unsettling about the image. Did it remind her that Eve was alone now? Liz was gone. Curt needed to be gone. What if he showed up while Eve was home alone?

"Come with me. You can see where I work and meet my work friends." Nora deflected. "Besides, then I don't have to come back home to get you, and we can get out of town quicker."

Eve nodded. "Okay. Will we leave in time to get to Simpson for dinner? The youth group is doing a pizza party."

"Plenty of time. Text your Uncle Phillip and let him know we'll be there by four-thirty. He knows about your plans for dinner, doesn't he?"

"I texted Aunt Judy on Wednesday when I found out about it. Last time, Uncle Phillip didn't tell her about my plans with friends, and it became a thing."

Nora smiled. "Welcome to lesson one in relationships—communication."

Eve gave Nora a confused look and went to pack.

A wave of comfort and familiarity washed over Nora when she stepped into the office. Work. Normalcy. Doing what she loved in a place she loved being. Interior design hadn't been her career goal. She was going to be a stay-at-home mom. After several miscarriages and multiple fertility doctors, it appeared God's plan wasn't for her and Seth to be parents. God used Nora's love of art to provide her with a career. God knew Eve would need Nora. And Nora would need Eve.

Betsy, the firm's admin and scheduler, was at the reception desk. "Nora!" The young Asian girl popped up from her chair and went around the desk to give Nora a hug.

"Hi, Betsy." Nora came out of the hug. "This is my niece, Eve."

"Good to meet you, Eve."

Eve shuffled her feet. "Good to meet you, ma'am."

"Betsy is studying design at Oakdale University and works here part-time."

Betsy smiled at Nora. "Just like you did. Good to see you." She looked toward the conference room. "Phoebe told me to let you know she has you set up in there."

Nora and Eve headed toward the conference room. Nora turned on the overhead lights to find Phoebe had pulled out some sample boards, including the ones used at the mayor's house. Nora picked up the board. Mrs. Watson had been her first big client.

"Whose house is that?" Eve looked over Nora's arm.

"That is the mayor's house."

"No way! You decorated the mayor's house?"

Nora smiled at the possibility that her coolness factor was on the rise. "Twice, actually. My first project was to design and decorate it for Christmas last year. Gave it a Charles Dickens theme. She liked it so much she hired us to come back and redo her daughters' bedrooms."

Eve nodded and walked around the table, looking at the other sample boards that included pictures of different furniture styles and fabric samples. "So, exactly what do you do?"

Before Nora could explain, Phoebe came in with her laptop. "Nora, thanks for doing this. Tony is thrilled with this opportunity. If Mrs. Preston likes our work, it could open doors to that entire group of country club families." Phoebe's fingers went up in air quotes.

"Well, let's hope we win her over." Nora put her hand on Eve's shoulder. "This is Eve. Eve, this is Mrs. Hays."

Phoebe reached out to shake Eve's hand. "You can call me Phoebe. It's good to meet you, Eve." Phoebe looked down and then back at Eve. "I am so sorry for your loss."

Eve looked at Nora, then back to Phoebe. They had survived the awkward expressions of sympathy in the first few weeks at church. Eve took a deep breath, her bottom lip quivering. "Thank ... thank you."

"Eve, Phoebe offered to give you a tour of the office and workshop while I meet with Mrs. Preston."

"Nora, I didn't know if you brought your laptop. But I've started Mrs. Preston's file. It's in the shared folder."

Nora pulled her laptop from her bag. "Got it right here. Thanks for setting up our file." She looked at her phone. "She should be here shortly. Let me take a look at your notes." She turned to Eve. "You okay with a tour?"

"Sure."

Eve followed Phoebe out of the conference room, and Nora settled in the chair at the head of the table to review the notes.

"You look in charge sitting at the head of the table." Tony Stanton was in the doorway wearing a tailored black suit and gray tie with purple diagonal stripes. He was always dressed in a suit and ready to meet the most affluent clients.

Nora stood and smiled. "Feeling more like jumping back in the deep end. Thought I was over the pre-first-meeting jitters with the mayor's wife. Now, I feel like the pressure is doubled with a referral."

Tony motioned for her to sit. "I didn't mean to interrupt. You're going to do fine. Just be yourself and listen to what she's looking for."

"Thank you for your vote of confidence." Nora fiddled with her laptop. "And thank you for all the time off. I know you didn't have to do that."

"For what it's worth, I know a little something about tragic losses."

Nora tilted her head with a slow nod. Other than meeting his wife at the Christmas party, she knew nothing of his personal life. He was a caring and encouraging boss who treated his staff well.

"Thank you. We're getting settled in, and if you're all right with it, I'd like to start back with some flexibility until school starts."

"Secure this client, and you're going to have to start back. She wants you." Tony pointed at Nora and smiled. "Yes, we'll work it out."

The conference room phone lit up with Betsy saying Mrs. Preston was in the reception area. Nora and Tony went to greet her.

"Mrs. Preston, it's a pleasure to meet you. I'm Tony Stanton." Tony and Mrs. Preston shook hands.

Maribel Preston was dressed in a summer knit pink dress, with a white jacket and matching purse. She wore low-heeled, white, open-toed shoes. Her gray hair was perfectly styled with soft curls off her face. Smile lines around her eyes deepened as she reached to shake Tony's hand. "Good to meet you as well. I've heard such wonderful things about your firm."

Tony returned the smile. "Our firm is only as good as our designers. I have to admit, we have the best." He gestured toward Nora. "This is Nora St. Claire. She's been with us close to two years. She started while she was in school. After she graduated and began working with clients, she earned a promotion to senior designer."

Nora looked into Mrs. Preston's eyes and saw it immediately. Jim's eyes. To stay focused, she shook the thought from her mind and extended her hand. "So good to meet you."

Mrs. Preston shook her head. "The mayor's wife raved about your work. I didn't know it at the time, but I saw some of your work when James and I were at their Christmas party."

Nora's eyes grew wide. James? Jim? She was Jim's mother. "Um ... Yes, we decorated their house for Christmas and then went back to do the girls' rooms."

"Hopefully, you can help me out. I'm looking to redo our living room and sunroom."

"Let's go to the conference room and you can tell me what you're thinking. Would you like something to drink?"

"A glass of water would be nice. It is blazing hot today."

Betsy took her cue to get the water. Tony stepped back. "I'm going to let you get started. You're in good hands, Mrs. Preston." He looked at Nora. "If you need me, I'll be in my office."

As they approached the conference room, Mrs. Preston looked at Nora. "St. Claire. I don't know any St. Claires, but I feel like I've seen you somewhere. What does your husband do?"

When a police officer was shot, it made the news. "I'm not married. My husband was killed in the line of duty six years ago."

Mrs. Preston snapped her fingers. "Yes, I remember that. It was all over the news. I remember seeing a picture of the two of you in the paper. What a horrible loss."

Nora's lips tightened. She looked out the window, giving the fresh knot in her stomach a second to settle. The media was so hard to take during the trial for the man who had shot Seth. "Yes, ma'am. Seth was my husband."

Mrs. Preston reached over and touched Nora's arm. "I'm so sorry."

"Thank you." Nora took a deep breath. "Let's get started on the vision you have for your home."

Nora and Mrs. Preston spent the better part of the next hour talking about Mrs. Preston's vision of updates to the living room and sunroom. When the doors that separated the two spaces were open, it would need to feel like the same space, and the sunroom to be more like a den, but also needed to allow for her to close the doors connecting the two rooms and still have a well put-together look. Their conversation flowed easily. Nora took notes about colors and furniture styles. Mrs. Preston was ready to empty the rooms and start with new wall color, carpet or flooring, and new upholstery or new furniture.

As they were wrapping up, Tony stepped into the room. "How's it going?"

Mrs. Preston stood and smiled. "I like her. She seems to understand what I'm looking for."

"Like I said, Nora's one of the best."

Nora shook her head. "Thank you both. Mrs. Preston, let me get ideas drafted, but I need to come out and do some measuring. Based on what you said, this is a large space. I'd like to do a drawing to help with the design. From that, we can do a formal proposal."

"Sounds great. Can you come next week?"

Nora smiled. "Certainly. What day works for you?"

"Tuesday morning. Would ten o'clock work for you?"

"I will see you then."

"Mrs. Preston, I'll walk you out." Tony and Mrs. Preston headed back to the reception area.

The sample boards were stacked and her laptop put away when Phoebe and Eve came in chattering. A guilty twang pulled on Nora's heart. For the last hour, she had put aside worries of Eve and dealing with Curt. *It felt good.*

Nora pulled into Frieda's Hair Salon with one minute to spare. After she left Eve with Phillip and Judy, she stopped by to check on her mother. Unfortunately, her mother wasn't having a good day. Even with her activities and friends, her heart hurt, and she was sad.

Mother dabbed a tissue to her nose. "Some days, I need to cry."

"I understand. As strong as I want to be for Eve, some days, I can't wait for her to fall asleep, so I can have a good cry."

What was going to be a thirty-minute visit became an hour. It was an important hour. Her mother shooed her out. "It's Friday night, surely you have someplace more fun than sitting with a blubbering old lady."

Nora shook her head. "Mom, if you need me, I'm here. Plans can change."

After Mom insisted she was fine, Nora left. But not before a hug and an "I love you."

The "I love yous" among Nora, her mother, and brother had increased in meaning with the loss of Liz.

On the thirty-minute drive back to Oakdale, Nora thought about her date the next night with Jim. *Jim.* He had been so accommodating and flexible with Nora's need to stay close for Eve. Any "date" time had been sitting on her back patio after Eve had settled in front of a movie, or they had taken her with them. He was trying, and she could tell. But tomorrow, it would be just the two of them. She had chosen a special outfit. Maybe she would have Frieda show her how to add a little curl to her hair.

Nora grabbed her purse and hustled into the salon. It smelled of perm solution and herbal shampoo. Fridays brought the buzz of busyness and chatter about the weekend. Frieda was at the front when Nora whooshed through the door.

"I'm so sorry, am I late?" Nora looked at her watch.

"You're fine, right on time. I was running a little ahead, so I thought I'd come up to greet you."

Nora seldom changed her hair style, but it was refreshing to have clean ends on her straight, dark brown hair. Frieda finished in about forty-five minutes and included a quick lesson on adding loose curls.

As Nora checked out and gathered her purse, she took another look in the mirror—curls, a fresh look, for a new beginning.

CHAPTER SIXTEEN

Jim linked his fingers with Nora's as they exited the Italian restaurant in downtown Oakdale. As they approached the end of the brick sidewalk, a horse-drawn carriage pulled to a stop. He led her to step up into the carriage. Nora looked at him in surprise.

"Care for a ride?" Jim winked at her as she accepted his assistance into the carriage, where she sat on the leather bench seat behind the driver.

The humidity of the afternoon had been overcome by the cool evening. Jim put his arm around her and drew her close. "Did I tell you how lovely you look tonight? I like your hair with curls."

Nora felt a blush crawl up her cheeks. She touched the curl at the end of her long locks and sighed. "Thank you. Thought I'd try something new." They rode in silence. With the rhythmic clop of horse hooves, Nora relaxed into Jim's side.

"I've missed our date nights. Having you all to myself."

His words pricked Nora's heart. *Eve.* For the second time in the last two days, she found herself not worrying about Eve, but his words ... was Jim getting tired of Nora's new situation?

"It's been an adjustment. I appreciate Phillip and Judy having her with them this weekend." Nora sat forward. "Don't get me wrong. I love having her with me. But usually when you become a parent ..." Her fingers made air quotes. "It's from the beginning, not from a teenager." She smiled and turned to look at Jim. "Lots of emotions even beyond her grief."

Nora noticed Jim's odd expression. "What's wrong?"

The carriage pulled to a stop back at the restaurant. Jim tipped the driver, took a long step down, and extended his hand to help Nora out. The valet had pulled Jim's car to the curb for them. Jim opened the car door for Nora without a word.

The question rolled around in Jim's mind. *What's wrong? Nothing with you, or you and me together. I don't want to have kids. But this is different. This is Nora stepping up to fulfill her dead sister's wishes. And now, I'm being selfish.*

They arrived at Nora's house. Jim pulled into the driveway and turned off the car. He took off his seatbelt and turned to Nora, reached for her hands. The streetlamp at the edge of her yard gave a soft glow. Jim looked into her eyes.

"Nora, we've had an amazing time together. I love being with you." He looked down. He had fallen for her. He didn't love being with her—he loved her. The undeclared emotion would have to wait. He needed to be sure. Not like the last time he thought he was in love. What a fiasco with him, Mandy, and his parents. "This has been an adjustment for me ... I'm not trying to be selfish. You have been through something no one should have to go through. Your entire family has. But I'm not sure how we move forward now that ..." He saw tears nudge the edge of Nora's eyes.

"Now that what?" Her voice was tight. "Now that I have Eve?" Her voice raised, "Are you telling me you don't like children? Or just me having Eve?"

Jim looked away. Nora continued, "Tell me, Jim. Are you breaking up with me because of Eve?" Her hurt tone turned into anger. "You don't want me to have to choose between the two of you. You will lose. She needs me. Liz ..." The tears slid down her cheeks. "My sister needs me."

Jim had no words. *How did this conversation go so wrong?*

"You have nothing to say? Fine."

Before Jim could say a word, Nora snatched her purse, got out of the car, and slammed the door shut.

Jim watched her deliberate steps to her front door. Inside, she closed the door. He was closed out. *What have I done?*

Nora couldn't get her keys into the lock and get into her house fast enough. Every ounce of her wanted to be away from Jim. *Jim.* He had been so patient. So kind to Eve. *It was all fake.* She paced around her living room, talking aloud to herself, or God, if he was listening. "I cannot believe I let myself get close to him. To love ... him. Now I see how selfish he is. Really, is that who you want me to be with? Seth was never ..." The sobs came. Nora melted onto her couch. "Oh, Seth, why did you leave me? Liz ... I want to call my sister and talk to her about Jim. Now Jim has left too." *Am I always going to be alone?*

Jim sat in silence. He shook his head. *That didn't go well. I am such an idiot.* He turned the key and slowly backed out of her driveway. He drove around the block. Should he go to her door or not? Would she even answer? "Lord, I am so bad at relationships. Always have been. But then you brought me Nora. She's smart, she's beautiful, and she loves you. And now I've blown it."

As if God was answering his prayer for help, Dan came to mind. Jim had gotten to know Dan through a couple of golf outings with Mark, church men's night out, and Dan and Maggie's cookouts. For a bank executive and an IT manager, Dan and Mark were handy with tools and had helped with a couple of projects at the theater. He checked the time, nine-thirty. Not too late. He gave Siri the command to call Dan Nelson. Dan answered on the second ring.

"Jim, what's up?"

Jim didn't know where to start. "Well, brother, I've blown it with Nora. Any chance you've got a few minutes to impart a little relationship wisdom on me?"

Dan chuckled. "Not sure about wisdom, but I've learned a thing or two in twenty or so years of marriage. What happened?"

Jim continued to drive home while he talked with Dan. At one point, he heard Dan tell Maggie it was him on the phone. In his heart, he prayed for clarity. His heart had been closed for many years. The years following the Mandy mistake. Mandy was a mistake from the start. It was a relationship that was approved by their parents. Mandy came from the right family. As if leaving med school for a higher degree in English literature wasn't enough, breaking up with Mandy solidified the wedge between Jim and his father. Their relationship came down to Mandy wanting the doctor husband, not the professor husband. Nora was different. She fit into his lifestyle. He loved her, and now, he was afraid he'd lost her.

"I think I blew it with Nora tonight. Completely blew it."

"I don't know Nora as well as Mags does, but I'd be surprised if you completely blew it. What happened?"

"Well, we had a delightful dinner and horse-drawn carriage ride through downtown."

Dan chuckled. "Nice romantic touch. You're making the rest of us guys look bad. Go on."

"We went back to her house, and ... well, let me back up. On the carriage ride, she said learning to parent a teen was not the usual start you get with a baby. With a teen, you have to just know how to parent. What you don't know about me is I don't want children. Getting parenting right without heaping your own expectations on the child ... it's too hard."

"Interesting take on parenting. But, go on."

"I tried to share this with Nora, but my words got stuck. And I didn't say anything, then she accused me of not liking children, or was it Eve I didn't like. There were tears, and she stormed out of the car and into her house." He took a deep breath. "I am so bad at relationships."

Dan left a long pause. "Do you remember last fall when Maggie wanted to volunteer at the theater, and I didn't want her to because it didn't work for me and my schedule? I was in my perfect world, and something she wanted rocked our orderly life."

Jim nodded. "Yeah, you and I didn't get off to a great start, with all I was asking Maggie to help with."

"That's true, but not where I was going. Maggie was sharing her heart with me. She was struggling with the amount of time she gave to the family—there was no time for her to be herself. For her to do something special. But what I heard in my selfish bubble was that she wasn't going to be available for whatever and whenever I needed her. We all come at relationships with our own needs and wants. But to make it work, sometimes we have to deal with whatever the block is. Sometimes the block is us, sometimes it's them, and sometimes the circumstances."

Jim was quiet. He pulled into his driveway, rolled the windows down and turned off the car. "I've blown it, Dan."

"Wait a minute. What did you say a few minutes ago about parenting and parents heaping their expectations on their children? Where does that come from? Maggie and I don't heap expectations on our kids. We love them and raise them with the appropriate discipline and guidance."

Jim explained his parents' expectations to Dan. "That's what my parents did. My brothers and I were expected to do well in school, date girls from the right families, and become either doctors or lawyers. My brothers did that. I didn't. I became a college professor. Which was enough status, not great, but enough. But when I resigned to take over Oakdale Theater and broke off a pre-engagement with Mandy Baldwin—that didn't sit too well with my parents."

"You were engaged to Mandy Baldwin, of the Baldwin family? The family that revived and restored our park system in Oakdale?"

Jim nodded. "The one and only. It's been ten, no, fifteen years ago. But we weren't engaged. We dated for quite a while, and our parents started talking about a wedding. Next thing I knew, my mother was giving me my grandmother's engagement ring. Mandy is beautiful and I enjoyed her company, but I knew we didn't want the same things in life." He looked at Dan. "We didn't want the same lifestyle. She was all about country clubs and social circles. I wasn't."

"It's good you figured that out sooner rather than later. Now, think about Nora. Think about where she's coming from. She's lost a husband, her father, and now her sister. She's stepped up to take care of her niece in the midst of her own grief. What do you think she heard when you were talking about family?"

Jim's cheeks expanded, and he blew out a sigh, shook his head, and swiped his hands across his face. "Of course, she heard me say I didn't like kids and didn't want them in my life. She marched into her house, and I left."

"Do you want to work it out with her? When you and Mandy came to a lifestyle crossroads, you broke up. You didn't want to figure out how to make it work to be together. Do you feel that way now?"

"No, Nora and I were having fun spending time together and getting to know each other before Liz's death. I didn't want it to end. And I've loved the time we've had, even with Eve here."

"Now the situation has changed. Nora's the same woman, but she has added responsibility. A responsibility she takes very seriously. Are you going to love and support her through it? Are you going to pray through the changes and how God is directing you both? Or will you let her go?"

"I don't want to lose her."

"That's a great place to begin. Admit what you want, how you messed up, and how you can do better. Talk to Nora. Open your heart to her. And be ready to hear what's in Nora's heart."

"You're right. Thank you for shedding light on what I was being too selfish to see."

"Glad to help. See you in church tomorrow?"

"Yes, sir."

They hung up. Before Jim got out of the car to go inside, he messaged Nora. *I'm sorry. Please forgive me. Can I take you to lunch after church?*

He had hoped to get an immediate response. But there wasn't one.

Curt had crossed into Oakdale on Interstate 65. The trip back from Florida was a success. He'd made the drug connection and had enough cash on him to cover Willy's part. He'd have a couple thousand dollars left to start over. *Again. But this time will be different. I'll have Eve and her money to start over with.* The ten-hour drive without air conditioning was boring, and he had finished the beer he'd bought in Alabama. The six-pack had barely given him a buzz. *Eve. I've got to see her again.* He picked up his phone and called Nora. No answer. No surprise. *She's going to keep my daughter from me. Great dad you were, hustling pool. Staying out all night.* A flare of anger pressed at Curt, and he pressed on the accelerator.

Halfway through Oakdale, Curt eyed the whiskey bottle lying on the passenger's seat. *No need to let the last of my whiskey go to waste.* He lit a cigarette, put his elbow out the driver's side window.

He popped over a hill when a police car pulled in behind him. Curt rolled his eyes. *Please just go around me.* No such luck. The red lights came on, and Curt slowed to pull onto the shoulder.

His heart raced, his eyes jetted around the car to see if there was a way to hide the whiskey. Curt reached over and shoved the bottle toward the gap between the passenger's seat and door. It got wedged halfway down. The top poked over the seat. *Maybe he won't notice.*

The officer approached the driver's side. "Sir, you came flying over that hill. I clocked you at ninety miles an hour."

Curt knew the drill. Until otherwise told, he kept his hands on the steering wheel. "Didn't realize that, sir. I'm on my way back into town to pick up my daughter. Her mother was tragically killed in a car wreck, and I need to get to her."

"License and registration, please."

Curt pulled his license from his wallet and reached into the glovebox for the car registration.

The officer leaned closer as Curt handed him the documents. "Here you go."

"Sir, have you been drinking?"

"I had a couple of beers with lunch three hours ago."

"Please step out of your car."

Curt followed his request, but when he stood up out of the car, he felt light-headed and stumbled. *A hangover, no food, and a six-pack of beer will do that.*

The officer looked at Curt's license. "Mr. Butler, please wait right there."

The officer walked back to his car, got in, and picked up his radio. Curt leaned against his car. The summer sun was hot, but the breeze from the whizzing traffic offered some relief. *Get it together, or this could be really bad.*

The officer got out of his car. As he walked toward Curt, two more state trooper cars arrived along with a tow truck. The officer stood on the white line at the shoulder of the road. The other officers stood opposite him. "Mr. Butler, would you please walk on the white line toward me?"

He took three steps toward the officers on the white line but stumbled on the fourth and fifth step.

"Mr. Butler, should I bother with the breathalyzer? I can smell it on you."

Curt knew defeat. "No." Curt shook his head in an attempt not to puke on the officer.

"You know the drill." The officer turned Curt around, handcuffed him, and read him his Miranda rights. Not the starting over Curt had fantasized about.

There's no one left to call.

CHAPTER SEVENTEEN

Nora walked into the church sanctuary and did a quick scan of the rows, looking for the one where she and Jim usually sat. Her eyes were immediately drawn to the back of his short, wavy, brown hair. Maggie and Dan were sitting behind him. Maggie had called her last night to check on her.

"I don't know exactly what the guys are talking about. Dan only had the call on speaker long enough for me to hear your name, and something about Jim feeling like he'd blown it with you. Want to talk about it?"

Nora's voice was tired. "Oh, Maggie. I've probably blown it with him. Maybe this isn't a good time for us to be in a relationship." She sniffed the last of her tears. "It's all so much to handle right now."

"I'm sure it is. I can't imagine."

"He's been so great this whole time. He's been there when I needed him and has given me space when I needed it." Nora was quiet for a minute. "But tonight, when he started talking about family and children and how he'd never wanted any, it hit me. I now have a child I'm responsible for." She pulled a tissue from the box. "Hearing that triggered something in me. I got upset and ran out of the car."

"Nora, let me ask you an honest question. If you don't want to answer it, that's fine, but I'd like you to think about it."

"What is it?"

"Do you think your response was out of fear? If Jim doesn't want children, are you afraid he'll break it off with you? So instead, you ran away from him."

Nora was silent. Maggie was silent. Nora shook her head. No truer words had been spoken. Maggie knew her well. "Mag, I don't know ... maybe. What I do know is it scares me how much I care for Jim. And right now, I'm in a storm and trying to do everything perfect with Eve."

"That's a lot to handle for anyone. But especially when you have old wounds."

"You're right. It's tiresome guarding my heart."

"Jim is as well, Nora. He's not had an easy relationship journey. Nothing as heartbreaking as losing a spouse, but he's guarding his heart."

Nora sniffed again. Her eyes ached. "Yeah. Maybe."

"I know it's late. I'm glad to stay on and talk more if you want, but you sound beat. Will you pray about what happened with Jim and how God is leading you?"

Nora sighed and pulled her feet under the throw on the couch. "I'm very tired and ready to sleep. Thank you for calling. You've given me lots to think about. I'll see you at church."

The next morning on the way to church, Nora thought about Jim's text. He had reached out with five humble words. *I'm sorry. Please forgive me.* This was Nora's moment of truth. Would she trust God's continued leading toward a renewed life? Or would she close her heart and not accept the blessing of a Godly man in her life?

The pre-service music was her cue to take a seat. She took a deep breath, a step of faith, and slid into the open seat next to Jim.

After church, Dan and Maggie slid out of their seats to leave. Maggie reached across the pew to hug Nora. Dan shook Jim's hand.

Nora sat down and turned toward Jim, who took his seat again. He looked into her eyes. The connection stirred in Nora's heart. *But I'm scared.* She sighed and looked down at his hands. She reached for them. His warm, strong hands. "Thank you for your text. I want to apologize to you for running into the house. I'm sorry."

Jim reached to lift her chin, bringing their eyes together. "Forgiven. Will you forgive me?"

Nora's lips curled into a grin. "Forgiven." Their fingers intertwined. Her voice was soft. "Now what?"

"Do you have time for lunch, and a conversation?"

Nora felt her heart begin to open. They needed to talk this out to move forward together. "Sure. Phillip's bringing Eve home tonight. So, I've got all afternoon."

"Do you want to get deli sandwiches and go down to the river?"

"Sounds wonderful. But I'd like to change clothes first. Do you mind picking me up at my place?"

Jim returned her smile. "Glad to."

Nora stood and took a deep breath. "I'll see you shortly ... and thank you."

Nora hustled home, changed into shorts and a cotton T-shirt. She brushed and braided her hair. As she finished applying sunscreen on her arms, the doorbell rang.

They found a shady spot on the riverbank where trees were growing out over the water. Jim spread a red blanket that boasted the University of Oakdale mascot. Nora set the box lunches and drinks on the edge and sat down. Jim sat next to her, and the two watched a barge loaded with shipping containers roll downriver. Nora touched her stomach to quash a rumble.

He leaned over to touch shoulder to shoulder. "Ready to eat?" He chuckled.

Nora's eyes widened. "You heard that?"

Jim laughed. "Yes, don't be embarrassed."

Nora felt her cheeks warm. "I'm sorry. Guess I'm hungrier than I thought."

They sat facing each other. Nora crisscrossed her legs. Jim handed her the box containing the turkey club and chips she'd ordered.

Jim opened his box and the conversation they both had shied from during the car ride. "Nora, I am sorry for last night. It wasn't a lie. I've never wanted children."

Nora stared out at the river. Here it comes. *He's going to break up with me. Did he bring me out today, to have a wonderful lunch, and break it off?* She shook her head. She began to say something, but Jim stopped her.

"Wait. Before you say anything, please let me finish." His voice was soft. "I've told you very little about my family and the way I was raised."

"All you've told me is that you and your parents aren't close."

"We used to be until I zigged, and my dad expected me to zag. When I didn't go into medicine and chose to teach at the collegiate level, Dad didn't like it, but it was good enough for my parents' status expectations." He looked out at the river, where jet skiers were weaving back and forth across the water. "Expectations. They were a big deal with my parents. The right schools, professions, and even who we'd marry." He reached for her hand. "That was the image of parenting I've carried. Loading kids with our expectations. I never felt like my parents took time to enjoy my brothers and me for who we were created to be. They had a plan for our lives and how we would live. I never wanted to be a parent, because that was the example I had of parenting." Jim shrugged.

Nora tucked a loose wisp of hair behind her ear. "I get that. You've made your own choices with your profession. Why don't you think you'd make your own choice on how to parent?"

Jim smiled and looked at Nora. "I love the way you look at things. No, I never considered I would parent differently."

Love. He'd never used that word. Nora's heart warmed. "My parents' methods were old school. When Seth and I were trying ..." Nora grew silent and sighed. "I read books and decided the parts of parenting I would adopt from them, and what I would do differently. When you boil down all the theories and psychobabble, children need to know they are loved, their needs will be met, and who they can count on." Nora looked directly at Jim. "That's what I'm going to do for Eve."

Jim took a deep breath. "I know. That's exactly what I would expect you to do. You are already doing a great job with her." A squirrel scurried close. Jim tossed the crust from his sandwich. The squirrel snatched it on his way to the tree trunk. The diversion gave the two a reprieve in the conversation.

Nora felt her heart rev. "Jim, please say it. Are you breaking up with me?"

"No." Jim sat up from leaning on his elbows. "I don't want to lose you ... I think ... I think I'm falling in love with you, Nora ... and it both excites me and scares me."

Nora looked around. He'd said it. Love. He was falling for her. The summer sun drilled into her warming heart, to pull it fully open. "Oh, Jim. I'm falling for you. And ... and I'm scared. After all the loss, I'm afraid to open my heart and risk loving you."

Jim reached over to caress Nora's face. "Look at us, a couple of scaredy-cats. You always seem so confident."

"If you could only feel how tight my stomach has been. I feel like I've been walking on eggshells, not wanting you to see my true feelings and questions about your feelings."

Jim leaned closer, and they shared a gentle kiss. "I do love you."

Nora took the full step of faith toward the man she knew God had brought. "I love you too." She sat back. "But I do have Eve now. I won't compromise what I need to do for her."

"I wouldn't expect you to. I need to support you in what you need to do for Eve. Can't promise I'll be great at it. But I'll try."

Nora grazed his arm with her hand. "That's all I can ask ... and what I will pray through and try better to do is not lump all my fears on you. That's not fair to you."

Jim held Nora's hand. "We both have some praying to do."

Nora pulled the iced sugar cookies out of the bag and handed Jim one of them. Each enjoyed the dessert in silence. Nora thought about what Jim had shared about how his parents had raised him. His mother hadn't seemed demanding or snobbish when they met at Stanton Designs. She finished her cookie and dusted the crumbs from her lap.

"I didn't tell you this, but I met your mother on Friday."

Jim's brow came together. "Where?" His eyes widened. "Don't tell me you're going to do her design work."

Nora sat up straight. "Is that a problem? She and I had a delightful meeting."

"Did you tell her who you ..." Jim rubbed the back of his neck. "Did you tell her about us?"

"No, I didn't. It wasn't appropriate for a professional meeting. And yes, I am going to be her designer. Is that a problem for you?" Her question was direct.

Jim sighed. "No. I don't think so. But ... but would you not say anything about us? I want to be the one to tell them."

Nora smiled. "Are you worried I won't live up to their expectations?"

"Remember, you just challenged me to decide for myself. I am, and I have. I choose you. It's that the dynamic with them gets weird sometimes. Please, let me find a time to take you over as my girlfriend, and introduce you."

"Okay, but I'm not going to lie. If she asks personal questions, I'm going to answer honestly."

"Fair enough." Jim grew quiet. Another barge, weighted down with coal, passed. The breeze lessened, and the heat grew intense. "We should probably head home. Eve will be there soon."

"Yes." Nora wanted to go back to the moment of sharing their love. "Thank you for a delightful picnic. You picked a great spot."

Jim stood and reached down to pull her up. Nora popped up and into him. They laughed and he pulled her close. The warmth wasn't just from the sun anymore.

CHAPTER EIGHTEEN

Nora hustled around her house picking up, straightening the throw pillows, and emptying the dishwasher. Eve had texted her that she and Phillip were on their way. From hearing Jim say "I love you" to looking forward to hearing how Eve's weekend went, she felt lighter than she had in several months.

Her phone buzzed. No caller ID. "Hello."

"We have a collect call from the Oakdale jail for Nora St. Claire from Curtis Butler. Will you accept the charges?"

Are you kidding me? How desperate is he to be calling me to bail him out? Nora shook her head. Before she thought twice, the word escaped. "No." With the one small word, the line went dead, but she was enlightened. No wonder there had been no word from Curt.

The rug got the brunt of her frustration over Curt trying to call from jail. She vacuumed the living room at least three times. By the time she realized what she was doing, emptied the vacuum canister, and put it away, she had calmed down. *Maybe I should be praying for him. That's pretty sad to only have me to call from jail.*

As she put the vacuum away, thoughts of Curt vanished, and the headlights from Phillip's SUV swiped across the living room as he pulled into the driveway. Nora headed for the front porch.

"Welcome back!" Nora called as Eve got out of the truck.

"Hi, Aunt Nora." Eve hurried to the door and into the house. Phillip followed her, carrying Eve's duffel bag.

"I'm delivering to you one teenager who has had a big weekend."

Nora looked at Eve. "Yeah, was it a good one?"

Eve nodded excitedly. "It was so much fun."

"I can't wait to hear about it."

Phillip dropped the duffel bag and hugged his sister. "I'd love to stay, but I'm going to head back. Need to take care of a few things before work tomorrow."

Nora tilted her head to try and read something more in his rush to get home. Eve went into the living room and plopped down on the couch. Nora walked Phillip to the door. "Everything go okay this weekend?"

"Everything with Eve went great. We had some family time with Mom, and she had time with her friends. She seems to be doing well." He put his hands in his pockets.

"How's Mom? I talked to her yesterday."

"Mom's doing all right. Her friends from church are trying to keep her busy. Judy has her over for dinner with us once or twice a week." He looked at his feet. "She misses Liz as much as we do."

"One thing you need to know. I got a collect call from Curt at the Oakdale jail a few minutes ago."

Phillip leaned closer and spoke in a hushed tone. "Are you kidding me? Did you take the call?"

"No. There was no reason for me to pay for a call to have him try and get me to bail him out."

Phillip rubbed the back of his neck. "I guess you're right. But why call you? He's got to know that neither of us would bail him out."

"You would think. But anyway, we know where he is and why we haven't heard from him."

"That's true. Are you okay?"

"Yeah. I'm fine." Nora hugged Phillip. Phillip left, and Nora closed and locked the door. She headed to the couch and dropped down next to Eve.

"It was a good weekend?"

"Aunt Nora, it really was. Busy, and fun. Let's see, Friday night was pizza with the girls from the youth group. Then Saturday afternoon, I got together with Zoe and Mary from school. Saturday night, Aunt Judy, Uncle Phillip, and I went to Grandma's for dinner. And today after church, I went to lunch with some of my other friends from the youth group."

"Wow, you really packed the weekend. Sounds fun." Nora patted Eve's knee.

Eve sighed. "It was good." Eve pulled her knees into her chest and wrapped her arms around them.

"Are you hungry? I went to the grocery store. Stocked up on your favorites."

"No, thank you. Uncle Phillip drove through for burgers and fries when we left Simpson. Aunt Nora, Zoe and Mary were talking about the classes they were taking this year in school. We haven't talked much about school or where I'll go."

"Oh, umm, school. I've been so focused on your mom's estate I haven't called the school district office to see where you'll go. I need to make sure of the documents they'll need from me as your guardian." Nora looked at Eve's drawn eyebrows. "We'll get it figured out. I promise. Do you know where any of the kids from the youth group here go?"

"Not really. I've heard a few talk about Oakdale East."

Nora's only experience with schools in Oakdale was when she redesigned the teachers' lounge at Anchor Academy, the private elementary school Maggie and Dan's kids attended. "Tell you what. I'll call Maggie and ask her about getting you registered for school. I do know school doesn't start until mid-August. So, you've got three weeks. Anything you'd like to do?"

"Uncle Phillip and I are going to run a mini-marathon on Thanksgiving. It's too hot to run outside. Do you think it would be okay for me to use Jen's gym?"

"A mini-marathon. That's a big goal. How many miles is that?"

"Thirteen point two. You want to join us?"

"Thirteen miles! Thanks, but no thanks. Your Uncle Seth used to run to stay in shape for the police force. I'll be your fan at the finish line."

"You think I can use the treadmill at the gym until the weather breaks?"

"I'm sure. Let me text Jen." She picked up her phone and texted Jen.

"I'm going to go unpack." Eve stood, picked up her duffle bag from the bottom step and went up to her room.

Nora dialed Maggie. "Hello, Mag." She chuckled. "One detail of being responsible for a child I've failed to cover."

Maggie echoed her laugh. "What detail have you missed, my meticulous friend?"

"School. I need to get her registered for high school. Do you know where or who I call?"

"I'm not exactly sure, but you can get on the Oakdale school system website. It should have deadlines for registration, and which high school is in your area."

"The website. Of course. I'll look tonight and make calls tomorrow. Do you know anything about any of the public schools?"

"Not really, but I know several of the kids from church go to Oakdale East."

"That's what Eve's heard too. I'm hoping she'll have some friends already to make the transition easier."

"She's a bright girl with a great personality. She'll make friends easily."

Nora and Maggie hung up. "Eve," Nora called up to Eve. No answer. She snagged her laptop from her bag and went upstairs to find Eve's door closed. She knocked. No answer. Nora slowly turned the knob to find Eve in the overstuffed chair with her headphones on—and crying. "What's wrong?" Nora hurried to Eve.

Eve pulled her headphones off, wiped her face with the back of her sleeve, and wrapped her arms around Aunt Nora. "Aunt ... Nora. I'm sorry."

Aunt Nora whispered in her ear, "What are you sorry for?"

Eve took a deep breath. Her eyes hurt from crying hard. She pulled away and wiped her nose. She stood up and walked across the room. "It's that I had so much fun this weekend. It almost felt normal for a couple of days. Then I ... I got back here, and it was quiet, and the memories flooded over me. It's overwhelming." She buried her face in her hands. "I'm tired of crying and being sad. I used to feel so free and light. Now it all feels heavy."

Aunt Nora looked at the floor. "I know how you feel. It's going to take time ... and giving ourselves grace and the space to feel what we're going to feel when the emotions hit."

Eve looked up with her tear-stained eyes. "Yeah." It was the only word she could say without sounding disrespectful.

I've heard that over and over. Does anyone have any other advice? Eve sighed. "I'm going to take a shower."

Aunt Nora stood up and picked up her laptop. Eve grabbed her robe and started for the bathroom at the end of the hall. "Why'd you bring your laptop up?"

"Maggie told me we might be able to get information from the school system website. But we can do it tomorrow."

"Is that ok? I'm tired and just want to shower and get in bed."

Aunt Nora nodded. "Not a problem. If you change your mind or can't sleep, I'll be downstairs."

Defeat followed Nora downstairs to the kitchen. She put the kettle on for a cup of tea and pulled a package of shortbread cookies from the cupboard. She heard the shower start above her as she sat down at the kitchen island and flipped open her laptop. Eve's emotions and words swished through her mind. Nora lowered her head into her hands. *Lord, I'm out of wise words. I understand. It all sounds trite and redundant. "It's going to take time. Give yourself time to grieve." She's fifteen. She shouldn't be burdened. This should be the most fun time of her life. I've got nothing new to say.*

The kettle whistled. Nora fixed her cup with a spoonful of honey and a tea bag and poured the steaming water. She grabbed another cookie and began to scroll through the Oakdale school system website. The first thing that stood out was that the application deadline was in three days. Ugh. Nora sighed. "We've got to get on this."

"Get on what?" Eve sat down on the stool next to Nora. "Got to thinking about what high school I would go to."

"Well, it seems the deadline to apply is Wednesday. That doesn't give us much time for visiting."

"Can we look at Oakdale East's website?"

Nora's brows furrowed. "Are you sure? I thought you wanted to go to bed."

"I did, but the shower was kinda refreshing." She fiddled with the pencil lying on the island. "Aunt Nora ... I'm sorry I got frustrated with you. I keep hearing the same thing from everyone. 'It's going to take time.' 'Let yourself feel your emotions.'" The teenager rolled her eyes. "It's getting old."

Nora nodded but didn't attempt to make it better with yet another cliché. She clicked open the map of the school district. "Looks like Oakdale East is in our area." She clicked on the school icon to open the school page and began to scroll through the pictures. She turned the laptop screen for Eve to get a better view.

Eve gasped. "Look, they have a drama club and girls' softball."

A surprised smile crossed Nora's face. "I forgot you'd been in the middle school play."

"Yeah. I really enjoyed it. The spring play was during softball, so I couldn't do that one."

"I'll call in the morning and see if we can go by tomorrow to tour. If you like it, we'll apply tomorrow. If not, it looks like there is one other high school we can look at. Do you know who from church goes to East?"

"Amanda and Patty."

"Do you want to text them and ask what they think of the school? Might be good to get a friend's opinion."

"Good idea." Eve grabbed her phone and began to text.

Nora's phone binged. A text from Jen. "Jen says she can get you a one-month guest pass for you to work out."

"Great. Yes, can we go tomorrow?"

"Probably. Let's start with seeing about school."

Eve's phone buzzed as she got up from the stool and headed toward the stairs. "Thanks, Aunt Nora."

"Not a problem. Glad I asked Maggie about it. We would've missed the deadline." Nora shut her laptop. "If you have any laundry, please bring it down."

"I will." Eve called over her shoulder on her way upstairs.

Nora put the cookies away.

Thank you, Lord, for calming Eve's spirit and helping me remember that I can't make it stop hurting. I just need to love her through it.

The bunk squeaked as Curt rolled over and sat up. His head clanged, and his mouth felt like he'd been sucking cotton balls. He wiped his hand over his face, thankful for no cellmates. When they processed him, he was offered a phone call. *There's no one to call.* In a moment of desperation, he dialed Nora. As if ...

"Butler. You've got a visitor." Curt stood as the officer unlocked the cell.

"Who is it?"

"No idea. He's in a suit, though. Probably not your fairy godmother." The door clanged as it opened. "Let's go."

Curt sat at the plexiglass booth across from a middle-aged man with grey hair, in a navy suit, white dress shirt, and a loose tie. He picked up the phone, as did the man.

"Curt, you don't know me. I'm Pastor Paul Sparks from the Baptist church."

A pastor. *Pretty sure I'm going to need more than you can offer.* "Why are you here?" Curt snapped.

The man sat against the back of the chair. "The question is, why are you here?"

Curt rolled his eyes and shifted in his chair.

"Hear me out. Every Sunday afternoon, I come to the jail and ask to visit anyone who was arrested and had no one to call. They can't give me specifics, so I have no idea why you're here. But if you'll listen, I'd like to share a story and an invitation."

"I've got no place to be." Curt crossed his arms in front of him and leaned back in his chair.

Pastor Sparks shared his journey of losing home, family, and career to his love of cocaine. The choices he made to have one more snort, or to stop at the bar on the way home. Something about the look in the pastor's eyes and his story drew Curt to lean in and listen. Much of his story sounded too familiar to Curt. He had lost everything.

"So I'll ask you again. Why are you here?"

When asked why he was in jail, there was one answer that came to mind. "Because I made all the wrong choices."

Pastor Sparks grinned. "How tired are you right now? Do you feel the burden of all those choices having caught up with you?"

Curt looked at the floor. His words were barely audible. "I am so tired." He looked up straight at the pastor. "I don't think your God is the answer."

The pastor stood. "What I just heard was a man who's tired of running. Well, my friend, that's right where God is willing to meet you. I've left a Bible with the guard with your name on it. If you'd like to talk again, ask for the Bible and tell the guard. The chaplain from the jail will call me, and I'll come back. Start with the Gospel of John."

Curt leaned forward and got close to the plexiglass. "God? Really, you think God is going to get my life straightened out?" He sneered. "I find it hard to believe that God wants to fish me out of this crap I'm sitting in."

The pastor didn't flinch. "That's exactly what he wants to do."

"Whatever, man."

"Curt, think about it. I'm guessing you're still in jail because you've run out of people to call. You've got no one."

The memory of hearing Nora say no to accepting his call echoed in his mind. *That was desperate. I had no one. But why does this preacher care?*

"It's hard to hear. Harder to accept. You're not alone, Curt. I'd like to stop by again tomorrow."

"How do you know I'll still be here?"

Pastor Sparks coolly spoke. "Maybe you won't be. Someone will come through with bail. Then, I will hope to see you at our church sometime."

Church. Curt almost laughed out loud. "I'm pretty sure your church people don't want me around."

"You're coming on my invitation. Don't worry about anyone else."

Curt stood. "Okay, preacher. You've done your good deed."

"Don't forget. There's a Bible—and a forgiving God—waiting for you. Just ask." Pastor Sparks hung up the phone and gave Curt a wave.

Curt watched him walk away. *Why does the man care about me?* As Curt turned to be escorted back to his cell, he had a revelation of his own. This preacher was the only person who cared enough to visit with him. He didn't even know him. When the guard took him back to his cell, Curt asked about the Bible. "Someone will bring it to you."

In his cell, Curt rotated from sitting on the cot to marching back and forth. After the pastor left, his case was called up by the judge for arraignment. With no bail money, and no one to call, they had him where they wanted him. His record gave the prosecutor enough ammunition to question him about dealing drugs for Willy again.

Willy had a way of always slipping free from the law. His attorney could create the right amount of doubt that kept a jury from convicting him. *Why couldn't that happen for me?*

"Butler," the guard called as he approached Curt's cell. "Time to see the judge."

Here we go. Another judge. Another opportunity for me to stammer around with no excuse. I'm all out of them.

The silver-haired judge leaned forward from his perch. "You've been in this situation before, Mr. Butler. I see here during your processing, they gave you a breathalyzer, and you blew a point nine. That's over the limit." He looked down his nose at Curt. "How do you plead?"

Curt wiped his hand over his mouth. His guilt clanked around his stomach. His hesitation opened another question for the judge.

"The facts tell us you're guilty, but you have the right to play this however you want. While you're considering your answer, the county prosecutor has an offer for you."

The attorney seated at the prosecutor's table, a woman with short, dark hair, stood. "Thank you, Judge. Mr. Butler, the state is willing to ask for one year's parole and community service in exchange for the names and locations of those working with a known local dealer, William Villow, aka Willy."

Curt looked directly at her, short, dark hair, dark eyes, well spoken, and about Liz's size. *Liz.* He locked his fingers together.

The public defender who had been assigned to him, Jerry Fleming, leaned over to Curt and whispered, "What do you want to do?"

Curt looked down at his hands. What if he gave up names? He had no home to go home to. No job. What did it matter if he sat in jail?

Mr. Fleming stood. "Your honor, I'd like some time to confer with my client on the options presented today."

The judge rapped the gavel. "Mr. Butler, you will spend another night in jail. I'll see you in the morning. The choice is yours—names for parole or risk a jury sending you to prison."

The rest of the day, the words from the preacher echoed in his mind. *Why are you here? Aren't you tired?* He stopped pacing and leaned against the cinderblock wall. "I'm here because I keep doing the same stupid things ... yes, I'm exhausted." Then the judge's words played out again, *The choice is yours.*

CHAPTER NINETEEN

Nora was up early to enjoy her coffee on the patio along with a prayerful quiet time. Her desperate prayers from six weeks before had softened to a conversation with her heavenly Father. With her Bible in her lap opened to Psalms, the warmth of morning sunlight was like sitting at his feet, sharing her thankfulness and needs. At the end of her quiet time, she called to schedule a tour at the high school. They could go at ten. A quick text to Jen solidified their plan to go to the gym after the school tour.

Eve was quiet as they walked out of the high school. Nora put the information folder in the back seat and slid into the driver's seat. "Eve, are you okay?"

Eve shrugged and slumped into the passenger seat. "I guess."

How hard do I push? Nora decided to push a little. "Did you see or hear anything that made you uncomfortable about going to Oakdale East? We still have time to—"

Eve whipped around in her seat. "Uncomfortable. Nothing was comfortable about the school. It's not my high school. Nothing felt familiar, and I don't want to go there." She crossed her arms in front of her and stared out the window.

Nora turned the car on so they would have air conditioning but left the car in park. With a voice just above a whisper, "Okay, I get that. It's not your school. I'm sorry. It's another change for you. But we need to choose a school here in Oakdale." She let there be silence for a minute. "What would you like to do, tour the other high school?" More silence.

Eve sat staring at the three-story, limestone high school. Oakdale East was huge compared to Simpson High School. Walking the long halls lined with hundreds of lockers made Eve feel small. The principal and guidance counselor tried to make everything sound great and wonderful. *It's big, and I won't know anyone. Now Aunt Nora is asking what I want to do. What do I want to do? I want to go home. I want to go to my high school. I want my friends. But here I am with another new thing to deal with.* She took a deep breath and looked at her aunt. "I'm sorry. This high school will be fine. Let's just go."

Thankfully, Aunt Nora didn't push. She put the car into gear, and they drove out of the high school parking lot.

Nora and Eve stood at the counter with their workout bags crossed over their shoulders when Jen hustled through the free weights area toward them. "Sorry to keep you waiting." She gave Eve a side hug. "How was the tour?"

Eve gave a tentative nod. "It was good."

Nora hugged Jen. "You okay? If this isn't a good time for you. I can bring Eve another time."

Jen adjusted her ponytail and clapped her hands. "Are you ladies ready?"

Nora's phone buzzed. "It's Tony from work. Let me take this and catch up to you."

Jen and Eve headed for the treadmills. "I hear you're training for a race."

Nora walked toward the smoothie bar and swiped across the screen.

"Nora, how are you and Eve doing?"

Nora smiled. It was kind of her boss to start by asking how she was doing. "We're doing okay. Went by the high school this morning to get her enrolled. School starts in three weeks. We barely made the deadline."

"Great. She going to Oakdale East?"

"Yes, she is. Your son goes there?"

"He'll be a senior. We're almost done. Then off to college. Anyway, we need to talk about how to proceed with Mrs. Preston's work."

"I'm scheduled to go by the house tomorrow to see the space and measure."

"I knew you'd be on top of things. Great. Do you want Phoebe to meet you?"

"Yes, if that works for her. I'll talk to her this afternoon when I come by the office to pick up some samples I want to take along. Mrs. Preston loved the soft green and light blue upholstery fabrics. I want to see how they look with the light in the room."

"That all sounds good. Thanks for taking care of everything."

Nora hung up. She hadn't yet figured out how to handle Eve when they had to go to a client's home.

As she went to meet Eve at the treadmills, her phone buzzed with another call. Jim. A smile warmed her lips when she saw his name and the photo she'd taken on one of their walks.

"What are you two doing this afternoon?"

"We're at the gym now, then I need to go by the office to pick up materials for a client meeting." Nora scratched her head. *Mrs. Preston is a client. It's business, not personal.* "One thing I need to figure out is what Eve can do while I'm working. Tony gave me flexibility until school starts, but that's still three weeks away."

"How about I put her to work here? I could use some volunteer help. And ..." Jim sighed. "And it would give me a chance to get to know her better. Would that be okay?"

It filled a need. But Nora didn't want to just dump Eve without first talking to her about it. "Thank you for the offer. Let me talk to her about it first."

"No problem. Consider it an option. I was calling to see if you wanted to come over for dinner tonight. Mark and Maggie and Dan are coming with their kids."

"Sounds like fun. No Jen?"

"Mark said she had to work late."

"Oh, I'm at the gym, I'll see if I can't encourage her to come by later if that's okay with you. What time, and what can we bring?"

"Please let her know she's welcome any time. Sounds like she's been working a lot lately. All you need to bring is your lovely self and your sweet niece."

"We'll be there."

Nora dropped her phone in her bag. No more calls for at least an hour. She stepped on the treadmill next to Eve, who was jogging with her earbuds in. Nora started with a warm-up walking pace.

After a few minutes, Nora was warm and turned the speed and incline up as Jen came through the area. "Is that the best you can do, Nora? Come on, you can go a little faster." She peeked over the side rail to see what Nora's speed was.

Nora swatted at her. "Mind your own business. It's been a bit since I worked out." She checked the time on her watch.

"What else are you doing today?"

"I need to run by the office."

Jen nodded toward Eve. "What's Eve doing while you're there?"

Eve noticed and took her earbuds out. "What are you two talking about?"

Nora's voice rolled up and down with the vibration of the treadmill. "I need to go by the office to prepare for a client meeting that's tomorrow. Jen asked if you were coming with me."

Eve's brow scrunched. "Am I?"

Jen leaned on the front of the treadmill across from Nora. "How about she stays here with me? After her workout, she can help me set up the training room for my class tomorrow."

Nora squinted her eyes with a question. "Will that help you be done in time to come to Jim's cookout?"

Jen looked away. "Guess you heard I couldn't make it because of work. Kevin keeps piling it on. Something's going on with all these meetings he's having. I can't say 'no' when he asks."

Nora's brow furrowed. "Sounds like your dream job is becoming a nightmare."

Jen looked at Nora and shrugged. "I don't know. Is this just one of those times when work is harder, and in a few months it'll lighten up again?" She sighed. "But having Eve with me this afternoon would be a delight."

Nora looked at Eve, who was already nodding. "Can I? I wouldn't mind staying for one of the boot camp classes, anyway. Didn't think you'd be up for that level of workout."

Nora laughed. "What are you saying, I'm out of shape? Guess I'm old too?"

Eve's eyes widened. "No, no, I meant ..."

Nora shook her head and grinned. "Please, I'm kidding you. Sure, if it works for Jen, you can stay. I'll swing back by and pick you up when I'm done at the office."

Nora slowed the treadmill to cool-down. "Thanks, Jen. And ... I appreciate your help." *The Lord provides.*

On the way to Jim's, Nora turned off the car radio. "Now that you've had a few hours, how are you feeling about Oakdale East?"

Eve twisted in the seat. "I'm nervous about a new school. But I know Oakdale East is probably the best option. I'm sorry about my outburst earlier. You didn't deserve that."

Nora sighed. "Forgiven. I know it's a big change and a daily reminder of not being in Simpson." She reached over and squeezed her niece's hand. "We'll get through this."

Nora and Eve pulled into Jim's short driveway and parked behind Dan and Maggie's van. Mark and Jen's car was first in the driveway. Jim lived within walking distance of the theater in an historic neighborhood not far south of downtown Oakdale. The small white-clad carriage house sat behind a three-story Victorian brick house. It was one of the few homes in the neighborhood where the carriage house had two bedrooms and a decent-sized yard. Other carriage houses were smaller and sat on an alley. Jim had purchased the carriage house from the family who owned the main house with the caveat that he could not turn it into a rental, and if he ever wanted to sell it, they would have first right of refusal to purchase it at market value.

Maggie's children, Danny and Emma, were playing cornhole in the side yard next to the driveway. Brian was watching. As she walked toward the front door, Nora heard the kids call out, "Eve's here, we can play teams." She knocked, and when no one answered, she let herself in. "Helloooo."

She walked through the rectangular living room that ran the front width of the house, the small square dining room, to the galley kitchen in the back of the house. Through the window over the sink, she could see Mark, Jim, Maggie, and Dan on the back patio. She set her purse down and carried the chips out toward the food table. When she stepped out the back door, Jim turned from the grill and hurried over to help her with the bowl of dip. "We didn't hear you come in."

"Sounds like the fun has already started." Nora relinquished her dish to Jim and put the bag of chips on the table.

Maggie gave Nora a hug. "No fun until you arrived. Jim and Dan were rehashing their last adventures on the golf course."

Dan gave Nora a side hug. "Good to see you. And adventure is one way to put it." He put his hands up. "I tried to help your guy out."

Jim interrupted. "Wait a minute. If we're going to talk about what a hack I am on the golf course, let me tell the story."

Dan surrendered. "Okay, but can I say that even the groundskeepers at the course didn't know about the woods that Jim's balls kept finding?"

They shared a laugh, and Jim hugged Nora while he whispered in her ear. "You look beautiful."

Nora's blush matched the tomato slices on the garden tray. "Maybe you and I need to get out and play."

"Nora, you could give him a lesson or two, I'm sure." Dan reached into the cooler for an iced tea. "Anyone want something to drink?"

Maggie reached for the tea Dan had pulled out. Nora waved him off. "No, thank you."

Nora looked around. "Mark, where's Jen?"

Mark reached into the cooler for a Diet Coke. "She's stuck at the gym, again." He popped open the can and changed the subject. "Okay, guys, sounds like I need to join you next time as the impartial judge."

"Just a few more minutes until the burgers are ready. Nora, are you set for your big client meeting?" Jim flipped the last of the ten burgers on the grill and closed the top.

Nora snapped a look at Jim. Did he know it was with his mother? Wait, I didn't tell him, he's merely asking about my day. "Oh, uh ... yes, ready to go."

"Is this another client that's among the rich and famous of Oakdale?" Maggie took a sip of her tea.

Nora's eyes widened. "Ah, well ... I wouldn't call them Oakdale celebrities or anything."

A glint of recognition crossed Jim's face. Nora closed her eyes. He realized who the client was. "Wait, is it a meeting with my mot—"

Before he could finish, the four kids came charging around the back corner of the house. "We're hungry. When do we eat?" They chimed in unison.

Jim stepped back up to the grill. "Looks like you are right on time. Who wants burgers, and who wants hot dogs?"

Eleven-year-old Danny was the loudest. "I'll have both."

"Get your plates over there." Jim pointed to the small table off to the side with plates and utensils. Danny, Brian, Emma, and Eve lined up to get the first burgers and dogs.

Nora and Maggie uncovered the side dishes and opened the chips. Maggie gave Nora a concerned look. Nora shook her head. In a hushed tone, she murmured, "We'll catch up soon."

Maggie turned as the kids walked up with their plates. "Anyone need help?"

There was a rectangular umbrella table on the patio that was large enough to seat the five adults, and a smaller round table that sat four under the aged maple tree in the grassy area where the kids took their food to sit.

Nora took her plate to the grill where Jim was serving. The grill was hot, but there was a cool vibe radiating from Jim. *Do I let it go? Or reassure him that he wasn't the topic of her conversation with his mother? Keep it light. Speak from your heart. No games,* the small whisper of her heart reminded her.

Jim's eyes were focused on the grill. Nora stood next to him and gave him a slight nudge with her elbow. "Chef, may I have one of those burgers with the perfectly melted cheese?"

Jim shuffled the regular hamburgers aside to scoop up a cheeseburger and slid it onto the bun on Nora's plate. He mumbled, "My pleasure."

Nora elbowed him a little harder. "Hey. Yes, it's your mother. We'll be discussing fabric swatches and colors, and I'll measure the living room and sunroom. Phoebe is going with me, if you want a witness."

Jim looked up from the grill. With a flirty smile, Nora turned to sit with Dan and Maggie.

Jim flipped his burger from the grill to the bun, loaded the tray with the remaining burgers and hot dogs, and sat next to Nora. Throughout the dinner chatter, his knee softly leaned into hers.

Eve was more talkative than usual on the ride home. It had been a full day with the high school tour, the gym, and dinner at Jim's. "Amanda texted me with her schedule. She's in my English class and Algebra II."

"That's great. I'm glad you'll have a friend in a couple of your classes."

"I know! And she knows everyone, so hopefully, she'll introduce me to others."

Nora felt a twang of parental responsibility. *What if Eve got mixed up with the wrong crowd?*

"Eve, honey. I'm so glad you'll know a few friends at your new school. Would you do something for me?"

Eve stopped talking at Nora's solemn tone. "Sure."

"Please be careful making new friends. It's easy when you go to a new place, or a new school, and want to be accepted so badly that you can make bad choices. Like—"

"Aunt Nora, Mom and I talked a lot about drugs, gangs, and boys." She looked out the passenger window. "Now I know why. She didn't want me to get involved with anyone like my dad." Her voice faded.

Nora's heart ached she even had to bring it up. Nora remembered Liz telling her she'd had a talk with Eve before her freshman year about the kinds of kids she would meet at high school. All kinds—good, bad, in trouble, out of trouble. Nora slid her hand over and squeezed Eve's. "You're right. She wanted to protect you as much as possible from even being tempted to make a bad choice."

They rode in silence for several minutes. Nora broke the quiet with a new subject. "How was the boot camp workout? Jen said you did really well."

As if relieved for the new topic, Eve twisted toward Nora, pulled her knee onto the seat, and unleashed her chatter box again. "It was so hard. But I could do all of the exercises."

Nora laughed. "That's great. What was the hardest one?"

"Burpees." Without hesitation.

"Ahh, burpees. Those are tough. Didn't have a chance earlier to ask you about an opportunity Jim mentioned. Would you like to volunteer at the theater over the next few weeks until school starts?"

"I don't know. Might be okay. What will I be doing?"

"I'm not sure exactly, but before you answer, we can call Jim and talk with him about it."

"Can we call him now?"

Nora handed her the phone. "Sure. Put it on speaker so we can both talk with him."

"Well, hello. What a pleasant surprise."

Eve and Nora smiled at each other. Nora pointed to Eve to talk.

"I'm glad it's a pleasant surprise." Eve giggled.

"What? Nora?"

Nora and Eve burst out laughing. "Sorry to confuse you. Eve and I were talking about her volunteering at the theater, and she had a few questions."

"You two are quite the pair. Sure, ask away, Eve."

"What would I be doing?"

"Great question. We're getting ready for our next production. There will be different things to do on different days. You'll help Sara with our social media posts, probably sort props, and help organize costumes. Things like that. You met her already, and Maggie will be around some. Was thinking maybe one or two days a week?"

Eve looked at Nora and nodded, then back to the phone she was holding. "Okay. I'll do it."

"Wonderful. I'll work out the schedule on Monday and I'll call you to make sure it works for you. I'm thinking Wednesdays and Thursdays, but I'll confirm."

"Sounds great. I'll let you and Aunt Nora talk now."

"Nora, if it's okay with you, can I call you in about an hour? I'd like to get the grill shut down and pick up the rest of the dishes."

"Sure." Nora couldn't resist smiling. She had been so concerned with Jim and Eve getting along. Now Eve was going to spend a couple of days a week at the theater.

"Aunt Nora, if I'm going to be at the theater a couple of days a week, that will help you with working and not having to worry about me."

Nora's heart sank. Had she made Eve feel like she was pawning her off? "Yes, but sweetie, if you don't want to volunteer, we'll figure out something else. I don't want you to feel like—"

"No, I don't. I was thinking maybe I could spend one of the other days at the gym with Jen. Then you could have three days, and I could be volunteering and getting ready for the mini-marathon."

Nora smiled. "You are so thoughtful. And mature. When did you get so grown up?" Nora handed her phone back to Eve. "Let's give Jen a call. Might be a little different since she's not in charge."

"I have her number. She gave it to me today."

They pulled in the drive, unloaded the leftovers, and went into the house. While Nora put the food away, Eve sat on a stool at the island and called Jen.

"I'd love to have you around the gym. Let's do Tuesday if that works for you. I'm actually returning some emails now, so I'll shoot one to my boss and ask. If you're willing to help with set-up and clean-up after the classes, I'll pitch it as a "professional shadow" program. I'm working so many hours right now, he's not going to tell me no. Never know, you might decide you like the gym life."

Eve looked at Nora for permission. Nora nodded. "If that's what you want to do, I'm all for it."

Eve smiled freely. "Aunt Jen, that all sounds great. Let me know what he says."

"Will do. Talk to you ladies later."

Eve leaned on the counter and rested her chin in her palm. "This all feels good. Like ... like I have some things to look forward to. The big high school is still a little scary, but like you said, we'll get through all the nerves of a new school." She sat back and looked down at her lap. "I don't want to forget Mom. I'm still so sad. But I'm also tired of being sad. Does that make sense?"

"It does. I have no doubt that we will cry more. But she wouldn't want us to get stuck only being sad. Do ya think?"

Eve shook her head. "My counselor encouraged me to try to look forward and not sit around being sad. But it's hard both ways."

Nora reached across the island and grazed Eve's cheek. "Sweetie, she would never want you to stop living or having fun with your friends. She wanted you to learn and grow and be the amazing person God created you to be." Nora walked around the island and hugged her niece. *Liz, I'm trying.*

CHAPTER TWENTY

Eve and Nora arrived at the Oakdale Community Theater early. Eve's nerves were dancing at her fingertips as she intertwined them. "Aunt Nora, what kinds of things do you think I'll be doing today?"

"Today may be more about you getting to know where things are around the theater and meeting some of the people who work or act in the plays." Aunt Nora reached for Eve's hand. "Are you nervous?"

Eve looked out the car window. Although the sun had been up for a couple of hours, there were still shadows from the trees dancing on the car hood. "I don't know." She took a deep breath. "I keep trying to think of all these new things as adventures. But, sometimes, it's hard."

Aunt Nora nodded silently. Jim's green Jeep pulled into the parking space next to them, and shortly after, Sara pulled in across the parking lot.

"Guess I can't back out now."

Aunt Nora smiled. "You could, but I don't think you want to. Last night, you were so excited. Tell you what—if at any time during the day you want me to come pick you up, text me. Otherwise, I'll pick you up at five, and we'll go to the gym."

"But what about your work?"

"It'll be fine. You are my priority. Adventures are fun, but they can be stressful too."

Eve smiled as Jim opened her door.

"Welcome to your first day."

Eve snagged her satchel from the back seat and stepped out of the car. Jim hustled around to open Nora's door. "Good morning." He gave her a wink and a gentle squeeze of her hand.

A smile slid across Nora's face. "I've never gotten this kind of service here. So, I bring free labor, and I get parking lot assistance."

Sara had her baby, Glenda, with her. She came alongside Eve as Jim and Nora walked ahead. "Eve, I'm so excited that you're going to be helping us out."

"I am too. Though kinda wondering what I'm going to be doing?"

Sara lowered her voice just above a whisper. "I've asked Jim if you can work with me today. I'm working on our social media plan for the fall."

Eve widened her eyes, and she straightened her stance. "Really? That'd be fun." She looked at Sara's baby and smiled. "A baby. How do you keep up with school and work with a baby?"

Sara gave a gentle adjustment to Glenda's hair bow. "It takes a lot. But I have the love and support of my mother, and Jake, that's the baby's father, and his parents. He comes over several evenings a week and we have dinner, take care of the baby together, and then study."

"Seems like it would be hard."

"It is sometimes. When I've got projects or exams at school, or our friends are doing fun stuff, and we aren't."

They were approaching the white wooden steps to the theater entry. "Sometimes, one of our parents will take her for an evening, and we can go out. But all the sacrifices are worth it for this little cutie."

Once inside, Jim flipped on the lobby lights. "Eve, do you mind working with Sara this morning?"

Sara parked the sleeping baby in her stroller by her desk and waved Eve to follow her.

"Sure." Eve followed Sara to the kitchen.

Over her shoulder, Sara began to let Eve know more about their morning routine. "First, we make coffee. Do you drink coffee?"

"Not really. But I'll learn to make it." Eve twisted a wisp of hair.

After showing Eve how to make the coffee and where the snacks and other drinks were kept, the two returned to Sara's desk to get started.

"Now, let's get to work." Sara pulled a stool over from the ticket counter for Eve to sit.

Jim turned his attention to Nora. "Sara's working on our social media plans today. Figured that's something Eve would be into."

Nora smiled and raised her eyebrows. "Very insightful."

He reached for her hand. "What does your day hold?"

"I'm going to work, but if Eve needs me, I told her to text." Nora's words were short and quick.

"She'll be fine. I'll keep an eye out. I'm having lunch brought in. And I think Maggie will be here too."

Nora nodded. They stood face-to-face. "Is this what mothers feel like the first time they drop their babies off at daycare? I feel like I'm just dumping her here."

With a gentle touch of his finger to her lips, Jim stopped Nora from rambling. "No, you're not dumping her. Remember, I offered."

"I guess."

Jim watched Nora look around. "Nora, I asked for Eve to volunteer not only for the things we need to get done, but I'd also like to get to know her."

Nora sighed. "I'm sorry. I guess I'm still trying to fit all the pieces together. Eve, you, me, work."

Jim reached to give her a hug and whispered in her ear. "Everything will be fine, and we're all here to love and support you."

Nora hurried to her car. There was that word again, love. *Nope, can't think about that now. I need to be sure he's going to accept that I'm responsible for Eve first.*

It took less than ten minutes to get to the Stanton Designs office. She arrived before anyone else. The office was quiet. She dropped her lunch into the kitchen refrigerator.

Their break for lunch wasn't much of a break. Nora and Phoebe ate in the conference room with both laptops on, notes, drawings, and diagrams for the clients Phoebe had been helping with. After lunch, Phoebe went to meet with one of her clients. Nora continued to prepare what she needed to pick up her clients' work again. It was three-forty-five when she checked her watch. Drawings and sample swatches, laid out around the conference room table, brought a refreshing sense of accomplishment. After being off work for so long, she was up to date on all of her projects and ready to move forward. *Moving forward*. A concept Nora had been struggling with. It was time. There would still be grief, but God had provided the support and encouragement she needed. *Today felt normal.* Nora gathered the samples and put them in the closet, then took her lunch dishes to the kitchen to rinse them. She met Phoebe at the sink. "I have missed working with you. Thank you for keeping all these clients' projects on track."

Phoebe smiled and picked up a towel to dry her mug. "Not a problem. I need to take care of a few personal errands, so I'm heading out for the day. Do you need anything else?"

"No, I'm good. Have a good evening."

"You too."

Nora double-checked the time. She had a couple of minutes to finish wrapping up. She headed back down the hall. Before she realized it, she was immersed in Mrs. Preston's work plans.

Nora looked up from the drawings she was working on and leaned back in her chair with a stretch, having no idea what time it was. Tony stood at the door and tapped the face of his watch. "You know you don't have to make up all the work you missed on the first day."

Nora chuckled and checked the time. Four-fifty-five? "Oh, my goodness. Look at the time." She grabbed her phone. No messages from Eve. "What a day." She paused and looked around the workspace. "It felt good to dive into normal stuff."

Tony smiled. "I'm glad. We missed having you around here. And I know Phoebe missed having you in client meetings. You have a way of putting clients at ease."

Nora felt the warmth of a blush move up her cheeks. "Thank you. I do love the work. And the clients." She looked back down at the drawing. "Do you have a minute to take a look at this concept for Mrs. Preston?"

"Sure." Tony walked around the worktable to look over Nora's shoulder.

"I'm meeting with her tomorrow and wanted to take these as options for furniture placement. What do you think?"

After Tony reviewed the drawing and made a few adjustments, Nora gathered her things and called Eve to let her know she was on her way. No answer. She tried Jim's phone. No answer. She pulled into the theater parking lot at five on the nose. No cars. Nora's heart quickened. *What is going on?* After checking the front door to find it locked, she tried Eve's and Jim's phones again. No answer. *Where are they? Has something happened?*

Nora got back into her car, trying to decide what to do next. Where could they be? As Nora was deciding between going to the hospital and trying Jim again, her phone buzzed. Jen.

Pastor Sparks stepped into the small room normally used for attorney-client meetings. Curt thought the public defender was back to discuss his plea deal.

"Good morning, Mr. Butler."

"What are you doin' here?" After asking the question, Curt felt a strange appreciation for the preacher returning. He leaned back in the chair and avoided eye contact.

"I wanted to see how things were going. You look a little better than when I saw you yesterday."

Curt scratched the back of his neck and leaned forward, allowing the four legs of the chair to rest on the floor. "Yeah, I was feeling pretty rough. Sorry."

"No need to apologize. How are you?"

In a humble voice, Curt replied. "I read the Gospel of John."

Pastor Sparks' chair scraped across the floor as he pulled it out to sit. "What'd you think?"

"Jesus got the crap beat out of him when he could of left—or had angels wipe out all those guys."

Pastor Sparks chuckled. "You're right. He did get the snot beat out of him. And ended up dead for a few days."

Curt sat up and rested his elbows on the table. "That's the amazing thing. I remembered hearing that story in church. Why did Christ make that choice?"

This time Pastor Sparks leaned forward. "He made that choice for you." He pointed at Curt. "And all people for all time. Curt, I hear you're going back to court today. Did they offer you a deal?"

Curt nodded. He'd made hundreds of bad choices that had led to this moment.

"I don't know. If I give up the names, what do I do then?" Curt sighed. "I got nothing. It's too late."

"It's not too late. God's mercies are new every day. I can help you start again." He slid a piece of paper across the table toward Curt. Paul Sparks, 812-555-0712.

"I'm friends with the guy who runs a halfway house for men trying to beat addiction. Choose to get clean, and you'll have the support you need, a roof over your head, and three meals a day. We'll also help you find a job. The choice is yours."

Pastor Sparks stood and walked out.

CHAPTER TWENTY-ONE

Nora tossed her purse in the back seat as the buzz from her phone vibrated in her jacket pocket. A text from Jen reported that Jim and Eve were at the gym and to please meet them there. Nora started her car and turned around in the theater parking lot. As she drove, a mix of anger and thankfulness wrestled in her mind. Guessing they would be on the treadmills, Nora walked sternly past Daisy at the front counter.

"What are you two doing?" Nora was both relieved and furious that Jim had taken Eve over to the gym. Neither of them had called or texted her.

Jim slowed the treadmill. "Right now, I'm proving to Eve that I'm not too winded to talk while running."

Nora wasn't smiling and said nothing.

Jim shrugged. "We're racing. I think that competitive streak that shows up when we play pickleball runs in the family."

"Jim, you scared me. I had no idea where Eve was."

"What do you mean? Eve texted I was bringing her to the gym and to meet us here."

Eve's eyes widened. She slowed the treadmill to a stop. "No, I didn't—you said you were going to call her."

She and Jim stared at each other while Nora stood with her hands on her hips. "Well, neither of you did any calling or texting, and I was worried."

Jim and Eve stepped off their treadmills, apologizing. "I'm so sorry. I thought ..."

Jen broke the apology circle. "These two showed up about an hour ago with some kind of bet on who could run the farthest."

Nora shook her head to realize what was happening. She'd gotten what she was hoping for, some bonding time for Jim and Eve. She smiled. "Who's winning?"

Eve squared her shoulders with a triumphant sparkle in her eyes. "I was."

Nora nodded, letting go of her frustration. "Way to go. We need to keep this guy on his toes." Nora nudged Jim. "I can't keep up running, but I dominate on the pickleball court. Now, about this communication gap, next time, would you both please risk overcommunicating? It wouldn't have been bad to get texts from both of you rather than neither."

Jim stepped toward Nora. "I'm sorry. I should have called you. You left Eve with me. I should have let you know our plans changed and made sure you were okay with it."

"Thank you. Forgiven. I'm going to change for the stretch class. Eve, do you want to come with me?"

"Sure. Let me wipe down the treadmill I was on first."

Jim had a towel and the disinfectant spray. "I'll take care of yours too."

"Okay. Thanks."

"Eve, thanks for all your work today. You did well."

"Thanks. It was fun."

Nora looked at the two of them. It had been a good day for all three of them. She turned to Jen. "Are you teaching class today?"

"I wish. Not today. Need to make some calls about our upcoming nutrition class. Ordering food, confirming the speaker. All the fun."

"Do I detect a note of sarcasm?"

Jen shook her head. "I don't know. There's a lot to do right now." She offered a polite smile. "We'll talk later. I'm looking forward to Eve coming tomorrow to help me with the high school athlete program. Several participants are coming from Oakdale East."

The early-morning-before-work crowd was at the gym when Nora dropped Eve off. She wore new running shorts and a T-shirt that boasted a geometric shape on the front. Nora pulled into a space near the door and released her seatbelt. Eve shook her head. "You don't need to walk me in."

"Really? I guess you know your way around here. If you don't see Jen, you can always ask Daisy."

"I know."

Nora started to say something else, but Eve was already out of the car and getting her gym bag out of the back seat. "I know, if my plan changes and Jen takes me anywhere, call or text."

Eve found Jen in the smoothie bar. "Hey, Aunt Jen."

"Hey, yourself, want a smoothie to start your day?"

"No thanks. What are we doing this morning?"

"Let's go to the training room. We need to get it set up. The athletes from Oakdale East should be here soon."

They walked down a hall with windows that looked into a gym, various workout spaces, and class studios. "What are we doing with these athletes again?"

At the end of the hall, they walked into the training room. It was set up in a classroom-style arrangement with six-foot rectangular tables and chairs on one side, all facing the front of the room. Jen gave Eve the handouts for the class on nutrition. "We've got twenty students, both male and female, coming in for a nutrition class, then we're going over to the yoga studio for a class on stretching."

"What sports do they play?"

"I think there are football and field hockey players today. I know a few of them from their parents coming in. I'll introduce you. Never know, some may end up in your classes."

My classes. The words hit hard. I'm going to a new high school with new friends. Not Simpson High like Mom and I planned.

"Eve, come meet Ashley and her friends." Aunt Jen called from the back of the room.

Eve joined the small circle of girls with Aunt Jen. They gave her the full up-and-down look teenage girls gave during the "new girl" inspection.

Aunt Jen put her arm around Eve's shoulder. "This is Eve. She's new to East this year. Right now, she's training for a mini-marathon."

Each of the five girls said hello. Ashley stood about two inches taller than Eve with sandy-blonde, curly hair. "I'm Ashley. I run cross-country. Got tired of sticks and all the field hockey gear."

Eve felt all their eyes on her. She remembered what Aunt Nora had told her when she was meeting new people, to stand up straight and speak up. They would respect her for it. "Hi. I'm Eve. Good to meet all of you."

"Okay, everyone, please take your seats," Jen called as she walked to the front of the room.

Ashley tugged at Eve's elbow. "Come sit with us."
Immediate inclusion. Maybe this will be okay.

CHAPTER TWENTY-TWO

Nora was washing lettuce for a salad. Jim had gone out back to see if he could get the charcoal grill started. "Why don't you own a gas grill?" he grumbled.

"I like charcoal. A gas grill makes me think I'm merely cooking on a stove outside. It doesn't have that charcoal-summertime smell."

Jim shook his head and dug through the damp charcoal bag to get enough briquettes to light the grill. Eve was making brownies for dessert and chatting about Ashley and the others she had met at the gym. But she and Ashley seemed to hit it off.

Hearing Eve's excitement about her new friend and that the other girls included her when they went to the smoothie bar after the nutrition class warmed Nora's heart. "What year will Ashley be at school?"

Eve stopped and thought. "I think a senior. She's already driving and has her own car."

"Her own car."

"Yeah, and Ashley doesn't live far from here. She said she'd take me to school some if you couldn't."

Nora's heart sank at the thought of letting Eve ride in a car with another teenage driver. Ugh. "We'll see. Let's get you started at school. And I need to meet Ashley's mom."

"Aunt Jen knows her. I'm sure she can give you her number."

Jim walked in. "Ladies, the charcoal is hot, and I'm ready for the burgers and dogs."

Nora handed him the plate with raw burgers and a clean one for when they were done. "We'll be out to set the table. What do you want to drink?"

"Sweet tea, please."

Eve put the brownies in the oven. "I'll get the drinks. Do you want tea also, Aunt Nora?"

"Yes, that'd be great. Thank you for the help tonight."

"No prob."

After dinner, over the embers of the grill, Jim, Nora, and Eve roasted marshmallows to make s'mores. Jim answered Eve's questions about the theater and its history. "It's been in that exact spot for nearly one hundred years. Can you imagine? The first theatergoers arrived in horse-drawn carriages or very early models of cars."

"No way! It's really old. Why haven't they torn it down?"

"They almost did last year. It was added to a list of sites in the area for redevelopment. But through the efforts of people like your Aunt Nora, Aunt Jen, and Aunt Maggie, we were able to save it. It's now on the national historic registry, and they can't take it down as long as it's being maintained."

"Seems like it needs a lot of work."

Jim grinned. "Yes, it does, and as we get the money, we're taking care of maintenance and doing improvements. We keep getting anonymous donations out of the blue. Next week, we're going to start upgrading the electrical wiring."

Nora carefully squished her marshmallow and chocolate between two graham crackers. "Anonymous donor. That sounds intriguing. Any thoughts on who it is?"

Jim wiped the melted chocolate from his chin. "No idea. I've speculated, but it's not something you can come out and ask someone. If they want to give generously with no recognition, I respect that."

Eve changed the subject to goad Jim about his running time. "What's your best mile this week?"

Nora watched and took it in. The bantering between Eve and Jim warmed her heart. *Maybe this will work.*

CHAPTER TWENTY-THREE

Nora had left another successful meeting with Mrs. Preston. They had easy, enjoyable conversations about Mrs. Preston's final color choices. There were a couple of choices Nora carefully questioned as was her practice with other clients.

"I understand you want to keep the look and feel light, but sometimes too many light colors can create a space that feels cold and unwelcoming. What if we bring a touch of warm pastels with the throw pillow, like this." She pulled a sage green and blue sample fabric from her bag and draped the swatch over the mid-century couch.

Mrs. Preston stepped back with her hand over her mouth, studying the slight pop of color. Nora said nothing. She would never try to sell the client on something they didn't like. They would either see and like the difference or they wouldn't.

Mrs. Preston began to nod. "Yes, I see it. You're right. And look over here." She walked to the water-colored painting on the far wall. "Those colors are in this painting. Yes, it will tie the room together."

Nora grinned. Mrs. Preston smiled and pointed at her. "You're good. You saw those colors the last time you were here and knew how to incorporate them." She shook her head. "Amazing."

"Thank you. And yes, true confession. I loved that painting and took a picture of it when I was here before to remember the colors."

"Thank you for being so insightful."

"This is my job. And besides seeing the end result, this part is my favorite. Getting to know my client, their space, and developing our plan."

Mrs. Preston sat next to Nora on the couch and patted her knee. "You do it well. You have a wonderful style. Are you sure I can't introduce you to one of my sons? I have three you could choose from." She winked.

Nora smiled. Mrs. Preston was such a sweet lady. Very proper, but bold enough to pepper several personal questions, attempting to find out if Nora was dating. Nora deflected the conversation to talk about Eve.

"Thank you, but I need to focus on Eve right now. I'm going to walk the relationship line carefully."

As she pulled out of the long driveway, her phone buzzed. Jim's picture popped up on the screen. It was taken during their long walk last Sunday.

"Hi."

"How are you doing?"

"I'm doing well, just now leaving your mother's house. Jim, it's getting more difficult to deflect her wanting to introduce me to any one of her three sons. I'm afraid she's going to be angry when she finds out I'm, in fact, dating her eldest. I feel like I'm lying to her."

Jim was silent. After the awkward pause, Nora continued. "Jim, please tell her."

She heard his sigh.

"You're right. I don't want to put you in a bad place with her."

"Or my boss. If she feels deceived, it could impact my job."

"You're right. I didn't consider that. I'll call her this evening, tell her about you, and explain it's completely my fault you didn't tell her we were dating."

"Thank you. And by the way, you never told me how dreamy you were in high school."

The phone went silent. Jim smiled and went for a run. *What am I doing? This wonderful, beautiful woman has more integrity in her little finger than I have guts to talk to my parents. Lord, why did you bother to bless me with Nora? I'm a silly, weak man. Time to man-up, James Preston III.* After a quick two miles, he took a shower, sat at his kitchen table, picked up his phone, and called his mother.

"James, what a wonderful surprise. Your father and I were just finishing dinner."

Dad's with her. Didn't consider talking with both of them. "Ah, okay, um, can you put your phone on speaker. I want to tell you both something."

"James, are you okay? In some kind of trouble?"

"I'm fine." The picture of Nora flowed into his mind. Her grace, infectious laughter, and commitment to family even when it wasn't easy. "Mom, everything is great. I have good news."

"Oh, well, let me figure out how to get your dad to hear. Where's that button ..."

Jim smiled, picturing his mother trying to find the giant button on her phone that said *speaker*. "Oh, here it is. James, can you hear us?"

"Yes. Hi, Dad."

"Hello, Son. What's your news? Everything okay at the theater?"

Asking about the theater again. Jim shook his head. *This is different.* "Yes, everything is going really well right now. But that's not what I wanted to tell you all."

"We're all ears." His mother was always ready to listen to him.

"Well, I've met a woman who has grown to mean a lot to me. Mom, you know her, and I think you like her. But before I tell you who she is, please know the reason she's not said anything to you is because of me. I asked her to let me break the news to you. I'm sorry I didn't do it sooner."

"Good grief, Son, who are you dating?" Mr. Preston Senior sounded a little put out.

"Well, it's Nora St. Claire."

Silence.

"Who's that?" His dad asked.

"My interior designer?" Mrs. Preston said a little too loudly.

"Mom, don't be mad. When I heard she was doing your design work, I asked her not to say anything about me." Jim paused for an immediate reaction that didn't come. "Look, you all have to admit, things have been a little tense between us. I've come to realize that's as much on me as anyone." *Not the time to accuse anyone of anything.*

His mother's voice caught. "Yes, we've had some bumps in the road with you."

More silence.

"I'm not mad at you or Nora," his mother finally replied. "She's been nothing but professional. Although I did notice her eyeing your picture in particular with the other family photos on the mantel."

Jim rubbed his forehead. "Thank you, Mom."

"Maribel, why don't we take Jim and Nora to the club for lunch on Sunday? I'd like to get to know this young lady."

"James, what do you think? Would Nora and Eve like to have lunch with us?"

"Who's Eve?" Jim's dad was in the dark again.

"Oh, James, it's Nora's niece she's raising since her sister died a few months ago."

The freedom of his parents knowing about Nora, and his mother already knowing some of her story, swept over Jim. He laughed.

"Dad, you've got some catching up to do. Thank you both for understanding. I'll ask Nora to lunch after church on Sunday. Mom ... she really is wonderful, isn't she?"

"I've been wanting to introduce you, and she kept changing the subject," his mother replied. "I think she's darling. And I look forward to meeting her niece."

"I'll call you back after I find out if they can join us."

"I'll go ahead and call for reservations."

My mom, always the optimist.

Nora shifted in the pew again. Eve and Jim gave her a questioning look. Biting her bottom lip, she looked up at the minister, who couldn't be done fast enough. Nora had spent an hour the night before choosing the perfect summer dress and accessories to wear to church and lunch. She played with her hair for another hour. Mrs. Preston had only seen her hair pulled into a tight bun. Should she wear it down? She decided loose curls would look good with the neckline of her dress. How do you shift from a professional relationship to a personal one? Unlike other Sundays, communion was served at the end of the service.

The minister concluded with a comment and the psalmist's words, "The world wants to distract us, and the enemy uses that distraction to keep us feeling anxious, alone, and sometimes worried about whatever is next. Let's take a few minutes as we take the Lord's supper to be still and know that our God brings peace, love, and guidance."

Nora took a cleansing breath and bowed her head. *Lord, I need your peace today. Calm my spirit. May I feel your love and guidance today. Forgive me for trying to rely on myself.* She swallowed the elements and opened her heart to God's peace and calm. The soft music gave her pause and quieted her nervousness about lunch with Jim's parents.

Outside the church, Maggie, Dan, Jen, and Mark met up with Jim and Nora. Maggie gave Nora a hug. "You seemed a little antsy in church. You okay?"

Jen fidgeted and kept her hand over her mouth.

Nora chuckled. "Since I blabbed the news when we were texting last night, go ahead and tell her."

Jen's eye grew wide, and she clapped her hands. "Nora's got a big day."

"What?" Maggie looked at Nora and back at Jen. "What are you doing today?"

Nora looked at her two closest friends. "We're having lunch with Jim's parents at the country club."

Maggie clapped her hands together. "That's great. What's so scary? You already know her. And you said she was great to work for."

Nora looked across the parking lot. "I know. But this is different. Now I'm going as a girlfriend. It's social, not professional."

Jim put his arm around Nora. "She's going to love you as much as a girlfriend as she does as her interior designer. I promise."

Nora looked into Jim's confident eyes. "You're right. It'll be fine."

Jen reached for Nora's hand. "You look great. It's going to be fine. I'm thinking a three-way call when you get home, though."

Maggie laughed. "Better yet, we'll meet you at your house later for tea and details."

The morsel of nervousness that hung on after her communion prayer had been encouraged away by her friends. "Sounds good. How's four?"

The clubhouse at the country club was flanked by the golf course and pro shop on the right and the swimming pool on the left. The two-story, red-brick building boasted white trim and columns on the front.

"Are you sure I'm dressed appropriately?" Nora straightened the skirt of her cream linen dress. Her loose curls fell softly next to the scalloped neckline of the dress.

"For the thousandth time." Eve rolled her eyes. "You look great, Aunt Nora."

The three walked toward the double front doors. Jim took Nora's hand. "You look perfect. And Eve, you look lovely too."

Eve wore a red cotton top that hung at the waist of her beige, wide-leg linen pants with pockets and tied in the front, creating a gathered effect, and strappy tan sandals.

Mr. and Mrs. Preston stood waiting in the lobby outside the dining room. Mrs. Preston smiled at Nora. "I'm so glad it's you." Her soft, aged hand took Nora's hand.

Mrs. Preston's touch was reassuring. Everything was going to be okay. "Thank you for the invitation to lunch. This is my niece, Eve."

"It's so good to meet you, darling. Your aunt has told me that you're going to our high school this year."

Eve smiled. "Yes, ma'am."

"Oh, and such good manners." Mrs. Preston turned to her husband. "James, this is Nora St. Claire and her niece, Eve."

He shook Nora's hand. "Good to meet you. I'm sure you're something special to capture my son's attention and please my wife's particular taste in decorating."

Nora nodded. "Not sure about all that, but I enjoy my time with both of them."

Mr. Preston shook Eve's hand. "And I understand you're a runner."

"Yes, sir. I'm training for a mini-marathon on Thanksgiving in Simpson."

"That's a big undertaking. I hope it goes well for you."

"Thank you."

An older gentleman in black pants and a white shirt interrupted them. "Mr. Preston, your table is ready."

Mr. and Mrs. Preston led the way following the maître d' to their table. Jim leaned over to Nora and whispered. "Who are these endearing people?"

Nora playfully swatted at him. "Hush, those are your parents. Your mom is always like that."

The round table was set for five. Mrs. Preston sat next to Eve, with Nora on the other side of Eve, and Jim on her left. That put Mr. Preston next to Jim. As he and Jim were taking their seats, he smiled. "She's beautiful, Jim."

Jim whispered back to his dad, "Inside and out. She's amazing."

"I'm hungry. What do you want for lunch?" Mrs. Preston leaned over to Eve. "You get anything you want. Our treat. And you'll want to save room—their sundaes are to die for."

Eve looked at Nora, who nodded. "What looks good, Eve?"

As lunch continued, the conversation flowed easily. Nora's nerves settled. Before she knew it, she was almost giggling over the stories Mrs. Preston told about Jim and his brothers growing up. "When James had to be out of town, I was outnumbered by those rascals. And your Jim here was their ringleader."

Nora felt the warmth in her cheeks growing. She reached for Jim's hand. "Oh, I'm sure he was just trying to reel them in."

Mrs. Preston threw her head back with a laugh. "I don't think so, but if it keeps you around, I'll agree with you."

Nora nodded. "Yeah, I think I'll stick around."

"Good, because I'm wearing out my knees praying for the Lord to bring him a good woman."

"Mother, I've been waiting for the best to come along."

Mr. Preston wiped his mouth with the cloth napkin. "Well said, Son. The young associates in our office are in such a hurry after getting their jobs to get married. They don't realize how hard a first-year associate's schedule is on a young marriage."

"I was so glad when we were past those hard, early years. James had his hands full trying to earn a junior partnership when Jim was born. Then Paul came along." Mrs. Preston grasped her husband's hand. "Those were busy years, but we survived." She looked at Eve, who was finishing her last French fry. "Do you know what classes you'll take this fall?"

Eve sat up straight. "Yes, ma'am, I'll have English III, Algebra II, Biology II, American History, and Spanish III."

"Oh, my goodness. You'll be a busy young lady."

"I guess. I'm looking forward to it."

"Would you like dessert?" She looked around the table. "Anyone else want dessert? What about brownies and sundaes all around?"

Nora put her hand on her stomach. "I don't know if I can eat another bite."

Mrs. Preston gestured to Eve. "I bet Eve will eat what you can't. James, why don't we order a plate of brownies with sundaes? That's always fun. Sound good, everyone?"

Mr. Preston gave a small wave to their server. "We'd like five hot fudge sundaes. Everyone okay with nuts and whipped cream?" Everyone nodded. "And a plate of brownies."

Lunch chatter continued through dessert. As they parted at the door, Nora leaned over and hugged Mrs. Preston. "That's from girlfriend Nora, not your designer Nora. Thank you for making this such a fun lunch. I wasn't sure what to expect."

"I'm glad we got to know 'girlfriend' Nora. I like you as much as or more than 'designer' Nora." Mrs. Preston hugged Eve. "Eve, if I don't see you before, I hope school gets off to a good start.

Mr. Preston gave Nora a side hug. "Good to meet you." He put his hand on Jim's shoulder. "Son, she's a catch. And keep me posted on the renovations at the theater. Glad they're going well."

"Thanks ... thanks, Dad."

Jim held the car door for Nora as Eve slid into the back seat. He took his place in the driver's seat. "Who were those people? And what did they do with my snooty mother and condescending father?"

"Your mother has always been kind to me. Maybe they're mellowing."

"Maybe. My dad has never been as interested in the theater as he's been lately. I don't understand. And my mother—no one outside their country club circle has ever been good enough for her."

"She'd not met me." Nora drew a sassy smile. "I'm kidding. Maybe working with her before meeting her socially helped."

"Maybe it did." Jim looked in the rearview mirror at Eve. "Eve, I hope you weren't too bored."

"Bored, no way. It was a blast hearing about all the trouble you and your brothers got into. Aunt Nora, can we go for a run this afternoon?"

"I can't. Maggie is coming over. I'd like to get our laundry finished before she gets there."

"I'll go for a run with you. What time?" Jim's offer surprised Nora in a good way.

As they rode home, the words of the minister settled again on Nora's heart. "Be still and know that I am God." The God who had guided her through so many peaks and valleys.

CHAPTER TWENTY-FOUR

The first day of school came with butterflies and a heat wave. In Oakdale, most schools began in mid-August. The weather didn't resemble fall in the slightest. The leaves were still green, pools were still open, and the grass still needed mowing. Nora and Eve had shopped for the school supplies from the list the school admissions coordinator had given them. Eve and Ashley had been texting every day. As they were choosing supplies from the list, Eve would give Ashley's commentary about not really needing this or that. Nora relented, noting that they could run out and pick it up if Eve's new friend was wrong.

"Are you ready for your day?" Nora slid a cup of hot tea across to Eve.

Eve scooted her scrambled eggs around her plate and took a bite of toast. She had taken a little longer to get ready this morning. Nora brought her plated toast and egg around the granite island to sit next to Eve. "Honey, are you okay?"

Eve continued the egg dance on her plate. "I guess." She looked at Nora.

Nora noticed a deep sadness in Eve's eyes. The last few weeks had been filled with Eve spending time at the theater and gym. They had enjoyed time together and with Nora's friends. This morning, things got real. Eve was going to a new high school. Nora realized it was a first—the first day of school without her mother.

"Aunt Nora, I'm sca ... I'm scared." The brave teenager couldn't hold back the tears. She leaned into Nora and sobbed.

Nora turned fully to Eve and wrapped her arms around her. She cried too. "I know. I wish she was here."

Eve sat back in the tall chair and wiped her eyes with the napkin. "Now I've spoiled my makeup."

Nora tucked a strand of Eve's hair behind her ear. "I noticed you're wearing a little more than usual. Sweety, you're hurting. I can't fix that. Something I think your mom would tell you today, starting a new school, is to be your wonderful self."

A small smile grew across Eve's lips. "She used to say that to me all the time ... my wonderful self."

"She was right. God created you with intelligence and beauty both inside and out. He's going to walk with you today into every class and be with you during the awkward introductions with classmates. Don't try to be what you think they'll like. Be yourself."

"You're right. But it's scary."

"Keep an eye out today for Ashley and some of the kids from church. How about we do something special for dinner ... Maybe go out?"

Eve took her half-eaten breakfast to the sink and scraped it into the drain. "That'd be nice. Mom and I always did either dinner or ice cream after the first day of school."

"You got it. Decide where. Did you have any other first-day traditions you'd like to do?"

"Not really. She always took a picture. I found all of them in a box. Guess we should do one for eleventh grade to keep it going."

"Sounds good. You go finish getting ready, and we'll take it on the front porch."

Eve started down the hall to the stairs. She stopped in front of a mirror. "I guess I did overdo the mascara and eyeliner."

Nora came in from taking her bag to the car. Eve met her at the bottom of the stairs. She had washed her face and toned down the makeup. Her long brown hair was braided, and her bangs lay loose on her forehead.

"Oh yes, much better. Before we leave, I'd like to pray for our day." Nora and Eve sat on the sofa. Nora took Eve's hands in hers and took a deep breath before she began. "Lord, today's a big, scary, nerve-wracking day. Please walk with Eve today. Bring the right friends into her path. The friends who will encourage her. Father, I pray she will find her classes and not get lost in a big high school. And Lord, thank you for bringing Eve to me. Help me to be the aunt she needs me to be. Amen."

Eve didn't let go. "Lord, be with Aunt Nora today. I'm sure she has a lot of work to do for her clients. I pray that it all goes well. And ..." She sniffed. "And thank you that Aunt Nora is here for me. Amen."

Nora looked up to see Eve dab a tear away. "Let's go take that picture. Do you have your backpack and lunch money?"

"I do. Oh, and are we going to Simpson this weekend?"

"Yes. Your uncle Phillip wants to finish at your house. He has some painters coming in next week."

"Can I plan on spending some time with my friends there?"

"Sure. Make plans for Saturday."

Nora pulled her keys from her purse.

Exhaustion from the morning of confession and testifying about Willie and his drug-running business weighed on Curt. When it was done, he was released.

In the hall outside the courtroom, Curt stopped the public defender who barely remembered Curt's name. "Hey, Jerry, um, I'm going to need an attorney to help me get visitation with my daughter. Can you help me?"

The public defender looked surprised. "Really? That story you told about your ex being dead wasn't a lie?"

Even his attorney didn't believe him. *Guess I deserve that.*

"Sure." Jerry gave him a doubtful look. "I'll find someone in family court to help you. Call me in a couple of days." Jerry shoved his file into the worn satchel.

Curt's thoughts of Eve and Liz had become less about the money and more about having a daughter who one day might want to know her father. When he walked out of the jail with only two duffle bags of personal possessions, he did so with an odd sense of freedom and a touch of fear. *Just make the next choice.*

His next choice felt odd, but right. He walked to the information desk in the jail lobby and asked to use a phone. Paster Sparks answered on the first ring.

The steps in the run-down apartment building creaked as Curt followed Pastor Sparks up to the room they'd offered. Greg Stump, the man who ran the house, reviewed the rules and assigned Curt a room. No alcohol, no drugs, no women, and everyone had to attend at least five AA meetings a week for their first month. After the first month, he would be required to have a job and attend at least three meetings a week, or as many over that amount as he felt he needed. There would be random drug testing and room searches. The church van left at 9:00 o'clock every Sunday morning. Those were the rules. If he didn't like them, he didn't have to stay.

The room was sparse. Not much bigger than his cell. A dirty window, a bed with sheets and a blanket folded at the foot, a wooden desk with a lamp and chair, and a closet.

Pastor Sparks set one of Curt's duffle bags down. Curt set the other one down and wiped his sweating hands on his jeans. He looked at the only person he knew who wanted to help him.

"Curt, it doesn't look like much, but it's a step up from the gutter."

Curt nodded. "A small step, but yes." He turned to Pastor Sparks. "He didn't say anything about a phone. I lost my cell. Any chance you could help me get another one?"

"There's a landline downstairs in a small room off the kitchen. If you need to make a long-distance call, you'll need to get a phone card to pay for the call. Otherwise, you can use it as much as you need. Just be considerate of others who may want to use it."

"Got it. And what about my car?"

"With a suspended license, you don't need a car right now. But I was told it's at the impound lot to be picked up. If you want, I can get a friend to go with us to get it. Most of the men here park in the lot behind the building."

Curt nodded. *No driving. No drinking. Only meetings, finding a job, and making new choices.*

Pastor Sparks clapped his hands. "I'm going to go, and you can get settled in." He looked at his watch. "They'll have lunch in a few minutes. That'd be a good time for you to meet the others. I'll see you Sunday for church."

Right, Sunday for church. Curt turned to Paul and reached out to shake his hand. "Pastor, thank you for picking me up, and getting me here."

"I'm glad to help. The next steps are yours, Curt."

When the pastor left, Curt stood in the middle of the small, dark room. *Yep, it barely beats the gutter.* Curt picked up the information sheet Pastor Sparks had left on the table. At the bottom was a Bible verse, "And my God will meet all your needs according to the riches of his glory in Christ Jesus." He looked around the dingy room. It no longer felt dark. *Today, this is all I need. If you're listening, thank you, God.*

CHAPTER TWENTY-FIVE

Located three blocks from the Oakdale Community Theater, Oakdale East High School was a three-story, rectangular building with wings jutting out from both ends. The stairs were marble, and the handrails were wood with brass fixtures. Eve had been told to report to the office to get her locker assignment. The office staff was buzzing around helping other students. The phone was ringing but wasn't being answered.

One lady, who seemed to be the office air traffic controller, was directing staff and students. "Sammy, you know the drill. Go to your homeroom class first. Mrs. Tatum will provide you with instructions for bookstore hours and submitting lunch money. Missy, here's your revised class list." When Missy took the sheet of paper from the lady, the school secretary caught Eve's eye at the back of the line. Over her shoulder she called for the principal, whom Eve had met on the tour. "Mr. Davenport, would you please come out here?"

Mr. Davenport was a seasoned educator and administrator. He stood over six feet tall with whispers of gray in his brown hair. He was thin, wore a long-sleeve shirt and tie, and looked students and adults in the eye when he spoke to them.

"Eve, it's so good to see you again. I've got your schedule and locker assignment." He stepped around the counter. "Here's your lock. Do you want me to walk with you or just point the way?"

Eve hesitated. "Point the way ... I'll find the locker and homeroom."

"I understand." He handed her the lock and class schedule.

Eve turned the schedule over to find a simple map of the school with room numbers. The smile lines around Mr. Davenport's eyes grew. "I added the map to help you find your classes. The room numbers are on the schedule. Turn left out of the office, and at the first hallway intersection, turn right. Your locker is down that hallway."

Eve nodded, still focused on the map.

"And Eve, if you need anything today or anytime, I'm always available."

"Thank you, sir."

Eve turned to leave the office. The hall outside the office was four deep across with students. Mr. Davenport's directions rolled over and over in her head. Left out of the office, right at the hallway intersection. *I can do this.* She stepped into the fray of students and bumped her way to the opposite side of the hall, so she'd be able to turn to the right. Following the numbers on the lockers, she found number 112. Not having any textbooks yet, she opened the door, looked inside, and closed it. She tried the combination to the lock, but it wasn't opening. She tried it again, and it didn't budge. The waves of students rolled faster as the first bell rang. Eve remembered being told on the tour there were two bells before class began. The first was a four-minute warning to get to class. She looked around and yanked at the stubborn lock.

"Eve!" Ashley came racing across the hall, with another girl following her. "You're here. How's it going?"

Eve gave a final yank at the lock. No luck. "Fine, I guess. Found my locker, next, homeroom."

"Here, let me help you with that. These locks are tricky. On the second number you always have to go back past zero again. What's your combination?" The other girl with Ashley looked bored.

Eve hesitated. Ashley took the lock. "We all share combinations. No biggy."

Eve read the numbers off the small piece of paper. Ashley whizzed through the numbers and the lock relented. "There you go."

Eve sighed. "Thank you. Where's your homeroom?"

"Seniors are down the other side. I came through here trying to find you. Hope your day goes well. Let's catch up after school. Meet me out front? Mom let me drive today." Ashley held her books with one hand and waved the other in the excitement of driving to school. "Where's your homeroom?"

Eve looked down at the sheet. Ashley peered over at it as well. "Oh, you've got Baker for homeroom and first-period math. He's great. All his exams come from his quizzes." She looked over Eve's shoulder and pointed. "His classroom is on the corner back from where you turned coming from the office."

Eve nodded. "Thanks. I appreciate you coming to find me." She looked around. "My high school in Simpson was the largest in the town. But this is even bigger."

"You'll get used to it. Hey, got to run. See you later." Ashley and her silent friend bopped down the hall.

Eve turned in the direction Ashley had pointed. Thankfully, the room numbers were easy to find without looking like you were looking for a room number. Eve bit her bottom lip as she walked into the classroom. The room was square with desks in rows facing the whiteboard. The wall opposite the door had windows across it looking out toward the front of the school. Everyone seemed to already know where they were supposed to sit. She took a deep breath and headed to the back when she heard her name from the other side. "Eve, over here."

Eve's eyes followed the voice calling her name. It was Torri, a girl from the youth group at church. Torri had long, blonde hair pulled back in a ponytail. She waved and pointed to a desk next to her. Eve released her bottom lip and zig-zagged through the other students to the desk. She didn't know Torri well, but she was a familiar face in a sea of the unfamiliar. *Maybe God did hear Nora's prayer this morning.* She slid into the desk, looping her purse on the back of the chair, and laying her notebook on the desk.

"Torri, thank you."

"I know, everyone has their spots." She leaned closer to Eve and in a hushed voice, gave her the lay of the land. "The jocks sit in the back, except Ben Milton. He's our quarterback, is pretty nice, and cares about learning something other than his playbook."

As Torri mentioned Ben's name, he looked at Eve with a small smile and nod. Heat flew up her face, and she looked away. He had blond hair, crystal blue eyes, and a friendly smile.

Torri nodded to the front right section of desks and students. "Those guys are the math and science guys. You'll see the six of them always together and talking equations and formulas. The two guys and one girl, here in front of us, are first, second, and third in GPA ranking for our class. They are competing for valedictorian. The rest of us just want to pass, you know?" She elbowed Eve.

Eve looked around at all the unfamiliar faces. "Yeah, I'm okay in math, but I don't need to talk about it all the time." The second bell rang, and Mr. Baker slid a pencil behind his ear and called the students to take their seats. While everyone was getting settled, he came by Eve's desk.

"Eve, I'm Mr. Baker. Welcome to Oakdale. Here's the textbook you need. Please let me know if you have any questions. I'm glad to help." He was very matter-of-fact. Like most math teachers.

With each class, Eve was given the textbook, a syllabus, and an individual greeting from the teacher. She took all her notes in the one notebook she'd brought, including additional supplies she would need. With each visit to her locker, she was thankful Ashley had helped her earlier. It turned out she and Torri were in several classes together. Eve noticed the other girls, the obvious 'clique,' and wondered if she would be included in a group of friends.

The final bell rang. Eve went to her locker to figure out what she needed to take with her. Torri stopped by Eve's locker. "How was your day?"

"It was fine. Thanks for asking."

"I know it's not your high school in Simpson. But I hope you start to feel like you fit in. Here's my number. Call or text me tonight if you want."

Eve took the bright pink sticky note from her new friend. "Thanks. I may need your help with that Spanish assignment." Eve smiled. "Really, find a recipe and translate it into Spanish?"

"I know. Be ready, I heard from someone who had her last year that we're going to exchange recipes and have to make the dish and bring it in."

Eve's eyes grew wide. "No way. Hope you and I can swap."

"That'd be great. See you tomorrow."

Eve pulled her Spanish and English books out of her locker to take home. She walked out of the school's front door to find Aunt Nora waiting in her car. To the right was the parking lot where Ashley and some of her friends were standing next to their cars. She started to walk over to the group when Aunt Nora waved. Eve shifted to walk to the car. She opened the rear door and put her books in. As she opened the passenger door, Ashley waved.

"Aunt Nora, do you mind if I go talk to Ashley? I saw her this morning and she asked me to meet her after school."

Aunt Nora nodded. "Sure, but I need to get out of the way of others picking up. What if I circle around and meet you in the parking lot?"

Eve's eyebrows crinkled. "Umm ..."

Aunt Nora took the hint. "I'll pull in away from Ashley where you can see me. Okay?"

Eve closed the door and headed toward Ashley.

Ashley pulled her wiry hair back to tame it from the breeze. "Eve! Come meet some of my friends."

The three girls standing in a semi-circle around Ashley looked over at Eve—with attitudes that shouted, "You are not welcome." One girl had long, wavy brown hair pulled back on both sides with hairpins. Eve recognized her as the silent friend with Ashley at her locker that morning. The girl chewed gum like it counted as exercise. The other girl had her hair pulled into a high ponytail that still hung below her shoulders. She stood with one hip cocked, balancing her books. The third one had perfect makeup and a sparkle to her.

"This is Crystal, Addison, and Olivia. Girls, this is Eve. She just moved here from Simpson."

"Aren't you a junior?" The gum-chewer asked. Eve thought that was Crystal.

Eve tilted her head. At Simpson High it didn't matter your class rank, everyone was friends. "Yes."

The next one, Miss Books-On-Hip, Eve couldn't remember their names in order, pulled her sunglasses off. "We beat Simpson High last year in football and basketball."

Eve twisted a loose hair. "Okay, I guess. Went to games but didn't keep up with who we beat or lost to."

"Not that hard when they're all losses." Gum-muncher added.

Ouch. Not a nice girl.

The third girl reached her hand out. "I'm Olivia. Don't listen to them. Good to meet you." Olivia was nice but not overbearing. "I hope you'll come to some of the games this year. They really are fun."

Eve made a mental note to be careful with Crystal and Addison but allowed a smile at Olivia. "Thanks. Sure." She noticed Aunt Nora's car a few rows away. She looked at Ashley and her posse. "Good to see you. Ashley, we'll talk later—I need to run."

"Sure. Talk to you later."

Eve hustled away from the gaggle of girls. When she wasn't far enough away, she heard either Crystal or Addison say, "I heard she has a tragic background. Both parents are dead, and she has to live with her old aunt."

A lump grew in her throat as she walked faster to Aunt Nora's car. By the time she got in and closed the door, all the good parts of her day became overshadowed by one statement from some girl she had only known for three minutes.

Aunt Nora reached over to hold her hand. Eve jerked it away. "Can we please just leave?"

Nora pulled out of the school parking lot. Tears rolled silently down Eve's face. Concern squeezed at Nora's heart. What seemed hours but was only minutes later, they pulled into the driveway at Nora's house. With the click into park, Eve bolted from the car and used her own key to get into the house. Nora went through the front door to see Eve's heels hit the top step. Wisdom kept her from taking steps two at a time to get upstairs. *Give her a minute.* Nora heard the bathroom door close. With a deep breath, she went back outside to check the mailbox. When she returned, Eve had changed clothes and was in the kitchen getting a snack. She set the mail on the counter. Eve pulled a bottle of water out of the refrigerator.

"Do you want to talk about your day?"

"It was fine. Typical first day of school."

Nora sat on a stool and crossed her arms. "It doesn't seem like it was a fine, typical first day of school."

"I don't really want to talk about it. Everything is fine. Okay?" Eve went back upstairs in a huff.

This was a new side of "teenager" that Nora knew nothing about. The statement and huff away. Had something happened at school? Should she call the school counselor? *Don't overreact.* To give Eve more time, Nora sat down at a small table off to the side in the den that she had used as her desk. She opened her work laptop and began to go through Mrs. Preston's color choices. She had met the movers there today to remove all the furniture from the spaces, storing everything in a temporary shelter outside. They left the carpet down until after they were done with the walls. Work helped her relax. *Eve will be fine. She knows I'm here when she wants to talk. What if she doesn't want to talk?* Twenty minutes later, Eve came downstairs in her running clothes.

"Aunt Nora, can I go for a run? And then ... I know we talked about going out to dinner ... and I need some school supplies."

Nora stood. *Okay, she's talking and not huffing off.* "Yes, you can go for a run. Did you decide what you wanted for dinner?"

"I don't care. Whatever is fine. Will you invite Aunt Maggie and Aunt Jen to come? Wasn't today Brian, Emma, and Danny's first day too?"

Nora's eyes narrowed. "Ah, I can call and see if they want to join us. If it's going to be a group, want to have pizza?"

Eve shifted. "Pizza's fine. I'll be back in about forty-five minutes."

Nora texted Maggie and Jen to see if their families wanted to meet up for dinner. Maggie said yes, but Jen was tied up with a work deadline. Nora snagged the mail off the counter—one of the thicker envelopes was from the county family court administration. After reading the first sentence, she called Phillip.

"No stinkin' way. Has Curt lost his mind? Petitioning for visitation with Eve."

Nora shook her head as she read the letter. "Looks like he wants weekends, and we have a court date late next week."

"I'll check with our attorney. He was probably copied on the letter. We'll need to meet with him before court." Phillip paused. "I can't believe he's doing this."

"Well, he is. And we're going to have to tell the story again. I'm sorry that Eve will have to go through this, but she's going to have to be there." Nora flipped the letter over to see if there were any more details.

"Eve's got so much going on."

"I know. But we'll be there with her."

"Nora, I've got to run to my meeting. Everything will be fine. If you want to wait until we're together to tell Eve, that'll work."

"No, I'll tell her. I may call and have you on speaker if that's okay."

"Certainly."

CHAPTER TWENTY-SIX

Jim whistled through the lobby of the theater, then broke into a hum. Sara lifted her eyes to see him flicking through the mail. Baby Glenda was sound asleep. Jim stopped at the counter. "Here's the mail. Looks like a utility bill and an invoice from the electrician."

"You're in a good mood. Usually, bill day makes you grumpy."

"I don't love the bills, but for the first time in a long time, the theater is running in the black and a tiny bit ahead."

"Oh, that reminds me. This came for you. The oddest elderly gentleman came in and handed it to me. He didn't say anything, then he turned and left."

Jim raised his eyebrows. The outside of the envelope simply had his first and last name, Jim Preston. He flipped it over and worked the sealed flap open. He looked inside and then reached in to pull out a banded stack of hundred-dollar bills. "What on earth?"

Sara's jaw dropped. "How much is that?"

"Not the point. Who was that man? What did he look like?"

Sara's eyes shifted, she looked down at the desk and over at her baby. "I ... I ... I don't know. I was getting the baby settled, and like I said, he just strolled in, handed me the envelope, said nothing, and walked out."

"This is our second anonymous gift. Are you sure he didn't leave a business card?"

"He was old. He had one of those flat hats on and wore a windbreaker jacket." She fingered her long brown hair. "I could see short whisps of grey hair. Kinda looked like someone's grandfather."

Jim fanned the bills. "There's probably five thousand dollars here. And he didn't say a word?"

"Not one word."

Jim opened the envelope further to see a small piece of paper wedged in the bottom. He pulled it out. All it said was 'for the needs of the theater.' He scratched his head. "Who is this guy?"

Sara shrugged. "Your guardian angel?"

Pizza wasn't only Eve's idea. The restaurant was full of families celebrating the first day of school. The hostess directed them to follow her.

Nora and Maggie sat across from each other. Eve sat next to Nora, and Maggie's daughter sat across from Eve. Danny sat at the end. Dinner went well. Nora noticed Eve chatting and laughing with Emma and Danny. She and Maggie talked about work, the theater, nothing too heavy. With Eve right next to her, Nora couldn't talk about what she'd noticed with the girls at school.

Eve was quiet on the ride home. Went inside and straight to her room.

Nora settled on the sofa in the den and called Maggie. "Got a minute now? I couldn't talk at the restaurant with the kids right there."

"Sure. I get it. What happened at school today with Eve?"

"Everything seemed fine this morning. She was a little nervous, but we talked about what she and Liz did for their first day of school traditions. We decided to continue the tradition she had with Liz, dinner out and a 'first day of school' picture. I was on time to pick her up from school, but she wanted to talk to Ashley before we left. I told her no problem, but I had to park somewhere else. I told her I'd pull into the parking lot. She was fine with that but didn't want me to pull close to where Ashley was. So, I pulled around to the parking lot away from where Ashley and the other girls were and let Eve go talk with them. Eve seemed fine before she went to talk with Ashley."

"Who were the other girls?" Maggie asked.

"I don't know. But Eve talked with them only long enough to meet them. They couldn't have said much. But whatever was said upset her. She got in the car, didn't want to talk. We rode home in silence." Nora put her hand over her heart. "It was killing me to see her hurting and not wanting to talk about it. When we got home, she went straight upstairs. She came down once for a bottled water, and I said it didn't seem like she had a good day, she said it was fine and huffed off. Then she came down and wanted to go for a run, then meet you for dinner." While she recounted the situation, Nora twisted a tissue around her finger until it was almost in shreds.

"First days someplace new are hard." Maggie paused and continued. "It's going to be okay. She still wanted to go to dinner."

"Yes, but she wanted you all there so she and I wouldn't have to talk."

"Today was a hard day for her. A few months ago, she thought she would be back at Simpson High School, and she's not. Eve is an extraordinary young lady, strong and smart. But she's hurting. Like you are, and your family."

Nora nodded. "I'm sure you're right."

"Every teenager is worried about being accepted. Then layer on everything else Eve is carrying. It's a burden for them." Maggie reassured her.

"What am I supposed to do? How do I fix this?"

"You can't. No parent can. All we can do is love and encourage them and be available when they are ready to tell us what's going on. That's why having the right friends is so important. They have a lot of influence."

Nora shook her head. "I'm not sure I'm equipped for this."

"You're more equipped than you think. You love her, you want to protect her, and you hurt when she hurts."

Such great friends. Not trying to solve the problem, just trying to help Nora through it. She shook her head. "I wanted Eve's day to be wonderful. And I don't think it was. Now she's not talking about it."

"She'll talk when she's ready. Be available and ready to listen."

"You're right. Thanks for talking to me."

"Always glad to."

Nora finished her conversation with Maggie and went into the kitchen to fix a cup of tea. Eve walked in texting on her phone.

"Who are you texting?"

"Ashley."

"Great. Did you meet some of her friends today?"

"Yes."

"What are they like?"

"They were okay. Ashley says they want to go to the mall after school tomorrow. Can I go with them?"

Nora pondered the request. She knew Ashley but not the other girls. All the things she had read and talked about with the counselor about teenagers rolled around her brain. Social interaction. Getting involved at school. A little freedom.

"I guess I could take you all and go do some other shopping while you do yours."

Eve's eyes grew large. "Uh, Aunt Nora, these girls drive on their own. I think she said Crystal would drive us."

"Oh. Hadn't considered letting you ride with a friend. What about volunteering at the theater? You told Jim you'd come a couple of days after school, and that covers the service hours you need."

"Please, Aunt Nora. We decided I wouldn't go back to volunteering until next week. I want these girls to like me. And I can't be like the little kid that needs to be driven by their par ..." Eve stopped short.

Nora heard an inkling of something in Eve's voice. Was it desperation? Nora had no words. She was at a crossroads on how to handle the situation. Eve opened the snack drawer and studied the contents.

It didn't seem like the best time, but Nora had to tell Eve about Curt's petition. "Eve, there's something I need to tell you."

"What is it?"

"Curt has petitioned the court for weekend visitation with you. Meaning you would have to go stay with him a couple of weekends a month."

Eve whipped around. "What? I don't want to. He's weird."

Eve wasn't wrong. Nora kept her voice cool, if only to help Eve remain calm. "I know. Phillip and I talked about it, and we feel confident that with Curt's record, and because he has been absent all these years, the judge will rule in our favor." She glanced at her niece, who was staring at her phone screen.

"I'm a little curious to get to know him, but I don't want to be made to go stay with him."

"That's fair. You should get to know him on your terms."

"So, what happens next?"

"Next week, we'll go to court. You're going to hear the entire story about him and your mom again. And the judge will decide. However, since you're over thirteen, you have the right to speak for yourself if you want."

"What would I have to say?"

"You would tell the judge what you just told me. That someday you'd like to get to know your dad, but you don't want to be made to spend weekends with him."

"And the judge will listen to me?"

Nora reached over and squeezed Eve's hand. "Yes, your feelings are the most important right now."

CHAPTER TWENTY-SEVEN

Eve went through her four bags of supplies for the next day at school. They'd found a backpack that was olive green with brown leather accents. Aunt Nora's phone buzzed. Eve saw it was Jim. "Go ahead and take his call. You've been ignoring them since you picked me up."

"I'll call him back. Are you okay? You got quiet after I told you about court. And I'm a little concerned about your mood after talking with Ashley's friends."

"Would you please quit with the questions?" Eve's hands waved and her face turned red as her voice rose. "I'll be fine ... with court and my new friends. You and everybody else told me to go to the new school, meet new friends, broaden my world ... You made me move here. Well, here I am, trying to get to know new people, and you want to treat me like a kindergartener." Tears threatened. Eve made an about-face and stomped upstairs with her bags.

ASHLEY: Will your aunt let you go?

EVE: Not sure. She didn't answer. I'll go back downstairs and talk to her in a few and ask again.

ASHLEY: Crystal, Addison, and Olivia really liked you. I know they can be a little snobby, but after you left, I told them how cool you are. Since Crystal's driving, she chooses who goes, and you are in if you want to go.

EVE: Thanks. I'll ask my aunt again.

Eve pulled out the new backpack and put her supplies and textbooks in it. Everything fit. She flung it over one shoulder and looked in the mirror. Yep, it looked like the backpacks several of the other girls had. As she set it by her nightstand, the picture of her and her mom caught her eye. *Mom. Why did you leave me?* Eve slid into a puddle on the floor next to her bed. Her eyes were locked on the photo. *I just want to get past all the new stuff and be comfortable again with friends ... and with you. I miss you, Mom. Why?*

Nora's heart raced, and she felt the heat climb her face. Something wasn't right with Eve. Was going to court going to be too much? Was moving and starting a new school too soon? Her phone buzzed. Jim again. Nora fell onto the soft couch and answered.

"Hello, my lovely Nora." Jim's mood was in direct opposition to Nora's.

"Hello." Her anger had subsided, leaving Nora with a rush of exhaustion.

"Are you okay? How was Eve's first day of school?"

"Don't ask. I dropped her off this morning, and she was nervous, but okay. This afternoon I picked up a moody, quick-to-anger teenager. I had to tell her about the court date. Now she's asking to go to the mall tomorrow after school with her friend Ashley and three of her friends."

"What's wrong with letting her go?"

"Well, for one thing, she would be riding with them. I don't know the driver or anything about any of the girls except Ashley. It's the second day of school. Never mind, you wouldn't understand."

Jim responded in a calm, low tone. "Nora, you've got this. I know you're trying to be perfect. Trust yourself to do what's best for Eve."

"What would you do? I want her to get to know new people. I don't want to treat her like a child. But something about this, her moodiness, doesn't sit well."

"Sweetie, sounds like you have your answer."

"She's not going to like it."

Nora hung up and called Eve downstairs. She heard a muffled "Okay" as Eve closed the bathroom door. A few minutes later, she came downstairs. Nora knew immediately she'd been crying. She reached for her niece. "Eve, are you all right?"

Eve pulled her arm back and walked past Nora into the kitchen. "What did you decide about tomorrow?"

"Eve, honey, I just don't have a good feeling about you going to the mall with Ashley and her friends."

Eve gave a restrained response. "Aunt Nora, these girls are friends of Ashley's, and you know Ashley."

"Come sit down."

Eve sat next to Nora on the couch. She drew her legs into a crisscross. Nora took a deep breath. "I'm not trying to be mean. You want to make friends. I get that. But something about those girls is nagging at me. I don't know them, but from what I could see when I picked you up today ... the way they were standing and looking at you. They didn't seem to be welcoming you."

Eve looked down at her hands and intertwined her fingers. "Ashley said Crystal and Addison are always a little stand-offish to new girls. She talked to them after I left, and they think I'm cool now." She looked up at Nora. "But Olivia was really nice."

Nora sighed. *Lord, what do I do? I just don't feel good about this.* Nora remembered Jim's words, you got this. She reached for Eve's hands. "Eve, I'm new at all this pare ... guardian stuff. And I'm sorry, but I can't say yes this time. Something about this doesn't feel right. I'll pick you up tomorrow. Maybe another time you can go with the girls."

Eve's shoulders slumped. She stood and turned to go upstairs. "Okay."

On her way upstairs, Eve's phone buzzed with a text.

ASHLEY: Well, can you go?

EVE: She said yes.

ASHLEY: Great. I'll tell the girls.

The next morning the house was quiet, the sun was rising, as were Nora's hopes that Eve wouldn't still be upset. After a solid night's rest, something about the scene she watched in the school parking lot and now these three other girls wanting Eve to go to the mall with them still didn't feel right. Her phone buzzed. Jim's grin on her phone brought her a smile.

"Good morning."

"How are things going with Eve this morning?"

"We haven't spoken yet. I hear the shower, so she's up and moving. I came down early."

"Prayed for you both this morning."

"Thank you. Sounds like you're in the car. Where are you going so early?"

"Headed to the theater. The electricians are coming to do the final wiring upgrade and connect the circuit box. I will be so glad to have all our lighting functional again."

"I hope it goes well. And Jim ..." Nora's thoughts turned to the change in Jim's attitude toward Eve. "Thank you for your encouragement about Eve and this whole friend thing."

"You're my best girl. I want to support you in whatever life brings our way."

"Your encouragement and efforts haven't gone unnoticed this last month. Thank you, it means everything to me." A skillet being set on the gas stove and the sound of a burner being lit came from the kitchen. "Sounds like Eve's making breakfast. Can we talk later?"

"Of course. Have a great day."

"You too." Nora set her phone on the coffee table and headed for the kitchen.

"Good morning."

"Hi, Aunt Nora. Hope you don't mind, but I'm really hungry this morning, so I'm making eggs and bacon."

Nora sat at the island watching Eve glide from the stove to the refrigerator, pulling out the eggs. Eve stopped. "What? Do you want me to make you some too?"

Eve's countenance was light. She was wearing the new jeans they bought with a peasant blouse. She added waves to her straight hair for the second day of school, and her makeup was still tame.

"No, thank you. I had toast with my coffee earlier."

"Yeah, I heard you up like an hour ago. Why so early?"

Now she's interested in me. Eve's behavior was going from energetic to maybe a little antsy. "Still having a few sleepless nights."

"I get it. Oh, and after school today there's a meeting about clubs this year. Can you pick me up a little later? I think it will last an hour and a half, maybe two."

"Sure. That helps with my work schedule a little better." Nora finished her coffee and walked over to put her mug in the sink as Eve pulled her egg out of the skillet onto a plate with two waiting strips of bacon. "Looks yummy. I'm going up to finish getting ready to leave." Nora stopped at the bottom of the stairs and turned back to Eve, who had taken her seat and was scrolling on her phone. "Eve, I'm glad you're not mad at me about the mall thing."

Eve pressed her lips together. "It's fine, Aunt Nora. There'll be other times. Did I tell you that Torri from church is in several of my classes?"

Two lies. Well, one and a half. How many more lies would today hold? Eve thought about trying to get out of leaving with Ashley and her friends. But then she'd be back to where she was, a loser in their opinion. She'd lied to Ashley about having gotten permission to go. Now she'd sort of lied to Aunt Nora. There was going to be a meeting about clubs, except Eve wasn't planning to go. It bought her an hour and a half to go to the mall and be back at school. Aunt Nora would never know.

Throughout the morning, the two lies rumbled around Eve's stomach. After lunch, she walked toward the cafeteria exit with Torri and some of her friends. Ashley waved at Eve. "Torri, I'm going to talk to Ashley. I'll see you later."

Torri's forehead wrinkled. "Okay, but Eve, be careful. Ashley's okay, but I hear her friends can be a little wild."

The advice from her mother, telling her to choose her friends wisely, echoed behind Torri's words. Eve smiled. "Thanks, Torri, but I think it'll be fine."

Eve walked over to Ashley and her friends. Olivia wasn't there, but Crystal and Addison were. Ashley stood. "I'm so glad you're going with us after school. We'll meet after the last bell at Crystal's car."

The lies pricked at her heart. *Tell them no.* Eve looked at Crystal, who chomped on her gum. Maybe that's how she stayed thin, gum instead of meals. Crystal raised one eyebrow. "You *are* going, aren't you?"

Two can play this way. Eve shifted her books to her other hip, cocked her head, and looked Crystal in the eye. "Yes, I'm in. See you at your car." *You can gnaw all the gum you want, but here's all the sass you want, girl. She turned and walked away.*

After the last bell, Eve went to put her books in her locker and figure out what homework she needed to do. She stood at her locker, staring at the books and a picture of her and her mom taped to the back wall. *If you hadn't died, I wouldn't be here. I'd be at home with my friends. Not trying to prove myself to Crystal.*

Torri walked by and turned around. "Eve, you okay?"

Eve shook off the knot of angst. "Yes, I'm fine. Just trying to remember all the homework we have."

"I know. It stinks they're giving us homework on the second day of school. Come on, let us ease into the year a little."

Eve pulled out her English, math, and biology books and shoved them in her backpack. "Yeah, it's going to be a long year."

"You still have my number. Call me if you ever want to study together. Or hang out. Oh, and did you hear the youth group is having a pizza and movie night this weekend? Are you coming?"

"Uh, no, didn't hear that. We're going to Simpson this weekend."

There was a weighty pause.

"Oh, okay." Torri looked around. "Maybe another time. See ya."

Eve closed her locker and headed for the student parking lot. Crystal, Addison, Ashley, and Olivia were standing around Crystal's navy-blue Toyota Camry. Eve took a deep breath as she joined them. Crystal hopped off the trunk. "It's about time. Let's roll."

Crystal and Addison were in front, Eve, Ashley, and Olivia fitted into the back. Olivia, as the shortest, got the center. As the rear tires left the parking lot, Crystal handed Addison a pack of cigarettes. "Fire me up one."

Eve turned a sharp look at Ashley and Olivia. Both gave uncomfortable grins. Addison lit both herself and Crystal a cigarette, and she opened the window to blow her first puff out. She turned to catch Eve's eye. "Don't worry, with the window down you won't smell like smoke when you get home."

Crystal glanced over her right shoulder. "Eve, want a drag?"

Eve shook her head. This was such a mistake. "No, no thanks. I don't smoke."

Cheerfully, Olivia changed the subject. "What are we shopping for?"

Addison looked at Crystal. "I need some new earrings. Don't you, Crystal?"

"Would love some. But I don't have the money right now."

"There's other ways to acquire what you want." Addison puffed a smoke ring out.

A sly grin crawled across Crystal's lips. "Ever lifted anything, Eve?"

The knot in her stomach from the two lies tightened. *How did I get here?* "No."

Crystal rolled her eyes. "Don't smoke, don't steal. What did you do for fun in Simpson?"

Eve looked at Ashley, who shrugged. Olivia swatted Crystal's arm. "Come on, give her a break. Besides, you don't steal either."

Crystal looked at Addison, and then back to the road. "Didn't you see my new leather purse? That's real leather, and not something my deadbeat dad is going to let me buy."

Olivia and Ashley were both wide-eyed. They turned onto Third Street. The theater was on the left. "There's the haunted theater," Crystal said.

Ashley finally had something to say. "Didn't you volunteer there this summer, Eve?"

"Yeah. And it's not haunted. I've been all over that building. No ghosts."

Addison threw the last of her cigarette out the window. "Really, you know the place? Let's stop. I want to go in. Eve, you can show us around."

Eve shook her head. "No, I don't think that's a good idea. Not today. Another time." The parking lot came into view. Sara's car was there. "Doesn't look like anyone is here."

Crystal pulled into the parking lot. "So, there's probably a back door or window we can get in."

"Really, Crystal. This isn't a good time. Let's go to the mall like you said. Please." Eve's heart raced. *Don't bring the theater into this circus of lies.* Before she could stop them, the five were out of the car and headed around back. Eve knew there was one backstage door that was hard to lock and might be open. She sighed and caught up with the others. "Okay, I know a door. We'll go in, you can look at the backstage, and then we leave."

Crystal gave Eve a wink. "I knew you were cool."

The door was ajar. Eve gently pushed it wider, looked at the others, and put her finger to her lips for them to stay quiet. Sara would be up front. They walked on stage and looked out at the dimly lit auditorium. The five of them wandered around looking at the rigging and curtains. Odd props were lying around from the latest acting workshop. Eve had been in charge of getting them out and putting them away before and after. In the middle of the stage was a 1920s fainting couch. Crystal plopped down, threw one leg on the couch, and leaned back. "Look at me, I'm an actress." She put an unlit cigarette between her lips. "See how glamorous I am."

Mortified, Eve turned around and grabbed it from Crystal's lips. "Are you nuts? You can't smoke in here."

Crystal stood up, grabbed it back from Eve. "Would you chill? I'm not going to light it." She draped the back of her hand on her forehead. "I was just being dramatic."

Addison, Ashley, and Olivia went out to the seats and scattered around. "We'll be your audience, Crystal. Perform something."

Eve's breathing sped up. This was not a good idea. *How did I get this far?* "Let's go. We really need to leave."

Addison went up to the balcony and did a princess wave to Eve. "Really, we need to ..."

There was a putrid smell coming from somewhere close. It was smoke. A smoky haze began to wash over the can lights hanging from the catwalk. *That's smoke, like from a fire.* Eve looked out from stage right and sniffed. "Do you all smell that?"

"Smell what?" Crystal danced across the stage.

A loud boom came from below the stage and dark billows of smoke emerged from between the stage floorboards. Eve and Crystal coughed and sputtered. Addison, Ashley, and Olivia shrieked and came running toward the stage. "We need to get out of here."

The five ran out the back door to Crystal's car, coughing the entire way. Eve looked back at the theater before getting in the car. Flames heaved from the rear of the building. Sara and her baby were still inside.

"I have to go back in."

"Are you crazy?" Ashley yelled at her. "We have to leave now before the fire department comes."

Eve coughed again as she headed for the front door. "There's people inside. I have to help Sara."

"Who's Sara?"

Crystal was behind the wheel. Addison was buckled in. The car was running, and she put her window down. "Ashley, you and Olivia coming? I'm not getting caught here."

Ashley jumped in the back seat. Olivia stood frozen in the parking lot. Crystal pulled out of the parking space. "Last chance." Sirens whirled in the distance. Olivia stared at her. Crystal stepped on the gas.

Flames jutted and danced across the roof. Dark smoke pushed out the old windows.

Olivia turned and ran toward Eve and the front doors. "I'll help you."

CHAPTER TWENTY-EIGHT

Nora checked her watch. Selfish as it felt, it was helpful that Eve had the club meeting after school. Not picking her up for another hour gave her time to get more accomplished. Phillip had called to confirm their plan for the weekend and the scheduled meeting with the realtor to list Liz's house.

"I think Eve will be okay with it, but let's talk with her again together. If she's not, we'll wait."

Phillip exhaled into the phone. "Okay. How are you both doing?"

"Good days and bad. Starting school here was pretty hard on her. I think something happened yesterday. She was in a foul mood, didn't want to talk, and snapped at me all evening."

"Sounds like a teenager to me. I've had to rein Phil in tight over the last month."

"My favorite nephew? He's an angel."

"You can think that. But that boy has skipped the second day of school, lied to me about having homework, and been late for his curfew."

Nora thought about having to tell Eve no to going to the mall. "How do you parent and discipline without him hating you?"

Phillip laughed. "Hating me is the least of my worries. We are raising him to be a man of integrity. I don't care if he hates me now—later he'll thank me."

"I guess. I had to tell Eve that she couldn't go to the mall with four girls from school. She was not happy."

"Why'd you say no?"

Nora sighed. "I don't know. I watched across the parking lot yesterday at how they interacted. I couldn't hear them but could see their expressions and how they looked at Eve. Something about them didn't sit well with me. So, I said no, another time maybe."

"You sound like Judy. She can tell when something's up with Phil before I notice. Usually, she's right. Sis, I know it's hard. You're doing great. You should hear Eve talk about you and your friends when she's at our house."

"She does?"

"She does. I think she likes living with you more than she's willing to admit."

"That's good. I know she misses Liz." Nora shifted her phone to the other ear.

"Sis, I've got to run. Remember when parenting, especially this early in the game, it's better to err on the side of caution. Trust your instincts and do what the rest of us veteran parents do."

"What's that? Any wisdom is appreciated."

"Pray every day, all the time."

"That I'm doing. Love you, Brother. See you tomorrow night."

Nora had time for one more call to Jim's mother to confirm their appointment. Betsy normally took care of confirmation calls, but Nora wanted to be sure Mrs. Preston was pleased with the painters' work. "Mrs. Preston, how are you?"

"I'm well. How are you?"

"Doing well. How did you like the new wall color?"

"I love it. To be honest, I wasn't one hundred percent certain when we chose it, but my friend Cheryl told me to trust your judgment when I hired you. Glad I did."

Nora blew out a breath of relief. "That's great. I've ordered the furniture. It should be delivered next Wednesday. I have decorative accessories to show you tomorrow, and I'd like to look at your artwork again so we can decide where to hang it. Does tomorrow still work for you?"

"I look forward to seeing you at ten in the morning."

Nora hung up and checked for a text from Eve. Nothing. She checked the time. The club meeting should be over by now. *Why hasn't she texted?* Nora packed her laptop and catalogs for her meeting with Mrs. Preston the next day and headed to school. If the meeting was still going on, she'd wait.

Nora pulled into the barren school parking lot. That was odd. There was one car parked close to the building. No students lingering around. No other parents picking up their kids. Something wasn't right. She went to the front door. It was locked. She shielded her eyes from the glare and looked through the window on the door. No one. She rang the after-hours bell a couple of times.

After what seemed way too long, the school secretary came to the door. "Can I help you?"

Nora's voice quivered. "I'm sorry to bother you, but I'm here to pick up Eve Butler, my niece. She said she was going to the clubs meeting after school and was going to text me when it was over."

The secretary's words were slow. "Well, there was a meeting, but they started it during the last period, and it ran maybe half an hour after school. Everyone has left."

Nora's heart hurt. "Where's Eve?" Her voice cracked.

"Ma'am, I don't know. Does she have a phone? Can you call her?"

"Her phone. Yes, I can call her. Thank you." Nora turned as the secretary closed and locked the door. She hustled to her car and snatched her phone.

She called Eve. Straight to voicemail. Nora's stomach lurched toward her throat. "Lord, where is she? Please don't let anything happen to Eve."

Nora tried Eve's phone again. Voicemail. She hung up and looked at the phone screen. She could track Eve's phone. The range wasn't exact, but it was something. She pressed the icon. It looked like Eve was at or close to the theater. *Maybe she got out earlier than expected and walked over there.* Nora took a deep breath and started the car. "This I can deal with."

Jim pulled over as the fire trucks raced past him. *Oh no, another historic home on fire.* He pulled back into traffic to turn onto the road to the theater. The same road the fire trucks raced down. His curiosity was piqued. Over the last year, and the challenges the theater had battled with the planning and zoning board, Jim had met several of the area homeowners. He supported the historic home association in their efforts to preserve the history of the area. As he drove closer to the theater, he saw the black billowing smoke and the fire trucks pulling into the parking lot. His breath caught. He stepped on the gas and swerved around other cars in traffic to follow the fire trucks. He parked at the end of the parking lot, yanked the car door open, and ran toward the building. Flames engulfed the back side.

Smoke stung his eyes. The stench from the ancient burning wood made him gag. Sara's car was there. She was inside. He coughed and headed for the front door.

A fireman lunged for him. "Sir, you can't go in there."

"There's a young mother ... and her ..." Jim pressed his hand to the side of his head. "Her baby."

"Sir, are you saying there's a woman and baby inside? Is there anyone else?"

Jim shook his head. "Only Sara and her baby."

CHAPTER TWENTY-NINE

The lights, firefighters, and hoses, like twisted spaghetti across the parking lot, seemed chaotic as Nora pulled into the theater parking lot next to Jim's car. *A fire. Eve. Eve's at the theater.* "Oh no!" She looked at the phone tracker again. The blue dot was in the middle of the theater. Nora grappled with her seatbelt and darted out of her car into the haze and smoke-filled air. She covered her mouth and nose with her hand and ran toward the building that was surrounded by firefighters and hoses showering the flames and dispelling the fire.

Nora raced over. "Jim."

Jim whirled around and saw Nora. "Nora, what are you doing here?"

Nora coughed through the strangling smoke. "It's Eve. She's ... she's here somewhere. I went to pick her up from school, and when she wasn't there and didn't answer her phone, I tracked her here."

Jim's eyes had fire in them. "What? She's here? Why?"

Nora yelled over the commotion. "I don't know why, but her phone is at least here, and she's nowhere to be found." Nora coughed again as much to clear smoke as to hold back tears. "Please, Jim, you have to find her."

Jim squeezed her arm and headed toward one of the firefighters who was calling commands. "There may be another person inside, a teenage girl."

The firefighter called to one of his men. "Joe, we may have another female inside. Go through the front. We have the fire contained in the back." He turned to Jim. "What's her name?"

"Eve."

Joe was hustling toward the front doors. The chief yelled Eve's name to him, and he waved as he and his partner disappeared into the smoke.

Nora stood frozen, watching the workers, the flames, and the smoke. "Lord, please, rescue Eve from the flames. Please don't take her away. Please let her be all right." She coughed and tried to catch whatever breath she could. *What was taking so long?* As she looked toward the front door, one of the firefighters came out carrying a young girl. Nora ran up to them.

"Eve." She followed them to the ambulance. The firefighter laid the girl on the waiting gurney. Nora ran to her side and looked at the girl's face. "This isn't Eve. Where is she?" Her loud, shrill voice caught Jim's attention.

"What? Who is this?"

The EMT asked the girl if she knew her name as he placed an oxygen mask on her. The girl coughed and pointed at the building. "Eve ... inside ..."

"So, your name is Eve?"

Nora couldn't take the confusion. She screamed at the girl. "You're not Eve. Where is Eve?"

"Ma'am, please calm down. Here, have a seat."

"I won't sit. My niece is still in that building."

"What?"

The girl on the gurney coughed again. "No. I'm Olivia. Eve is inside. She ran in when we saw the smoke."

"What?" Nora's head began to swim. She couldn't catch a breath, and her knees began to buckle. She immediately felt Jim's strong arms wrapped around her.

"Take a deep breath. They'll get them out."

Daisy hurried into Jen's office. Jen looked up, startled at Daisy's entrance. "What's wrong?"

Daisy's hand was on her breathless chest. "It's the theater. One of the members came in and said they passed the old theater near campus, and it was on fire."

Jen bolted from her chair. "What? On fire? Maggie was working today." She grabbed her purse from the bottom desk drawer. "I've got to go. Tell Kevin I'll finish the report he asked for and email it tonight."

Jen slung her bag over her shoulder, pulled out her cell phone to call Mark, and assured Daisy she would be in contact.

"Answer, Mark ..." The phone went to voicemail. "I'm headed to the theater. There's been a fire, and I have to be sure Maggie and Jim are safe. I'll call you when I know something."

She hung up and immediately tried Maggie. Straight to voicemail. Jim. She called Jim. After three rings, he answered.

"Yeah."

"Jim, it's Jen. I just heard. Is everyone safe? What can I do?" She heard him yell over to someone.

"There's at least three people still inside. One is an infant." Jim began to cough.

Jen's mouth went dry as the call transferred to the car Bluetooth. "Jim. Is Maggie..."

"Jen, I've got to go. I'll let you know when I know more. Can't believe my theater is on fire."

Jen tried to turn onto the road that led to the theater, but it was blocked. She stopped, and a police officer approached her window.

"Ma'am, you can't go any further."

"I need to be sure my friends are safe."

"I understand, but we need to keep the area clear of extra people."

Defeated. Her phone buzzed. She thanked the officer and answered Mark's call. "Mark, there's a fire at the theater. Maggie and Nora aren't answering their phones, and Maggie was supposed to work today. I got through to Jim and overheard him say there were at least three people inside."

"Take a breath. I'm sure the firemen are doing everything they can. Where are you?"

Jen paused. Took a breath. Mark was always steady when she needed his strength. "I'm about half a block from the theater. I can't get closer."

"Sweety, there's a reason for that. They have to control the number of people at the scene."

"I know, but those are my friends. Maggie's like a sister to me." Her efforts to not cry failed.

Mark whispered into the phone, "I know this is scary. I'm on my way."

Jen pulled her car over and turned it off. The officer gave her a sympathetic nod. Jen watched in the direction of the theater but didn't have a clear view. Her phone buzzed. It was Maggie. Jen snatched her phone to answer it.

"Maggie, are you okay? Were you still at the theater?"

"I'm fine, but Sara and the baby were there when I left."

"When I called Jim, I heard him tell someone that there were at least three people still inside?"

"No idea who could've been there."

"I was so afraid you were inside. I came right over, but they won't let me close to the theater."

"Where are you?"

"On Third Street. There's a barricade but the officer let me pull over and wait for news."

"I'm on my way. We'll wait together."

Jen, Maggie, and Mark were waiting in Jen's car when Maggie's phone buzzed with an unknown number.

"Hello?"

"Is this Maggie?"

"Yes. Who's this?"

"This is Phillip. Nora's brother."

Maggie felt her breath catch as her hand went to her chest. "Phillip, is Nora okay?" At the mention of Nora's brother, Jen leaned forward. Maggie pressed the speaker button. "Phillip, you're on speaker with Jen and Mark. We're about a block from the theater. They won't let us closer."

"Jim called me. Nora's at the theater. They think Eve is inside, and Nora is terrified. I'm on my way, but it'll take me thirty minutes. Is there any way you can get to her?"

Jen looked at Mark and Maggie. She nodded. "Phillip, we'll do our best. They've blocked the road. But we'll find a way."

Phillip's voice broke. "Thank you. Jim's call was brief. It sounded chaotic. I ... I don't want Nora to feel alone."

"I'm sure it sounded worse than it is." Maggie nodded. "We'll see you shortly."

The call ended and Jen looked out the driver's side window. The police officer was leaning against the other side of his car, his head down, probably scrolling on his phone.

Maggie looked at the two and sighed. "Let's slip around the other side of the courts and across the park."

The three doubled back around the tennis courts, across the park to the theater's parking lot.

"Oh my goodness." Maggie's hand drew to her mouth. The fire was almost extinguished, but the pumper truck continued to douse the historic building.

"Nora's probably over there near the ambulance." Jen pointed toward the edge of the parking lot where the lights of the ambulance still swirled.

When Nora came into sight, Maggie and Jen ran to her. Nora was sitting on the back edge of the ambulance drinking some juice. Her face lit up at the sight of them. "Jen. Maggie." She grabbed their hands and the three fell into a tight hug.

Maggie pulled away, not letting go of Nora's hand. "What do you know about Eve? Is she inside?"

Nora looked at the front door and then at the ground. "They haven't come out yet. The firemen went in forever ago. What if? Oh, Maggie, nothing can happen to her." She buried her face in her hands.

"Ssshhh." Maggie rubbed her back. "They're going to bring her out any minute. Eve will be fine."

Jen flanked Nora's other side. "Maggie's right. Eve will be fine."

"I want them to get her out of there." Nora's voice rose with a hysterical strain.

Mark hustled over to the huddle of friends. "I found out they located Eve. She's in the conference room with Sara and the baby, but there's debris blocking the door. The firemen were able to get a window open. They have a ladder up to the window and are helping them to climb out."

CHAPTER THIRTY

Jim stood with fisted hands, staring at the fire-ridden destruction. How had this happened? The fire was extinguished. The firefighters were clearing the hoses and packing their equipment. He looked over at the ambulance where EMTs examined Sara and the baby. Eve came down the ladder coughing, but unharmed. Relief washed over Jim, only to be replaced with frustration and anger. What had Eve been doing there? He dragged his hand through his hair and wiped it over his face. *How can we afford to rebuild?* The fire chief approached, and Jim turned to him.

"We need to have our arson team investigate the cause of the fire. At this point, it could have been a careless match thrown behind the theater or something in the electrical box. We'll know more tomorrow."

Jim's eyes grew as wide as spotlights. "Arson. You think this was done on purpose?"

"We have to look at all possible causes."

Jim nodded and shook the chief's hand. "Thank you for everything you and your guys did."

"Glad we could get everyone out. The building can be rebuilt."

Jim huffed. *Easier said than done.*

Phillip arrived and parked across the street. At the sight of Nora, he yelled to her and ran over to the ambulance. "Are you and Eve all right?"

Nora stood and sank into a hug with her brother. "Oh, Phillip, I was so scared. Eve was the last one out. I was so afraid we had lost ..."

Phillip held his sister and spoke softly. "Sssshhh ... everyone is safe and alive. We didn't lose anyone ... everyone is safe."

Nora pulled away and wiped her eyes. "How did you know to come?"

"Jim called me."

She leaned into her brother again. "Thank you."

"How's Eve?" Both looked over to the EMTs.

"She appears fine. They said she ran into the theater and helped Sara get the baby, and they shut themselves in the conference room where they were able to open a window. We couldn't hear them yelling because it's on the other side of the building. The firefighters couldn't get to them from the lobby."

Phillip shook his head. "What was she doing here? Last night when we were texting, she said she wasn't volunteering this week."

"She wasn't. I have no idea why she was here. Or why she was with her friend Olivia. Lots of questions."

The two walked over to the EMTs who were checking the baby. Olivia had been cleared to leave with her mother. Jen and Maggie were talking with Eve. Her eyes were laser-focused on the ground. Nora gave her friends a questioning look, only to have them shrug in return. She sat next to Eve and grasped her hand.

"Eve, are you okay?"

Eve nodded through the oxygen mask they put on her for good measure, but she didn't look up. Nora rubbed Eve's back. "I know that was scary. But you helped keep Sara and her baby safe. That was quick thinking to get close to a window."

The EMT walked over to Nora. "How are you feeling, ma'am? Any more lightheadedness?"

"I'm fine." Nora tucked a wandering hair under Eve's oxygen mask. "Sweetie, are you okay? Any pain or difficulty breathing?"

Eve swatted Nora's hand away without looking at her. "I'm fine. I just want to go home."

"We'll go once they tell us you're all right to leave."

Phillip stepped beside his sister. "Why don't I go pick up some dinner and meet you both at your house?"

Eve looked up and pulled the oxygen mask off. "No, I want to go home to Simpson." She looked at Phillip. "Uncle Phillip, can I go back with you tonight?"

Nora felt the sting of Eve's words.

Phillip knelt close to Eve. "I know you're scared. Let's go back to Nora's, have some dinner, and talk about this."

Eve stood next to Phillip. "Can I ride with you?" Phillip draped his arm around her. "Of course." He looked at the EMT. "Is she okay to go?"

"Yes. Her breathing is normal, oxygen level is normal, and no signs of injury or burns. But please call 911 or get her to a hospital if anything changes."

Mark walked back over from talking with Jim. "Jen, why don't you drive Nora home. I'll follow, and then we can come back for your car."

Jen grimaced and pulled Mark aside, but not far enough for the others not to hear. "I kinda need to go back to the gym. In the hurry to leave, I forgot a curriculum manual I need to finish tonight."

Mark leaned forward. "Are you serious? Your best friend needs you."

Maggie walked over to them. "First of all, we can hear you. I'll take Nora home. Dan and the kids can meet me to come back for the car."

Jen walked back over to Nora and hugged her. "I'm so thankful you both are safe. I'm sorry I have to go, but call me tonight if you need anything."

Nora turned to hug her friends. "Thank you."

Sara's mother, Mrs. Biddle, hugged Nora again. "I'm so thankful Eve was here. They're taking them to the hospital to examine the baby, but they said there was no apparent injury."

Nora returned the hug. "We have a lot to be thankful for."

Mrs. Biddle turned her attention back to her daughter and granddaughter.

Jim said goodbye to the fire chief as Nora walked toward him on the way to the car. "Jim, are you all right?"

With a sharp turn, Jim flashed an angry look toward Nora. "I'm fine. Great. Never better. My theater has burned down. No clue how I'm going to rebuild. But yes, I'm peachy."

Nora stepped back with her hands in surrender. Maggie turned to see Jim's red face as Nora said, "Not sure why you're mad at me."

"I'm mad because my theater is a wreck. And I have no clue how I'm going to rebuild. And why were Eve and her friend messing around here today?"

Nora felt her own internal flame expand. "Now wait just a minute. Eve had nothing to do with the fire."

"Really? Are you sure?" Jim's jaw clenched. "What was she doing here?"

Nora looked him straight in his bloodshot eyes. "Yes, I'm sure." She turned and walked away.

The distance between them grew with each step Nora took. Eve needed the benefit of the doubt. Something had happened. Eve had made a mistake, and she had lied. In Nora's heart, she knew Eve had nothing to do with the fire. Jim ran to catch up to Nora.

"I'm sorry. You didn't deserve that."

Nora sped up. His words burned her. She had opened her heart to love Jim. *And this is how he responds during a crisis? Not for me.*

Jim kept up with her. He reached and grazed her elbow. Nora kept walking. Much to her surprise, and in everyone's hearing, Jim shouted to her.

"Nora, please stop. I'm an idiot. Forgive me. You didn't deserve any of what I said. Please."

His words squelched but didn't extinguish the hurt. Nora stopped and cautiously turned. Her love for him won over the hurt of his words. She walked back to him.

"Thank you for apologizing. But I'm not your verbal punching bag. You can't talk to me like that."

Jim raised his head and eyes to hers. "You're right. I'm so sorry."

"I heard you the first time." Nora looked around. "As did pretty much everyone."

"I don't care as long as you heard me." Jim looked back over at the charred building. "It's all such a shock. The theater ... well ... you ... Eve" He rubbed the back of his neck and looked at Nora. "What if I had lost all three of you? It scared me." His voice softened. "I need you to understand what this theater means to me ... to my life."

Jim's remorse wafted into Nora's heart. She loved him, and she heard him. "Thank you for apologizing." Nora reached for his hand.

Jim looked into Nora's tired eyes. "I meant it. I am sorry I spoke harshly. You and Eve mean so much to me. I love you."

She squeezed his hand and let go. "I know what the theater means to you. But remember, I'm on your team in the good and bad times."

"I'm so thankful for you and Eve. It won't happen again."

With a gentle kiss and hug, the two parted. Nora handed Maggie her keys. She was too shaken to drive.

Jim turned to meander his way back to the theater. It was quiet. All the pandemonium of firefighters and EMTs was over. He opened the back hatch of his Jeep and sat looking at the mangled building. The fire had consumed the back of the theater, from the rear door to the stage. The setting sun shone through the burnt wood planks. He crouched to see inside. It looked like the seats had escaped fire damage but were soaked. Several windows were broken. But the walnut front doors with the beveled glass and brass pulls stood strong. He raked his hand through his hair. A few flakes of ash floated out. He was alone. No one stood with him in the mess that stood before him. *Helpless.*

"Son, are you all right?"

The familiar voice pulled Jim around to see his father standing behind him. "Dad, what are you doing here?"

"Your mom and I saw the fire on the news. She's worried sick about you. And ... well ..." He looked beyond Jim to the building. "I am too."

"Dad, don't start with the theater being a bad career decision. I was a disappointment when I didn't go into law or medicine. I disappointed you when I left the university. And now the one thing I loved doing ... running a theater ... has been destroyed. There's no way I have enough insurance to cover all this." Jim waved his hand toward the burned structure.

His father put his hands up in surrender. "Whoa, hold on with the big speech. I said I was worried about you. I came down here because I wanted to know you were safe, not to rehash old disagreements. Jim, you may find this surprising, but I've watched what you've done with this old theater, and I'm impressed. You've overcome the odds to build a vibrant organization."

Jim shook his head. "I can't seem to say the right thing. A little while ago, I shouted at Nora out of frustration. And I immediately assumed you wanted to gloat." He looked at his dad. "What's wrong with me?"

His father squeezed Jim's shoulder. "It's been a hard day. Come home with me so your mom can feed you and see that you're okay. Give yourself time to take it all in. You'll be ready to start rebuilding soon."

Jim swiped his hand over his face. "Rebuild ... I can only hope."

The setting sun ducked behind a cloud, leaving a haze that loomed over the theater. Jim walked up to the front doors and pulled to make sure they were locked. He looked at his dad and shrugged. "Doesn't really matter, but it's what I do every day. Just need something to feel right."

"I understand."

The two men walked in silence to his dad's car. "I'll come by the house to see Mom. Not too hungry though."

"Be ready, she'll have food." His dad opened the car door. "And Jim, you and Nora will weather this storm. I'm confident of that."

Jim drove in silence behind his dad's car. There was something different in his dad's spirit. He was supportive and understanding, not condescending. Even wise about making things right with Nora. *Nora. Will she ever forgive me? Do I know how to be in a true, loving relationship?*

CHAPTER THIRTY-ONE

Nora had no words. Dan pulled up to Nora's house as Maggie dropped her off with a hug and a promise to call. Eve and Phillip pulled up in front of the house and got out with a couple of fast-food bags. The three entered the house in silence. Nora pulled out plates. Eve did everything she could to avoid making eye contact with Nora. Phillip filled the silence with light conversation, insisting they both eat. Nora and Eve picked at their burgers and fries. When Phillip pushed back from the table, Eve took that as a cue to pick up the dishes. Nora thumbed through the mail as if it was imperative to read it immediately. Her conflicting emotions of worry and anger twisted like the smoke over the theater. Eve had lied to her. Hurt at Jim's harsh words even though he had apologized. Not a good day. Eve mumbled that she was going up to take a shower. Nora nodded without looking at her.

Phillip clapped his hands together. "Yes, a shower will make you feel better. And, by the way, you both kinda stink." Nora flashed a smirk at his attempt at humor.

When the shower started upstairs, Phillip snatched the letter that Nora was pretending to read from her hands. "Outside, sister. We need to talk."

They walked out on the patio and closed the sliding glass door. Nora paced around. "Did she tell you what happened? Honestly, Phillip, I don't know whether to be mad at her or thankful she didn't get hurt." She stopped and leaned on the back of a chair. "What am I supposed to do?"

Phillip took a deep breath. "No, she didn't say anything. I asked what happened and she just stared out the window." Phillip rubbed his forehead. "Keep doing what you're doing. Everything will be fine. She's safe. She didn't get hurt. Let's count that blessing for now. She'll be ready to talk soon."

Nora nodded. "You're right." She drew a deep breath.

Phillip looked at his watch. "If you're okay, I'm going to head home."

Nora stood. "Of course. Thanks for coming. We'll see you at Mom's tomorrow night for dinner."

Nora and Phillip walked into the house. From the bottom of the steps, Phillip called up to Eve. "See you tomorrow, Eve. I love you."

Eve poked her head around the corner at the top of the steps. "You're leaving?"

"Yeah, I've got to get back. But you and Nora are coming tomorrow. I'll see you for dinner."

Eve came downstairs. Phillip gave her a hug. "I'm so glad you're safe."

Eve looked at her mismatched socks and nodded. Phillip hugged Nora. "I love you, Sis. See you girls tomorrow."

Nora closed the front door and locked it behind Phillip. As she leaned against the solid wood door, the day washed over her, and exhaustion set in. Eve had disappeared upstairs. Nora closed her eyes and took a deep breath. *Lord, give me the right words. Help me hear and understand Eve.* She opened her eyes and headed upstairs to Eve's room.

The door was open. Eve was curled up in the overstuffed chair with the crocheted blanket pulled around her. Nora sat on the bed. Eve looked at her.

"This chair still smells like mom's perfume. I feel so close to her when I sit in it."

Nora spoke softly. "I'm sure you do." Nora looked around the room and sighed. "Eve, are you ready to tell me what happened today?"

"Do I have to?"

Nora pursed her lips and paused. "Eventually. You were in a dangerous situation. How did you get there?" Silence. Nora moved closer to Eve. "Honey, I love you. Nothing will ever change that. If I don't know what happened, it's going to be harder for me to ... guide you through all of it."

More silence. Nora stood. "You think about it. If you don't want to talk tonight, that's fine. We can talk tomorrow." She walked to the door. "We didn't eat much dinner. I'm going to go get us a snack and something to drink. When I come back, we'll either eat in silence, or you can tell me the story."

While Nora made a plate of cheese cubes, peanut butter, and pretzels, she prayed in her heart for wisdom. As she pulled two sodas from the refrigerator, her phone buzzed. Jim. Sent straight to voicemail.

Eve tossed her phone onto her bed. Crystal and Addison wouldn't stop texting her. They were desperate to know what she'd told her aunt. Confusion and fear played tug of war with her emotions. *Aunt Nora is going to hate me. Why did I do it? For those girls to be my supposed friends? People I'm not even sure I like.* A call lit up the screen on her phone. Olivia. Eve rolled her eyes. Not her too. At least, *she*

didn't run off. Seconds later, a text from Olivia. "I want to know if you're okay. I know you're mad."

Eve snagged the phone and texted back. "I'm fine." And tossed the phone back on the bed and slid to the floor. She was sitting with her legs crossed, back against the bed, when Aunt Nora came in.

"Here you go. Your favorite peanut butter and pretzels." Aunt Nora pulled Eve's lap desk off the shelf onto the bed for the plate. "I brought a couple of sodas too."

Eve didn't look at her. She shook her head and rolled her eyes. *How do I tell my aunt, who has done so much for me, that I lied? Not once, but multiple times.*

"You know, Eve, we all make mistakes. Nothing you have done or could do will change the way I feel about you."

Eve felt the cool soda can Aunt Nora tapped on her arm. "I know." Eve could barely say the words. She wanted to believe her. The silence was broken by the "pfssst" of a soda being opened. Eve took a drink. The pressure of the silence forced her guilt deeper into her heart. Now it hurt. *Why isn't Aunt Nora saying anything? Think, Eve. You've got to talk with her. What's the worst thing that could happen? I could lose her too.* Her eyes made their way to the overstuffed chair; the chair where she and her mom had snuggled and talked about everything. *But she's gone.* The pain in her heart twinged harder. Eve sighed. She fiddled with her soda can.

"Aunt Nora, I'm so sorry about today." Eve didn't look up and around at her aunt.

"I know you're sorry. How do you feel about going to school tomorrow? If you want to stay home, you can."

Eve slid around and up on her knees to reach for a pretzel. With a small dip into the peanut butter, she popped it in her mouth and joined Nora on the bed.

"You don't hate me?"

"Of course not. I could never hate you."

"I'll go to school. We didn't start the fire at the theater."

Nora sighed and allowed a faint smile to appear. "I didn't think you did. Let's start a little earlier, when you told me there was a club meeting at school and never went." The truth stung, but Aunt Nora spoke in a calm, gentle tone.

Eve twisted her hair with her right hand and wouldn't look Nora in the eye. She took a deep breath and began. "I wanted to go to the mall with Ashley and her friends. They're older and popular." Eve shrugged. "Maybe I thought it was a shortcut to making friends. I thought we'd be back by the time the club meeting was over, and you would've thought I'd been at school the whole time." As she spoke, her words came faster. "We were driving to the mall when we passed the theater, and Addison wanted to stop and see it. They knew I'd volunteered there."

With each confessed word Eve felt the burden lift from her. She risked a peek at Aunt Nora and was encouraged by the grace reflected in her eyes.

"We went in through the back and walked out on the stage. Kinda goofed off there. But then, we smelled smoke, and by the time we ran back out toward the car, it looked like the whole place was on fire. Smoke was everywhere. I saw Sara's car there and was afraid she and the baby were inside. When I started to run in the front door, Crystal, Addison, and Ashley said they were leaving." Eve's voice caught, and tears threatened. "I couldn't leave with Sara inside. Olivia followed me back in, but I lost her in the smoke. I thought she'd run out. Sara was trying to gather the baby, and I pulled her into the conference room and shut the door. We were trying to figure out how to climb out the window when the firemen showed up." As she told the story, Eve took another deep breath and looked directly at her aunt. She wasn't saying anything. *What is she thinking?*

Nora reached over and grasped Eve's hand. "That was a very brave thing to do. I am so thankful you didn't get hurt. That no one got hurt. So, so thankful." She blew out a breath and brushed the crumbs off the bed. "Eve, we need to talk about why you lied to me. Why did you disobey me?"

Eve looked down. "I don't know. I was feeling nervous about school, and all my friends back home were texting me about their first day." She scrunched the napkin in her fist. "I'm sorry. It's all so hard, and I wanted Ashley's friends to like me."

Nora lifted Eve's chin, so their eyes met. "It *is* hard. But that's no excuse for lying or disobedience. Is that the person you want to be?"

Eve's shoulders slumped. "No."

"Sweetie, you have always been a kind, honest person. You love Jesus. That's how you live, and in the last forty-eight hours you abandoned some of that … for what? Friends who ran at the sight of getting caught in a lie?"

"Olivia didn't leave."

"No, she didn't. But you need to know that her mother is blaming you for her being there."

Eve's eyes grew wide. "What? But it wasn't my fault."

Nora raised her hand and nodded. "I know. And I think she'll calm down. But that's what I'm saying about lying and choosing the wrong friends. You could be accused by association."

Eve stood, walked over to her dresser and picked up a picture of her and her mother. "Everything made sense when Mom was alive. Now I feel like everything is scrambled. I've messed up already, and I've only been in my new school for two days. I'm so sorry, Aunt Nora. You're right, I'm not a liar. My friends and I at home have all kinds of fun without needing to sneak around."

Both sat in the midst of Eve's confession. The silence began to weigh on Eve. She turned around to face her aunt. "I'm so sorry. Will you forgive me?"

Aunt Nora smiled at her. "Yes, of course I will. But I have a question for you."

"What is it?"

"If you hadn't got caught, would you continue to hang out with those girls?"

Eve shook her head and sat back down on the bed. "I don't think I would have. You know, all day I worried about lying to you about the mall. Crystal and Addison were smoking in the car." She grimaced. "Even when we were in the car, nothing was fun. And when we sneaked into the theater, I felt like I could puke."

"I'm a little glad it was a miserable day. Eve, I have to be able to trust you. Today you broke that trust." Nora looked into Eve's eyes.

"But I'm sorry. I promise ..."

Nora rubbed Eve's arm. "I know. I believe you're sorry. Now, you need to rebuild my trust, which I'm sure won't take long. That's the way it works when you lie. You've apologized, and in the coming days, you'll show me you're trustworthy."

"What do I need to do?"

This was the difficult part after a conflict. Rebuilding trust. Eve was a young person whom Nora was now charged with guiding into adulthood. *How do we rebuild trust?* The answer came as a whisper in her heart. *Only God restores.*

She reached for Eve's hand again. "Every time you're honest with me, trust is built." Nora gathered their plate and soda cans. "In other words, time will heal this hurt. I love you." She stood to leave. "Did you have any homework?"

"A little reading for English." Eve pulled out her pajamas. "It shouldn't take long."

"Okay. Don't stay up too late."

"Good night. And thanks, Aunt Nora. I love you." Eve walked around the bed and hugged Nora from the side, tight enough that she almost dropped the plate.

"Good night. I love you too."

Nora took the dishes and soda cans to the kitchen. As she opened the recycling bin, she was startled by a pounding on the front door and someone yelling.

She ran to the front door as Eve came downstairs. "Who's that?"

The man yelled his slurred insults. "Nora, you little miss fancy pants. You're a nobody. I want to see my daughter. You can't keep her from me. I've changed."

Nora looked through the peep hole in time to see Curt stumble and fall off the porch. He was drunk. She grabbed Eve's hand and pulled her back into the kitchen. "Do not go near or open the door. I'm calling the police."

Nora kept Eve close while they waited for the police and listened to Curt yelling.

Eve covered her ears. "Make him stop. He's horrible."

Nora called Phillip to tell him what was going on.

"Do you want me to come?"

"Let me call you back, I think I hear the police out there with him now."

Nora and Eve watched from the front window. After Curt was put in one of the two squad cars, two other police officers rang the doorbell. Nora invited the officers inside.

Nora and Eve gave the police their account of what had happened and told them who Curt was.

"He won't bother you anymore tonight. But if you want to take out a restraining order, you'll need to come downtown."

Nora looked at Eve. "I think we've had enough excitement for one day. Curt's locked away tonight."

Before he left, the officer gave Nora the report number and a card with the phone number to call to get the final police report.

"Thank you."

"Aunt Nora, why did he come here like that?"

Nora hugged Eve. "I have no idea. But one thing is for sure, I don't think we'll have to go to court over visitation anymore."

Nora called Phillip to recount what the officer had said.

"What does Eve think?"

Nora looked at Eve, who had a shocked expression over the whole ordeal. "We haven't talked about it. The whole thing was a little much. Curt was about as drunk as I've ever seen him and yelled the most horrific things."

CHAPTER THIRTY-TWO

"Have you lost your mind?"

Curt slumped in the chair across the diner table from Pastor Sparks, who was again the only person he could call. "Hey, man, is that any way for a man of God to talk?" The waitress came by and refreshed both their coffees.

"Even Jesus had righteous anger. For the last three weeks, you've been doing great … going to your meetings, helping around the house, looking for a job. And you've got a court date for visitation coming up next week. It's … it's almost like you wanted to ruin your chances."

Curt rolled his eyes. "I didn't do this on purpose. I thought I could have one drink, shoot a little pool, get back to my room before curfew, and no one would know."

"How'd those choices work out for you? Oh, and you may not have a room to go back to, you know that, right?"

Curt looked beyond the pastor. "Would you stop with the choice thing? Yes, I made some choices tonight. Probably not the ones you would have made, but they're my choices to make. I'm tired of waiting for some judge to tell me I can see my daughter. I'm tired of everyone else's rules. I'm a grown man. I can decide for myself."

"Curt, you sound like a child." The pastor sat back, crossed his arms, and said nothing more.

The silence lingered long enough to make Curt uncomfortable. He looked at the man who'd helped him in a hundred ways—with clothing for job interviews and leads for jobs. He took a swig of coffee. "You're right." He looked at his friend. "I'm sorry. Please forgive me."

"I'm not the one you need forgiveness from." Pastor Paul pointed at Curt. "I am going to do something I shouldn't for an addict. I'll call Greg and see if he'll let you stay. But, Curt, this is it. No more."

Curt took a deep breath. Most of the time, drinking would reduce the pain in his life, but this time it didn't. Even drunk, he'd still felt it. "Thank you."

"You're welcome." Pastor Paul caught the waitress's attention. "Now, how about a burger and fries. Might help with tomorrow's hang-over."

"Sure. Thanks." Curt shook his head and took another drink. "I've probably blown any chance to see my daughter again."

"First things first. A day at a time, one choice at a time, but with God's strength, that relationship will come together."

Jim arrived at the theater early. He had called Sara to check on her and ask her to email the cast and crew to let them know they were shut down for the foreseeable future. He exited his SUV with coffee in hand and slowly walked around the entire building. The fresh, cool morning was squelched by the smell of burnt, dusty wood. His stomach wrenched at the gnarled back third of the building. The front had some missing windows, had been soaked by the sprinklers, and smelled of smoke, but had escaped fire damage. The insurance adjuster and fire inspector were scheduled to arrive soon. Jim sat on a wrought iron bench under an oak tree to wait, drink his coffee, and pray.

Lord, you have brought me through so many storms and disappointments. I've always felt your peace running the theater. Forgive me for lashing out at Nora. Forgive me for being so tied to this wonderful building that I forgot to focus on you and the people who mean so much to me. Lord, show me what's next for the theater, and I will follow. Give me the words and the actions to make things right with Nora and Eve. Father, give Nora the encouragement she needs to deal with Eve. And Lord, I do pray for Eve to continue to settle into her new life here. Thank you that no one was hurt in the fire. Amen.

Jim had begun his prayer looking at the mangled building. By the time he said amen, his head was bowed, his eyes were closed, and complete peace had washed over him. He looked up as the fire inspector and insurance representative walked toward him.

After the introductions, the three men began walking around the building. They walked in through the front door and stood at the back of the auditorium, seeing that the stage and most of the structure beyond it had been destroyed. The fire inspector began to explain the investigation process.

"We'll need two to three days to complete the inspection and give you our findings. Wish it could be faster. I know you're anxious to know the cause and begin to rebuild. I should have a crew here after lunch."

Jim nodded. "No problem. Let me know what you need from me."

"We just need access—and besides you, the area needs to remain clear."

"I've let the staff and crew know we're closed until further notice." He looked at the insurance adjuster who was scrolling through a document on a tablet.

The adjuster nodded. "Jim, you have comprehensive and fire coverage. Also, since the building was designated as a historic landmark last year, there are additional grant funds from the city you can apply for. Be ready, those applications can take months."

Jim blew out a deep sigh and smiled. The insurance adjustor put up his hand. "Hang on, I can't tell you how much insurance will pay until we know what caused the fire."

The peace Jim felt while he prayed plunked at his heart. *Lord, show me what's next for the theater, and I will follow. Yes, I meant that.* "Okay, we'll take it one step at a time and see where we land." He shook both men's hands and thanked them for coming.

Jen, Mark, and Brian sat at the circular wooden kitchen table. Brian struggled to shove the additional school supplies he and his dad had purchased into his backpack. Mark stirred cream in his coffee, and Jen added honey to her tea.

"You were up late talking on the phone."

"Yeah, I was talking with Maggie when Nora called, and we ended up on a three-way call."

"How are she and Eve doing?"

"Sounds like a rough night, but I think they'll be fine in time."

Mark reached for Jen's hand. "Honey, we need to talk about your work schedule. It's too much. It's all you're focused on."

Jen sighed. "I know. But what am I supposed to do? Kevin keeps giving me projects. Looks like he's going to sell the gym. I don't want to lose my job."

"It was never our plan for you to work full time. What are you worried about?"

"I know. But so far, I've liked the job. Up until recently with all this extra stuff piled on." Jen reached across and took Mark's hand. "The accountant is coming in to do a … an … a valuation. I think that's what he called it. Then we're supposed to know more."

As vice president of operations at an IT consulting firm, Mark knew exactly what a business valuation was. "Sure, a valuation is like an appraisal, only using accounting methods to determine the value of a company."

Thankful for a business-savvy husband, Jen perked up. "Do you know about this? How long will it take to do all that?"

"A valuation can take a month to six weeks. You've done so well this last year, I'm sure you won't lose your job. And if something does happen, you can find another gym. But, please, let's try to put a little more balance to our lives and not bring work home as often." Mark got up and put his mug in the dishwasher.

Jen knew he was right. She was a personal trainer, teaching all these healthy living workshops, and working upwards of sixty hours a week. Mark grabbed his leather backpack and kissed Jen. "Brian, finish up and let's go. You've got Brian this afternoon, right?"

"I do." Jen threw her tea bag away and rinsed her cup. She grabbed Mark's arm before he headed out the door. "I love you. We'll get this figured out."

Nora was awake after a restless night. Not since Liz's death had sleep been this elusive. She wanted to call Jim. Her conversation with Jen and Maggie last night replayed in her mind. *He is a great guy, loves the Lord, but is in an extremely stressful situation.* Jim had called multiple times last night, and each time, she sent the call to voicemail. Maggie called her on it.

"If you want to talk to him, what's with sending the calls to voicemail? Sounds a bit like a power play. That's not fair to him."

She wasn't wrong. Nora's frustration was quickly squelched by Maggie's wisdom. "Mags, you're right. But I've had as bad a day as he has. I'm hurt, disappointed, and exhausted. The Curt incident didn't help."

Jen empathized. "It's been a long, emotional day. Perhaps both of you could be thinking of the other a little more. Get some rest and return his call in the morning."

The three were silent. Nora rolled around in her thoughts the difference between Maggie calling her on a power play and Jen's comment about it being an emotional day.

A thought pricked Nora's heart. "My relationship with Jim is a gift. An answered prayer I didn't know my heart was ready for. Do you remember last year, when I was praying for a renewed life? God delivered me from grief. I finished design school and got a job. I prayed for renewal. The blessing came when Jim and I became friends, then started dating."

"You and Jim were so cute." Jen chimed in. "Both so guarded."

"He had thrown himself into his work after his breakup with Mandy," Maggie added. "You're right, Nora, we all prayed for how God would renew your life."

"He told me about Mandy. The pressure from his parents to marry her. Their break-up added to the stress on his relationship with his father. The theater was all he had." Nora sighed. "Today, he watched it burn. Thank you both. I think I know what I need to do."

Nora picked up her phone to call Jim when Eve came through the kitchen.

"Hi."

"Good morning." Nora went over and gave Eve a hug. "Did you sleep well?"

"Okay." Eve poured a glass of juice. "I laid there and thought about the day. Crazy. The fire, then Curt showing up. Thanks for talking last night."

"Of course. We're good. And please don't worry about Curt."

"I won't. Are we leaving right after school for Simpson?"

"Yes. I told Mom we'd be there for dinner."

Eve took a deep breath. "There's a Simpson High home football game tonight. My friends want me to meet them. Can I?"

"Probably. This is one of those opportunities for me to trust you again. There will be rules about going."

Eve gave a fast nod. "I know. You name the rule, I'll follow it."

"We'll talk about it on the way. Games don't start until seven, right? Plan to have dinner with us at Mom's, then I'll take you to the game."

"Great. I'm going to text my friends." Eve dashed upstairs.

Nora called behind her, "Please be ready to leave for school in thirty minutes."

"Got it."

Nora pulled into Mrs. Preston's circular drive and parked. The September air had turned cool enough to whisper a hint of autumn. The seasons were changing. Her morning devotion had left her feeling calm and optimistic. The entry to the home boasted a large wooden door with frosted glass in the center. At the bottom of the porch steps was an urn with a burst of yellow mums. Mrs. Preston answered after Nora's first knock.

"Good morning, Nora."

Nora stepped into the foyer. "Good morning." It suddenly occurred to her she didn't know what Mrs. Preston knew about the fire. Should she say something? No, keep it professional. They'd managed to get through the project without crossing the line of Nora dating Jim. Mrs. Preston took her hand.

"Before we start, how are you doing? It sounds like yesterday was a horrible day for both you and Jim."

Nora sighed at Mrs. Preston's warm touch and the spirit of her words. She cared about Nora as a person. Nora looked at the floor and back at Mrs. Preston. "It was a hard day. Jim was devastated to see the theater burn."

"What about you, dear? Sounds like you had a scare with Eve."

"It was very scary." Nora shook her head. "I don't know what I would have done if something had happened to her."

Mrs. Preston patted her hand and released it. "Looks like the Lord was watching out for everyone. Jim was beyond upset last night."

"You saw him last night?"

"Yes, when we saw it on the news, his dad darted out of here to go check on him. He talked Jim into coming home for dinner—although he didn't eat much."

"The theater means everything to him."

Mrs. Preston looked at Nora with a questioning look. "The theater. That can be rebuilt. He was worried about you and Eve. He loves you both, and evidently, words were said—he lashed out, and now he's afraid he'll lose you."

"Yes, words were said in the heat of the moment. Jim and I'll work it out."

"Good. Before last night, I honestly haven't seen him so … happy. No, more than that, so at peace with his life." Mrs. Preston looked into Nora's eyes. "You are a big part of that. You've given him a new outlook on his future."

Nora's throat tightened. The thought she had made a difference in Jim's life hadn't occurred to her. She smiled at the nod from God that everything was going to work out. "Thank you for saying that."

"I only speak what I know to be true. Now, let's get started." The two walked into the living room, which had been expanded to include French doors leading to the back sunroom. "I love how this has come together."

Nora walked around the room, examining the furniture placement and adjusting the pictures they'd hung. "I agree. We've opened the space, tied the two rooms together, and with the doors, you have the option of more or less space as you need it." She turned to Mrs. Preston. "Are there any adjustments you'd like to make?"

Mrs. Preston sat on the beige couch with new throw pillows that added a touch of color and surveyed the space. "It's simply lovely, Nora. It's light and warm. I love it all. There is one thing that I'm disappointed about."

Nora's eyes widened. "What? I'm glad to fix it."

The corners of Mrs. Preston's sparkling eyes lifted. "You and I won't be spending time together."

They both laughed. Nora slid her notepad back into her bag. "How about we plan to meet for coffee or lunch next week?"

CHAPTER THIRTY-THREE

Nora and Eve arrived in Simpson in time for dinner at her mom's house. During the drive, they discussed the rules Eve would need to follow to attend the football game.

"I will drop you off and pick you up. You are not to leave the school grounds for any reason. Do you understand?"

"Yes. I promise. We're meeting at the game. We'll be there the entire time."

"How were Addison, Crystal, and Ashley today?"

"A little distant. But that's fine. I'd like some friends, though."

Nora patted her hand. "I understand. But I'd rather you have two or three friends you can count on than five, most of whom will lead me into trouble. Olivia's mom is having a similar conversation with Olivia. Not sure about the other moms."

Eve nodded. "Ashley texted me that her mom had the big trust conversation with her. She really wasn't the one starting trouble. She just followed Addison and Crystal."

"Good to know. To be honest, it surprised me she would be hanging out with girls like Addison and Crystal." Nora smiled at Eve. "You'll get all this figured out. Choosing friends who build us up and do not lead us into trouble is important."

"I get it."

Nora took a deep breath. "Okay. One more thing."

Eve's eyes widened. "What?"

Nora smiled and squeezed her hand. "Have fun tonight. We'll get past the events of this week."

Eve's face beamed with a smile. For a second, she looked like Liz when she and Nora were teenagers. For the first time, the memory came with a warm, happy feeling instead of the thump of grief.

After dinner with Phillip, Judy, and her grandmother, Eve ran upstairs to get ready for the game. Phillip stood and pushed his chair in. Judy helped Vivian clear the table.

"How are the two of you doing?"

Nora nodded. "Better. We talked last night. I was a little worried about her going to school today. It seems the rumor mill has made her a legend. Eve understands rumors like those shouldn't be an encouragement to behave that way again."

"Glad you both are getting back to right."

"We'll be fine. I spoke to Olivia's mom, who was as shocked at Olivia's involvement as I was Eve's. We agreed to let them try to be friends again. Crystal, Ashley, and Addison's moms were much more dismissive about the incident. At first, they didn't believe their little angels could have possibly pulled such a stunt." Nora stood and picked up her plate. "Is that how parents are? They really think their kids are incapable of finding trouble?"

"Some are. They think as long as the grades are good, their kids are doing fine. What do you think about the Curt situation?"

"I don't think we need to pursue a restraining order. He's all bark."

"As long as you all feel safe."

"We do. Thanks."

Nora picked up pints of ice cream on her way back from dropping off Eve at the football game. She and her mother enjoyed the sunset and munched on their respective favorite flavors of ice cream. The front porch swing creaked with each swing.

"You remembered my favorite. Thank you." Her mother sighed as the swing returned forward. "Your dad and I used to have dessert out here." Their feet dangled as they went back.

"I miss Daddy." Nora took a bite. "And Seth ... and Liz."

In the soft light of sunset, Nora saw her mother's eyes glisten. "I'm sorry, Mom. I shouldn't have gone there." She took another bite. "Lately, it seems too easy for me to go down the grief trail."

"Sweetie, we're all grieving. I miss ... I miss them too. Never would I have thought my daughter and son-in-law would go before me."

"Aren't we a blast tonight? Both wallowing in our sadness."

"Yes, but it will pass. Some days, I hurt so much with grief that I don't want to get out of bed. But then, I remember I promised your dad that I would take care of you all and try to find some joy in every day."

Nora nodded. "What's today's joy?"

Mother looked out across the yard. "Today has had several joys. I had dinner with my kids and granddaughter, and now I'm eating my favorite ice cream with you." She smiled with gratitude. "It's a good day."

The rhythm of the swing relaxed Nora. She finished her ice cream and set the empty container on the small table next to the swing. Her mother handed hers to Nora to set with the other.

"Tell me how things are going with Jim."

Nora bit her bottom lip. "The fire has him pretty stressed. And ... I don't know. Everything feels a little scrambled."

"He's a good man. You both have a lot weighing on you now. Stay focused on the most important things, and you'll soon see the pieces of the puzzle fall into place. Can I tell you a story about a similar time your dad and I went through?"

Nora pulled one knee up to her chest and turned toward her mother. "Sure. I love hearing about you and Daddy."

"I found out I was pregnant the week before your dad shipped out to Vietnam. We were so excited."

Nora's brow furrowed. "But ..."

Her mother put her hand up. "Let me finish. We celebrated that night and knew in our hearts everything was going to work out. He'd serve his military duty and come home to me and our first child." She shifted in the swing. "A month after he left, I had a miscarriage. I didn't know how to tell him I'd lost the baby. We'd hung our future hope on the start of our family, which was not where it should be."

"Why haven't you told me this before? When I went through two miscarriages."

"Because those were your losses. Every woman is different, and you didn't need to hear my story. Your father and I were able to talk to one another for very short periods of time every now and then. I never knew when. I wrote to him and told him. He finagled a call to me as soon as he got the letter. Fortunately, I was home, and we talked. He was loving and gentle, but there was also an edge to him I'd never heard. We finished our call with 'I love you.' A week later, I got a letter where he told me how angry he was. How helpless he felt being so far away and not being with me to go through the grief of losing a child." She took Nora's hand. "Sweetie, men are created to protect, provide for, and love their wives. When life spins out of their control, they don't know what to do, or sometimes, how to react."

"What do I do when that happens?"

"You let them have a little space to sort it out. When it's true love, they settle down, the two of you realign and can move forward together."

Nora looked at her mother's aged hands. Hands that had held her when she lost two babies and then Seth. In their frailty, there was the strength of life's ups and downs. "I haven't returned Jim's calls. He was pretty angry yesterday. I think I know why now." Nora looked into her mother's eyes. "His world was spinning out of control, and he was powerless to protect us or the theater."

"How are you feeling? You had a scare yesterday too. Then Curt showing up."

Nora bit her bottom lip. "It was intense. Curt was more startling than scary. I knew he couldn't get into the house. He didn't even really try. We got through it. Eve and I talked last night. She's got a lot on her right now. I keep praying for wisdom."

Nora's mother patted her on the leg. "That's a good start. Don't forget to take care of yourself."

"I won't." Nora's phone in her hoodie pocket buzzed. "It's a text from Eve. The game is in the fourth quarter, probably another thirty minutes."

Her mother stood. "Looks like she's trying to win your trust."

Nora picked up their ice cream containers from the side table. "She is. What she doesn't know is that she already has it. Before I tell her, I want to be sure she continues to make good choices."

Her mother laughed. "You're catching on to all our parenting tricks. What about her new friends? Will you let her spend time with the girls involved?"

"What would you do if I had been involved in something like this?"

Her mother laughed again. "Oh no. I can't tell you the answer to that. The time and situation wouldn't have been the same. Eve is struggling with all the changes in her young life ... the loss, the move, the new school." Mother shifted in her seat. "I will say this, you are the constant for Eve. We're here to support you, but you have Eve every day. Her friends will come and go. Be the stability she needs, and pay attention to who Eve is meeting and wanting to spend time with. You'll notice things about those friends and know how to guide her."

"Mom, thanks for talking. I want to go call Jim." Nora's phone buzzed again. It was a text from Jim.

The church youth group was getting together for volleyball and pizza. Eve asked to go, and Nora agreed with the same rules as the night before. When Nora returned to her mother's house, Jim was already there. He had called to ask if he could drive to Simpson to take her to dinner. Nora's heart warmed hearing his placid voice and his gentle words, stepping out in faith that she wouldn't hang up on him. "Yes."

They went to the only white-tablecloth restaurant in Simpson. It was a quaint, family-owned restaurant that served outstanding Italian cuisine. The soft music and candles set the mood for the evening. Jim held the door open and made sure to pull Nora's chair out for her. He was trying. Nora noticed. Once seated, to squelch the awkwardness of where to begin the conversation, they both buried themselves in the menu. When the waiter took their drink order, they had to come out of hiding.

Jim took another step and reached for Nora's hand across the table. Their fingers slid easily together. The warm connection ran through Nora. She smiled through the candlelight.

"Nora, I love you. I was all messed up the other day." Jim looked across the restaurant and back to Nora. "I was scared, and it was like ..."

Nora squeezed his hand. "Like your entire world was spinning out of control?"

Jim's eyes brightened. "Yes, exactly that. How did you know?"

"Let's just say I have a very wise mother."

"Remind me to thank her." Jim smiled. "How do we get back to where we were?"

"This is a lovely start." Nora winked.

The waiter brought their drinks and took their dinner order. Over dinner, Jim told Nora about meeting with the fire inspector and the insurance adjuster.

"Sounds like you're going to be able to rebuild. That's great."

"Yes, now I'm trying to figure out how to pay the staff through all of this. We won't have a fall production. No income. Dr. Crosby told me not to worry about giving back the internship sponsorship and that we'd work it out. I could keep the interns busy and teach about theater management and rebuilding after a crisis."

"That's a great idea. They'll have real-world experience."

"Enough about me. How's Eve?"

Over their lasagna Nora told Jim about her conversation with Eve.

"Sounds like you've handled it wonderfully."

Nora sighed. "It's not easy figuring out teenagers."

Jim paid the check, and they left. Nora noticed the time. "Oh, Jim, I'm sorry to have to do this, but I need to pick up Eve. Can we go straight to Mom's so I can get my car?"

"Would it be okay if we both went to pick her up? I'd like to say hi."

He cared. "Sure. She's at church."

He reached across the seat and hooked his fingers around Nora's. "And selfishly, I'm not ready for our evening to be over."

This felt good. Nora's heart opened and took in Jim's warmth, love, and care for Eve. As they pulled into the church parking lot behind the other parents picking up, Nora texted Eve that they were in Jim's Jeep. While they waited, she turned in the seat to face Jim. "Let's not talk about the fire with her. Can we keep it light? She is really trying to get past that day."

"Sure."

Jim and Eve chatted about last night's Simpson High School football game. Nora didn't expect Eve to have paid that close attention to the game. She thought all high schoolers did at football games was hang out and eat food from the concession stand. When they got back to Nora's mom's house, Eve ran in to talk with her grandmother. Jim and Nora lingered on the front porch. He pulled her into an embrace. A mixture of musk and something outdoorsy, the smell was still fresh. She loved the scent of his aftershave and the strength of his hold on her. Tight enough for her to feel secure—to be wanted.

"Thank you for going out to dinner. It felt like a new start after a very bad day."

Nora pulled back but stayed within his arms. "Agreed. I look forward to navigating the theater rebuild with you."

Jim grinned and tweaked Nora's nose. "And I look forward to supporting and encouraging you in navigating high school with Eve."

Their foreheads touched, and their lips met in a sweet kiss goodnight.

CHAPTER THIRTY-FOUR

The coffee shop chatter hummed as Jim chose a table in the far back corner for his makeshift office and a meeting with Maggie and Sara. He was a man without a place to work. Sara had taken on additional administrative tasks, and Maggie had volunteered to research possible government grants. While he waited, Jim reviewed the results from the fire inspector. Faulty electrical wiring—the wiring the electricians were coming back to fix. Nobody's fault, just bad timing. The electricians would get to start over after the architect, demolition, and framing crews. Starting over seemed to be Jim's theme. The insurance adjuster had given him instructions to get three quotes on the project. They required him to use a general contractor to manage the project. He had one in mind he wanted to work with— George Mason, a friend from church with an outstanding reputation—but Jim would still need to get three quotes.

As Jim was finishing his call with George, Sara and Maggie took their seats across from him at the four-top table.

Maggie pulled her laptop out of her bag. "Is this your new office?"

"It would appear." Jim pulled out a gift card for each of them. "Where's little Glenda?"

"Thank you." Maggie went to place her order.

Sara slipped her light jacket off. "My mother has her this morning. Jake will pick her up this afternoon."

"I admire you both for making it work. Here, get something if you'd like."

Maggie rejoined them after placing her order. "Before we get started, Dan told me to tell you to call him if you have a gap in cash flow while the insurance is being worked out. He said the bank is ready to help."

Jim raked his hand through his wavy hair. "That's great. We're good for now, but I'll probably call him anyway to talk through all of the financial implications of this disaster."

Maggie tilted her head to the left. "Are you okay?"

Jim took a deep breath. "Everything is going to be fine, but right now it feels pretty chaotic." He looked across the table and managed a polite grin. "Thank you for asking. I appreciate you and Sara."

Sara returned to the table. "I have messages."

"Messages? How'd you get messages from the theater phone?"

"Our voicemail is a cloud-based system. The day after the fire, I dialed in and retrieved the messages. Then I Googled how to forward the phone to my cell so I wouldn't have to keep calling in."

"That's great. Thank you." Jim ran his hand through his hair. "And ... um ... I'm going to continue to pay you. There's going to be plenty to do while we're rebuilding."

"Thank you. You saved me from pulling out my poor, single mother monologue." The three shared a laugh.

"Save it." Jim shuffled some papers. "You may need it another time."

Sara went to the counter to pick up her drink and returned to the table. "My uncle rents trailers to construction companies. He agreed to donate one big enough for us to work from. We could put it in the parking lot at the theater."

"Sara, you're a genius." A place to work for the next several months close to the theater where he would watch the reconstruction. "Thank you. Give me his number and I'll call him."

"No need."

"Why?"

Sara sat back with a grin. "Because I already called him. He said if you want, he could deliver one tomorrow and hook up the electric, water, and bathroom by the end of the day."

Jim laughed. "Well, okay then. Should I have you grab a toolbelt, so you can rebuild the theater too?"

"Guess I'm used to having a lot more to do. I've been a little bored for the last week. Yesterday, I started to make calls, figured out the phone ... and I called my uncle." Sara sat up straight. "On to the messages. There's a reporter from the university newspaper who wants to do a story on the fire. She's talked to some of the students in the internship program and wants to talk to you."

"Might be a good PR move." Maggie opened her notes on her computer.

"That's fine. Do you both still have access to my calendar?"

Sara raised her hand. "I do. I had packed my bag right before Eve came running in to find me and Glenda."

A twinge of guilt pinched Jim's heart. "I'm sorry you two were put in danger."

"Jim, you've already apologized a dozen times. We're safe and healthy."

Jim nodded. "Will you schedule the interview and add it to my calendar? Dr. Crosby wants to meet on Friday. Maggie, can you be in that meeting?"

"He's not going to pull the plug on the university's support, is he?"

"No, I talked to him about my idea for doing a semester of theater management. The interns learn about insurance claims, working with vendors, and how to reopen after a disaster."

"Great idea. I can be there Friday."

Sara adjusted in her chair. "Also, I was thinking we should track our rebuilding progress on social media, you know, post pictures of before and after, along with an email campaign to keep fundraising."

"Great idea! Will you put a plan together? Let's talk about it."

As promised, Sara's uncle delivered and set up a trailer complete with a bathroom, a small kitchen sink, half-size refrigerator, and counter. Jim moved his desk from the office inside the theater into the trailer along with two smaller desks for Sara and Maggie. It was far nicer than he expected. When Sara's uncle's crew were leaving, Jim asked about an invoice or leasing agreement. The supervisor said there wasn't one. The use of the trailer for as long as he needed was a donation. "This theater is a jewel. The trailer is a donation from Mr. Pepperdine. He said it's his way of supporting the theater."

The messages of well-wishers had been overwhelming—way more than Jim ever expected. Dr. Crosby loved the change in direction for the interns, which justified the continued university grant funding.

Meetings and conversations each day helped Jim untangle the mess. Friday afternoon, while Sara was setting up the printer, Jim ran out to get them lunch. When he returned, he noticed his dad's car in the parking lot. He pulled his sunglasses onto the top of his head and took the two steps up to the trailer door. He opened it to find his dad handing Sara an envelope.

"Dad, what are you doing here?"

Sara's eyes widened. "This is your dad?"

"Son, uh, hi, when I called, Sara said you were out to lunch."

Jim shook his head. "Wait. Why would you come here if you thought I'd be gone?"

Sara stood still, holding the envelope. "Looks like your dad is our anonymous donor."

"Dad, what is this?"

Mr. Preston put up his hands and grinned. "Guilty."

Jim looked at the floor and back at his dad. "I don't understand. All this time, you've been donating to the theater?"

"Yes, Son. I told you last week after the fire. I'm proud of the work you've done and are doing here. We wanted to contribute, but I wasn't sure you would take our money."

"Our money? Does Mom know about this?"

"Yes. It's from both of us." He looked out of the trailer window and back at Jim. "She's the one who opened my stubborn mind to see what you were really doing here. You're not wasting your talent or intelligence. You're sharing it. You've kept this place alive for the community."

Jim had no words. When he thought about the timing of the anonymous donations and how his dad's attitude toward his work had changed, the pieces of the puzzle came together. "Last year, when planning and zoning threatened to demolish the theater, and we got the gift to help us pay to fight it—that was you?"

"Yes. That's when your mother told me what was going on. I went back and read the articles that had been in the news. And I heard things through the grapevine. The fact that you remained calm, built the alliance with the university, and gained the support of the community was impressive. I knew you would never take our donations straight out."

Jim dropped the fast-food bag into Sara's hands and agreed. "You and I are equally stubborn that way ... Thank you."

"Our pleasure." His dad clapped his hands together. "What do you hear on rebuilding?"

"Let's take a walk, I'll show you what I'm thinking." Jim and his dad walked out of the trailer across the parking lot to the theater. They walked around the building talking about the plans. "I want to keep the original feel but make some updates to increase our auditorium capacity along with sound and lighting system updates. There's some great technology we could build in." Jim explained the three bids he was waiting on, but that he'd like to use George Mason.

Jim's dad stopped walking and turned to Jim. "George Mason. I know his father. Now there's a potential donor for you. He built a successful construction company through the recessions and the height of the market, then taught George the business. Made that boy work summers and weekends from cleanup crew to now running the business. Solid company."

"I met George at church. Didn't realize his dad started the company."

By the time they circled the building and stepped through the lobby, Jim and his dad were talking freely and exchanging ideas about taking advantage of the rebuild to reconfigure the office space. Jim walked his dad to his car.

"Dad, thank you. I'm sorry. Will you forgive me for my part in the barrier we've had between us? I hope we can move forward."

"Forgiven. Forgiven before you asked. Will you forgive me?"

"Forgiven."

The two most stubborn Preston men hugged, and Jim said, "I'll see you and Mom soon."

Sara came running out of the trailer. "Jim."

Jim turned around. "What's up?"

"The story the girl from the university paper did has been picked up by the local news. Two stations have called to come interview you."

Mr. Preston grasped his son's shoulders. "Looks like you better go freshen up. Your mom and I will watch the news."

After meeting with her counselor, Eve practically fell into Nora's car. "I'm exhausted."

"Rough session?"

Eve tossed her backpack over the seat. "Kinda. It's emotionally draining to talk about ... emotions."

"I understand."

"You do? Have you ever seen a counselor?" Eve had always seen her Aunt Nora as having it all together.

"Yes. I saw one early in my marriage to your Uncle Seth. I had a miscarriage, and then when we found out I couldn't have children after my second miscarriage, I went into depression. It was a difficult time for both of us."

Eve said nothing for a moment. Her drama with friends paled in comparison to losing a baby. "I'm sorry you went through that."

"It was only after I was willing to ask for help that I began to heal and be more myself. I would leave those sessions exhausted."

Eve nodded and let silence linger between them. "What's for dinner?"

"Jim's coming over to grill. With the weather turning, this may be our last weekend to grill." They rode in silence. "Do you want to tell me about your session?"

Eve watched the passing houses and neighborhoods. "We talked about my new friends at school and how I was feeling about living in Oakdale." She didn't have the energy to say much more. Maybe later. Aunt Nora didn't ask a bunch of questions, which made it easier to share. Oakdale as her new home. Eve had begun to get used to the idea. Olivia and Ashley had become her friends. She avoided Crystal and Addison, who were rumored to have gotten caught hiding alcohol in their lockers and drinking at the football game. Eve, Ashley, and Olivia joined the school drama club.

When they arrived home, Jim was already there getting the charcoal ready to light. "Hello, ladies. How was your day?"

Aunt Nora laughed. "A handsome man greeting us."

Eve slid her backpack over one shoulder as the three walked to the front door. "Hey, Jim, I joined the drama club at school. When we decide on the play for this year, could we borrow a few props and costumes from the theater?"

"I think we can make that happen. Get a list, and I'll see what we can do to help. Most of the props are in the warehouse."

"Thank you." Eve bounded upstairs.

What a difference a few weeks made. Nora couldn't believe the change in Eve's attitude since the fire. Jim noticed it as well.

"Who was that? She's come out of her shell, hasn't she?"

Nora tucked her work satchel in the front hall closet. "Isn't it great."

Jim pulled Nora close for a quick hello kiss. "It is. The grill is ready, but I need matches."

Nora went into the kitchen and opened the drawer where the long matches were kept. There was one of her extra house keys. Should she offer it to Jim? Was it too soon? She picked the key out of the drawer and turned around as Jim came into the kitchen. With a quick reverse, Nora put the key back and handed Jim the matches. "Here you go. I'll get the chicken out."

The three had dinner and talked about the news coverage on the theater, the fire, and its historical significance to the city. Jim had done four interviews with TV stations and local podcast hosts after the story was picked up by the local newspaper. Jim asked Eve about school and her upcoming audition for the play. Jim offered a few tips.

"Eve, are you ready to resume volunteering at the theater? Sara's working on our social media fundraising campaign. I'm sure she'd love your help."

Silence. Eve's shoulders fell. Jim shot an awkward look to Nora who shook her head and changed the subject.

"Did I tell you that I've added two Christmas clients?"

"Let me get this straight, these people pay you to create a theme and design for their Christmas décor, and they pay you to put it up and take it down?" Jim shook his head.

"Yep. Remember? That's how your mother found me. I did the mayor's house for Christmas last year. The Dickens theme. Your mom and dad went to their party. Then we did the mayor's second floor bedrooms after the New Year. When your mom was there for the spring tea, she saw the renovation and loved it. That's when she got my number."

"I'm still shocked people pay you to decorate their homes for Christmas, then you go in and take it all down."

Eve sat forward. "Jim, I'd like to come back, but I don't think I'm ready yet. Is that okay?"

Jim smiled. "Of course. You let me know. We can always use your help."

They finished their meal with brownies and chocolate chip ice cream. Nora served it in glass short-stemmed dessert bowls from her grandmother. "My Gran always said to give desserts a name. I'm calling this creation the 'chocolate double whammy.'"

Jim sat back and rubbed his midsection. "Wow, you could have named the entire meal a triple whammy. I'm going to have to run an extra mile in the morning. This meal was worth it. Those brownies with ice cream were the perfect dessert."

Nora gave a shy point to Eve. "Our baker here made them last night."

"Amazing." Jim stood and collected their plates. Nora and Eve picked up their glasses and the other dishes and took them to the kitchen.

"I'm going up to watch some TV," Eve announced.

Nora gave Eve a hug. "Okay. I think Jim and I are going to sit out on the patio if you need us."

"See you later, Jim. Thanks for offering to let us use stuff from the theater when we do our school play."

"No problem, kiddo."

The evening grew cooler, and the stars began to poke through the navy sky. Jim and Nora sat in the quietness of the evening. Nora leaned against him with her legs stretched out on the cushioned bench seat. Jim wrapped his arms around her. The two melted into each other. "I love you."

Nora closed her eyes and felt their breathing ease into the same rhythm. "I love you too. Thanks for grilling."

"Glad to. That was an odd shift with Eve at dinner. Should I not have mentioned her coming back to the theater?"

Nora ran her finger along Jim's forearm that hung over her shoulder. "She's done that a couple of times lately. Something will be said, and it's like she pulls back into her shell. Then, after a little while, she comes back out and is ready to talk about how she feels about whatever sent her into her shell. Maybe it's something she's learning in therapy."

"I didn't mean to say anything wrong."

"You didn't. We need to be sensitive but not tiptoe around things we would normally talk about."

The crickets began their nightly performance. Nora closed her eyes and enjoyed the warmth of Jim's closeness, a peaceful reminder that Eve was doing better and confidence that a renewed life was ahead for both of them.

CHAPTER THIRTY-FIVE

The mid-October leaves swirled around the parking lot in front of Nora's car. She parked next to the trailer and gingerly lifted the cup carrier, which contained four steaming coffees and a box of fresh donuts, from the passenger-side floor. Across the parking lot, near the front entrance to the theater, a second trailer sat with a large banner, "Mason Construction," hung from its side. Parked next to the trailer were open-bed trucks with tools and lumber. Reconstruction had begun. Nora loved the excitement in Jim's eyes when he'd shared the plans George Mason had proposed.

A couple of times, he had asked Nora for her opinion on the new layout and color scheme. He had taken most of her suggestions. Nora poked her elbow out to rap on the door to the temporary office. Sara opened it and reached out to help with the coffee and donuts. The motion of one of the workers who lugged rubbish from the building caught her eye. She blinked and looked again. It looked like ... no, it couldn't be ... haircut, clean-shaven ... Curt?

"Jim?" Nora entered the trailer. "Have you seen who's working on George's crew? Is Jim in?"

"He is." Sara nodded toward his makeshift office, then called to the back of the trailer. "Nora's here, and she brought donuts."

Jim looked up from an unrolled blueprint. He had a pencil behind one ear, and a tablet with his construction plan. "Good morning. What a wonderful surprise." He got up and walked around the desk to give Nora a soft kiss on the cheek.

Jim pulled back. "Donuts, what a treat."

Nora walked to the window. "I think I saw Curt in the parking lot."

Jim walked the two short steps to the window. "Really? It's George's crew. I haven't met any of them."

"I know you've only seen him a couple of times—would you go ask George? I knew he'd turn up again somewhere." Nora's voice caught. "Please."

"I will. But if it is Curt, remember, he's George's employee. I can't tell him who to hire."

Nora nodded and looked out the window.

As Jim approached the construction trailer, George emerged from the door, talking on his phone. Jim stood away from him, looking at the theater that was in its second week of rebuilding. It had taken over a month to obtain quotes, secure building permits, and finalize the budget with the insurance company.

George finished his call. "What's up, Jim?" He was a stocky man in his forties. He wore jeans and a collared short-sleeved shirt. A pen and a folded piece of paper peeked out of the chest pocket.

Jim rubbed the back of his neck and looked away. "I need to ask about one of your guys."

"Sure. Who?"

"Curt Butler."

George nodded. "You know him?"

"Sort of. He's Nora's former brother-in-law."

George winced. "Ouch." He looked over at the hive of workers. "Jim, I met Curt three months ago. Can't tell you where—that's confidential. I know what you're worried about. All of my employees go through random drug testing. Our HR group goes to each job site to perform them. They say 'random.'" He raised his fingers in air quotes. "But it appears to happen sometime every month. Random days of the month. Any sign of using, and the employee is immediately let go. Zero tolerance policy."

"You do random testing." Jim looked back over at the window Nora was peeking out of. "How did you meet ..."

George put his hand up. "Let's just say I've been volunteering with a men's group at church on Thursday nights ..." George emphasized Thursday nights, and Jim caught the look on George's face. "Curt started coming, like I said, several months ago. I've spent a lot of time with him, and he's on the right path." He checked his watch. "I need you to trust me on this."

Jim nodded. He knew exactly which men's group met on Thursday night. It was a recovery group. "Thanks, George. Would you mind not saying anything to him? I'll handle this with Nora."

Nora jerked away from the window when she saw Jim turn from George and walk back. She skirted over to the plans on his desk. When Jim stepped inside and closed the door, she could no longer hold her curiosity. "Well? Is it Curt?"

Jim glanced outside and then back to Nora's waiting expression. "Yes." Nora started to say something, but Jim interrupted. "Wait. Let me tell you what George said." Jim gestured for her to sit. They sat knee to knee, and he took her hands, leaning close. "It is Curt. George met him at church at a men's group about three months ago ... on Thursday night."

Nora shook her head. "There are no men's group at our church on Thu ..." Her eyebrows rose. "On Thursdays. Aren't those the recovery support groups?"

Jim grinned. "George couldn't tell me directly, but he said all of his employees are drug tested and if they aren't clean, they are fired. The testing is done randomly. Curt has to be clean to be working for him."

Nora's stomach churned at the thought of Curt being so close to Eve. Had he been here last week when Eve was helping Sara? She looked down at her fingers intertwined with Jim's. She ran one finger along the outside of his hand. His forehead almost touched hers. He understood how hard this was for her.

Jim reached over and lifted Nora's chin. "I trust George. Can you trust me to keep an eye on things?"

"Yes." Nora's comment was barely audible. "I don't like it, but I guess ..." She looked into Jim's hazel eyes. Those warm, loving eyes. "This would have been better on another day."

A sympathetic smile raised the corners of Jim's eyes. "No, it wouldn't. Today is harder because it's Liz's birthday. I'm sorry."

"You don't have to be sorry. You didn't hire him. I'd hoped he had disappeared somewhere."

"Sounds like he's trying to clean up his life." Jim caressed her hand, which was still folded in his. "Everyone deserves a second ... or third ... chance. We all fall short, Nora."

Nora snatched her hand away. "What are you saying? Should I forgive him for all the hurt he caused my sister? My family?" She stood and walked back to the window.

"No, I mean ... well ... yes, eventually, you'll need to forgive him." Jim walked up behind Nora and put his hands on her shoulders. He leaned close in almost a whisper. "We all need forgiveness and the chance to start again."

Nora whipped around. "Forgive me if I'm not feeling that generous today." She grabbed her purse. "Why are you so willing to forgive him?" Nora didn't wait for an answer. She bolted out the door.

Jim's words, "Nora, wait," were hammered out by the door banging shut. Nora raced to her car, digging in her purse for her keys. She fussed at herself for letting them fall to the bottom of her bag. Jim caught up.

"Please wait. I don't expect you to be glad he's shown up. Nor do I expect you to want to have anything to do with Curt." He grimaced and looked over at the construction crew. "It's hard to forgive the kind of hurt Curt has caused. I have some personal experience with the hurt that comes from substance abuse."

"What do you mean personal experience ... you?"

Please say no. Nora didn't want to turn around. She wasn't mad at Jim. She was hurt and felt like she could vomit. Jim was right. Everyone deserved forgiveness. She wasn't ready to lay it down. It was easier to hold onto the hurt than to give Curt freedom to live under the same grace she did. She looked at the ground as she turned around.

Jim caught one stray hair from Nora's perfectly wrapped bun. "My brother John started down a dark road for a few months when he was in college. It was so hard not to swoop in and try to fix it for him. I couldn't. I'll tell you the whole story some other time. He's been clean since then." Jim bent down enough to catch her eye. "I'm sorry. I didn't mean to hurt your feelings."

Nora nodded and reached further into her leather purse to find her keys. "Eve and I are leaving for Simpson as soon as school's out."

"Okay. Will you call me when you're on the road?"

"I'll have to see. With it being Liz's birthday, I don't know how Eve will be after school. We were both pretty melancholy this morning."

Silence.

"I understand."

Jim stood back and put his hands in his pockets. Nora wanted him to pull her close and hold her. Make the hurting stop. Nora hesitated, opened the car door and dropped her purse on the driver's seat. She turned around as Jim turned to go inside.

"Jim, wait."

The distance between them closed, with two steps from each of them. "You aren't wrong. It stung to hear the word 'forgiveness' when it came to Curt. It's so hard."

Jim pulled her close. "I know. You'll get there. But probably not today."

His embrace gave her the security of being vulnerable with Jim. Her faith overcame the fear and anger surrounding Curt's presence. "No, but I will commit to praying about it."

Jim winked at her. "I'll be praying for you. Nora ... I love you."

"I love you too. Thanks for speaking the truth, even though it hurt."

"I don't ever want to hurt you."

"I know. Eve and I will call you from the road."

CHAPTER THIRTY-SIX

Phillip met Nora and Eve at Vivian's house. Eve staying with Phillip and Judy for the weekend gave Nora and Eve a short break from each other. Other than a few incidents of grief-ridden emotions on both their parts, Eve and Nora were becoming comfortable with each other. Spending time with Phillip, Judy, and her cousins provided Eve with an opportunity to connect with her family and friends in Simpson. Phillip and Eve moved her overnight bag to his car and then stepped onto the porch to say goodbye.

Nora's arms encircled Eve. "I love you. Have fun."

Eve returned the hug and hugged her grandmother. As she bounced down the three concrete steps, she called back, "Bye, Aunt Nora, bye, Grandma."

Nora and her mom waved and turned to go inside. The stillness of the house swept over Nora. "Mom, did you feel the same unbalanced quiet when we all left after a visit?"

"Unbalanced quiet?" Mother pulled silverware from the buffet in the dining room and went into the kitchen to get their dinner. Nora followed her.

"You know—when the house goes from having the energy of a teenager to total stillness. It feels odd."

Her mother laughed. "Oh yes. When all three of you moved out and were on your own, your dad and I looked at each other and laughed at how still the house became. Grilled pimento cheese sandwich okay with our potato soup?"

"Sounds great."

Her mother stirred the soup and pulled out the bread and a bowl of pimento cheese spread. "We had many conversations as we saw the end of raising kids on the horizon about what our life would be like as empty-nesters."

"What about when we were away at college and would come home for the weekend and then leave again. Was it weird?"

Vivian spread butter on both sides of the sandwich and laid it in the skillet to grill. "It felt a little weird at first. Then you all would come home for a weekend or holiday, and our lives would get swirled up. You'd leave, calm would come, and we'd go on. During that time, your dad and I talked a lot about what our lives would be like when there were no more kids home for the weekends, when you would be out on your own."

Nora sat at the Formica-topped, two-chair kitchen table, leaning with her hand under her chin. Her mother pulled two plates from the cabinet. "Will you pour us tea? And we'll go ahead and sit in here instead of the dining room."

The two sat across from each other with their soup and sandwiches. The salty-sweet aroma of the soup lingered in their silence. After a bite of her sandwich and a taste of the soup, Nora's mother laid her soup spoon on the edge of the plate. "Nora, where are all these questions coming from?"

Nora stirred her soup and looked out the window next to where they sat. "I don't know. Every time Eve leaves to come here for the weekend, it's like shifting gears from guardian to simply being me ... doing what I want and not having to worry about where Eve is, picking her up, keeping her safe ... it almost feels like when she's home, I'm holding my breath, and when she leaves, I get to exhale."

"Sounds about right."

"But then the house is too quiet. I miss having her there."

"Yep." Her mother grinned and kept eating.

"Is that all you've got? Sounds about right, and yep?"

A laugh came next. "Oh, Nora, when Eve's with you, you feel 'on' and responsible for everything. Which is what a good parent or guardian does. That feeling will ease as time passes. In the meantime, take the time when she's away to give yourself permission to relax." She tilted her bowl to scoop the final spoonful of soup. "How are you and Jim doing?"

Nora rolled her eyes. "I think we're doing fine. He's trying very hard to get to know Eve."

"That wasn't my question. I asked how you and Jim were doing. You answered he's trying to get to know Eve. Which is good."

A timid smile rose on Nora's lips. "We're good. Talking about a future, most of the time it feels right and wonderful, but something inside me niggles at the thought." She wiped breadcrumbs off the table onto her hand. "Our relationship is an answer to prayer. And with Eve moving in, we've overcome a lot. But then I think of Seth. He was everything to me."

Her mother softened her tone and reached across to touch Nora's arm. "Sweetheart, you grieved over Seth for years. You've started a career, and your prayer was for the Lord's direction and renewal of your life. He's provided that. I'm not pushing you toward Jim if you don't love him or want to build a life with him. I'm telling you to consider if it's the desire of your heart, and God's will, to open your heart more fully to a new life with a godly man."

Nora let her mother's wisdom linger. She picked up their dishes and began to rinse them for the dishwasher. She turned to her mother. "I know you're right. Jim is who I prayed for. I want to feel the freedom to love him."

Nora's mother put the butter in the refrigerator. "'Create in me a clean heart, O God, and renew a right spirit within me,' says the psalmist. Life flows in and out of seasons, highs and lows. With each, God is there to refresh and renew our hearts. Think about it."

"I will." Nora finished hand-washing the skillet. "Do you mind if I turn in early?"

"Of course not. We've got a lot to do tomorrow."

"Yes, the realtor and Phillip are going to meet us at ten."

Nora went upstairs and turned the bath water on to fill the clawfoot tub. *Create in me a new spirit. Let me feel the newness of you, Lord.*

The silence didn't feel so odd anymore.

Sunday evening, Jim and Nora sat on her sofa. Eve was in her room doing homework with her earbuds in. Jim wrapped his arm over Nora's shoulder, and she snuggled into his side. "Thank you for coming to the church service this morning honoring Liz."

"It was lovely. Phillip did a great job speaking."

"He did. I'm thankful one of us isn't afraid of public speaking. We have all come a long way since June."

"You have." Jim pulled Nora a little closer. "I'm sure you would have done just as well."

"He, Mom, and I talked about Curt showing up on the construction crew." Nora sat up and shifted one knee up on the sofa. "My mother, in her infinite faith and wisdom, agrees with you."

"With me?"

"She said we need to find it in our hearts to forgive him. He's as much of a sinner as we are. We all have flaws." Nora twisted a piece of hair in her fingers. "Phillip is struggling as much as I am."

"You still need time. Nothing wrong with that."

"Mom did say something else. She said that because we forgive someone, it doesn't mean we're ready to let them back in our lives. There can be guardrails."

"Guardrails. Kinda like when you and I first started dating. You were like a scared cat."

Nora sat up straight and swatted at Jim's arm. "Maybe. But you were too."

Jim threw his head back in laughter. "Fair enough. I was too. But both of us prayed, asked for God's guidance, and opened our hearts a little at a time."

Nora leaned back onto Jim and thought about her mother's words. "We did."

"I'm thankful we did. I don't ever want to be without you."

Nora's heart thumped. *Was Jim talking about what she thought he was? Marriage? It was a big step to open her heart to love him, but marriage?* Nora took a deep breath. It wasn't a bad thought.

"What are you saying, Mr. Preston?"

She felt Jim shrug and take a deep breath. "I'd like us to think about a future together."

They were both venturing into a new stage of their relationship. The thought of a future with Jim wasn't a foreign thought. A feeling of warmth, like the autumn sun through a window, fell over her. She smiled. *Create in me a new spirit.*

"A future together. I like that thought." She sat up again and turned to face Jim. "Remember, it's not only me in this scenario."

"I know. I've had time to think about Eve coming to live with you. My stupidity about children and parenting has been squelched by conversations I've had lately with my dad. I'm so thankful we've put our disagreements behind us and forgiven each other."

"I'm glad you and your dad have reconciled." Nora ran her finger along Jim's arm. "Your mother is sweet."

"I guess that's where my comment about forgiveness came from the other day. I've felt the burden I was carrying lifted."

"I understand."

Jim pulled Nora close and into a warm kiss.

"What are you up to?" Eve called from the kitchen.

Jim and Nora scrambled to their feet and rushed into the kitchen. "Nothing." Saying it in unison didn't help.

Eve grinned. "Okay." She pulled a snack out of the cabinet. "Jim, I'm supposed to come help Sara with a mailing or something after school tomorrow."

Nora and Jim joined Eve in the kitchen. They sat on the stools at the island. "Sounds great. How about I have your favorite milkshake waiting for you."

"Great. Is it okay if Olivia comes too? She'll help, and she needs service hours toward graduation next year."

"Sure. Text me her favorite shake as well, and I'll treat you both."

Nora's stomach felt like she'd eaten gravel at the thought of Curt being near Eve. "Eve, when you get there, please don't go near the construction. Just to the trailer with Sara and Jim."

Eve scrunched her nose. She'd been there several times since construction began and had never gotten in the way. "Okay, Aunt Nora." She called over her shoulder as she went back upstairs, armed with Oreos and milk.

"Real smooth, Aunt Nora." Jim smirked.

Nora raised her hands. "I know. Now I'm going to worry that she's going to see him."

"She's a teenager. Don't they live in their own world?"

"What if he sees her? What if he says something to her?"

"I promised I would keep an eye on things at work, and I will. Trust me."

Nora nodded. Jim slapped his knees and stood from the stool. "It's getting late. I should go."

After Jim left, Nora immediately missed him. A future with Jim. The thought danced around her mind and heart as she floated up to bed. Pleasant dreams ahead.

CHAPTER THIRTY-SEVEN

It took two weeks for Nora to run into Curt at the theater. Each time she was there to pick up Eve, the temptation to walk up to Curt and question his reason for being there, for choosing this construction company to work for, for not asking to be put on another project poked at her. But she didn't. She kept her distance from the workers and remained focused on Eve. The construction was progressing well. All the exterior walls were in place. To ensure the building's color was consistent all the way around, the white siding was replaced around the entire exterior. With the exterior completed, the construction workers moved inside the theater to begin the interior renovations. This squelched Nora's angst about Eve running into Curt. That was until she pulled in at the end of the workday as workers were walking out of the building. Nora barely noticed she had pulled in next to a black Chevrolet truck. She got out of her car and walked to the back to get boxes of fabric samples Stanton Designs was donating to the upcoming production of *Joseph and the Amazing Technicolor Dreamcoat*. She juggled the box to close the back of her car.

"Here, let me help you with that."

Curt. She didn't have to see him. She knew his voice. Hearing it brought the hair on her arms to attention. "No. I have it. Thanks." She didn't have it. The box of samples toppled out of her arms and spilled onto the ground."

"Are you sure you don't need some help?" Curt stooped down to pick up a few samples that were out of Nora's reach. He stood and handed her the fabric. "Nora?"

Heat rose to Nora's face, either from anger or embarrassment at dropping the box. She wasn't sure. "Curt, what are you doing here?"

Curt laid the fabric across the top of the box. "Nora, I'm just here to work. I don't want any trouble."

Looking into his steely eyes, all the words of wisdom and forgiveness evaporated. She was left with anger. "Really, Curt? Of all the places you could be working, I'm supposed to believe that a job twenty-five yards from where Eve volunteers two days a week was the only place you could find work."

Curt took his hat off and shook his head. "I know you don't believe me. That's okay. I deserve that. But it's true. I met George at church a couple of months ago. He gave me a job as long as I ..."

"As long as what? What empty promise did you give him, Curt?"

Curt nodded. "Empty promises. I deserve that too from you. I've made more mistakes than most in my life. Hurt a lot of people, you being among them. But I'm trying. I'm trying to rebuild my life. Until I was further along, I wasn't going to contact you. My word to George was no more drugs, no more dealers. I celebrated sixty days sober last Wednesday."

Rebuilding his life. Renewal. New spirit. Where is mine? Nora looked at the ground and took in a cleansing breath.

"We all fall short, Curt." Nora hardly believed the words came out of her mouth. "But do not ask to see Eve."

Curt waved his hands in front of his chest. "I wasn't going to. I've seen Eve coming and going. It took everything in me not to try and talk with her. I still have some messes to clean up."

Nora nodded.

"But, Nora, I do want to spend time with her when I'm ready. And she's ready. It's too late for me to really be a dad to her ... but she's my daughter. I love her and would like the opportunity to get to know her."

"We'll talk when the time comes. But in the meantime, do not let her see you here or around Oakdale. Agreed?"

"Yes."

Nora snatched the box from the ground and walked toward the office trailer. She felt her heart thumping in her chest as she tried to take a deep breath to stay her churning emotions. The question would be coming soon. *Can I forgive him?*

"Didn't you decorate the mayor's house last year for Christmas?" Eve sat at the island and leaned forward while Nora made breakfast. She looked around the kitchen and den.

"Yes. Why do you ask?"

"I remember you decorating your house for all the seasons. And you did that big house for Christmas last year. Thanksgiving's next week and you don't have the fall stuff out."

Aunt Nora turned around and slid Eve's egg onto the plate beside a slice of buttered toast and handed it across the counter. "Must have slipped my mind."

"I'm no designer, but doesn't it look weird for the cushions on the front porch to still be blooming flowers? Didn't you have fake pumpkins or something last year?"

Nora flipped her egg and dropped her bread in the toaster. "Yes, you're right."

"Tonight, when I get home from the theater, can we get all the decorations out? I know we'll turn around and switch them for Christmas, but it might be fun."

Home. Aunt Nora's house was Eve's home now. Not the one she grew up in with her mom, but a place where she felt loved. Eve continued to meet with her counselor, who gave her coping tips for the first holidays without her mom. One was to think of something about the holidays that she loved. Eve remembered Aunt Nora's decorated home always being something she looked forward to.

"That does sound like fun. Do you want to invite Olivia over?"

"Can I? I've been wanting to invite her to spend the night. What about Ashley too?"

Aunt Nora pulled a fork from the drawer. "I don't see why not." A sly grin crawled across Aunt Nora's lips. "Can I invite a friend over too?"

"If it's who I think it is, yes, but no sleepover for you."

Aunt Nora's eyes grew wide, and she swatted at Eve. "Young lady. I'm not that kind of girl. And you aren't either."

Eve giggled. "I know. Yes, let's include Jim."

They finished breakfast in silence. Eve's heart was warmed by their teasing. She pulled her phone from the side pocket of her backpack and texted Olivia and Ashley.

"Looks like they are in."

"That was fast."

Eve nodded. "You've been great about driving us around and taking us to the mall. Thank you. But I need to tell you something. I think I saw someone ... someone on the construction crew ... the other day when we went by the theater."

Nora patted Eve's arm. *How do I get around this?* "Who do you think you saw?"

Eve shook her head. "It was probably no one. Never mind. Anyway, thanks for driving us."

"Glad to. I'm glad Ashley's chosen you and Olivia over the other girls who seem to find trouble. You're at the theater after school, right?"

"Yep, we're doing a social media campaign for the Christmas reveal of the renovations."

CHAPTER THIRTY-EIGHT

Nora arrived at Oakdale East High School as the bell rang. She knew it would be several minutes before Eve came out. A gentle smile grew on her lips as she recalled her days at Simpson High School—chatting with her friends after school, making plans for the upcoming dance, and trying to stay out of the latest drama among the girls. Upcoming dance ... she hadn't heard anything about dances at Oakdale. She made a mental note to ask Eve. Hopefully, after Eve heard she'd been volunteering twenty-five yards from where Curt had been working, she would still want to talk to her. *Breathe, it'll be fine.* With her next deep breath, Eve pulled the passenger door open and plopped into the seat.

At home, Nora went into the kitchen to make a snack, all the while praying in her heart for the right words, wisdom, and discernment.

"Aunt Nora, you're quiet today. Is everything all right?"

Nora realized she had barely said hello. "I'm sorry. Must have been lost in thought. Everything's fine. But I need to tell you something."

"Okay." Eve slid onto one of the stools at the breakfast bar. "Aunt Nora, did I do something wrong?"

Nora's shoulders dropped. She reached over and touched Eve's hand. "No, sweetie. You've done nothing wrong. In fact, I'm so proud of you for making better choices, and choosing to spend time with friends who are not trying to drag you into trouble."

"So, what's going on?"

Eve's stomach churned. "Aunt Nora, please. What's going on?"

Her aunt faced her. She looked troubled. "Eve, I need to tell you something about your dad, Curt. I'm worried it's going to upset you. I did what I did to protect you, but ..."

Eve stood and paced into the den. Nora followed her. A deep cleansing breath. *It's about Curt. Okay, I can handle this.* She turned back toward her aunt. "What is it?"

"The other day you thought you saw someone on the construction crew ..."

"Yeah."

"It was him."

Eve's eyes grew wide. "Has he been following me?"

Nora waved her hands. "No, it's nothing like that. But that was my fear as well, at first. It seems Curt met the owner of the construction company at a support group meeting at church. The man got to know him and offered him a job. Curt had no idea he'd be working on the theater project. I found out from Jim that the owner's rule for his employees is they have to stay out of trouble. That includes drinking and using drugs."

Eve looked at the floor. *Maybe he was trying to straighten out his life.* "Did he know I was there?"

"Yes. But he assured me he would not try to contact you. He told me he was trying to clean up ..."

"Wait a minute. You talked to him? How long have you known he was working there?" Eve's shaky voice rose.

Aunt Nora was silent.

Nora had no words. How could she explain the timing, the need to protect Eve? "Eve, I'm sorry I didn't tell you sooner. He's been on the job the entire time."

Eve threw her hands up. "Are you kidding me? For months I've been across the parking lot from my dad, and no one told me?"

"I asked him not to talk to you. He agreed and said he wanted to wait."

"What is he waiting for? It's been fifteen years. I don't understand. Him not wanting to tell me. You not being honest with me. I guess Jim knows too. Anyone else keeping secrets from me?" Eve's voice cracked, and tears threatened. "I'm going upstairs."

Nora straightened up and grabbed Eve's arm as she tried to pass. "Let's slow down. The whole world is not out to lie to you. Come over here, and let's sit down and talk about this."

The tension in Eve's arm relented as Nora took her by the hand and walked to the couch. "Let me start from the beginning. I noticed Curt the way you did. He looked familiar, but with a haircut and shave, I wasn't quite sure. To be careful, I asked Jim to talk with the owner of the construction company. So, yes, Jim knew too. As long as he wasn't drinking or doing drugs, came to work on time, and worked hard, he'd have a job. I later found out that those were the requirements of his parole."

"His what? He went to jail?" Eve wiped a rebel tear.

"Evidently. Then one day, I ran into him when I was at the theater. That's when we agreed he shouldn't try to contact you. It was as much my demand as it was Curt's choice. He said he wanted to wait until he felt more confident in his life choices." Nora reached for Eve's hand. "All of us were trying to do what was best for you. Even Curt." With those words, a thought pierced Nora's heart. Even Curt was trying to protect Eve. Maybe it was time to release her pent-up anger and forgive him.

Eve fiddled with a stray strand of hair and looked at the floor. Nora couldn't stand the burden of knowing she might have hurt Eve. "Eve, I'm sorry. I never meant to hurt you or deceive you."

Eve mumbled, "I know." She looked up at Nora with dark, sad eyes. "It feels like you all were being so controlling. But I understand why. You love me, and you were protecting me just like Mom did all those years." She looked back at the floor and then at Nora. "I forgive you."

Nora closed and opened her eyes. *Forgiveness.* How quick Eve was to extend it to her. "Thank you. Will you trust there will be a time for you to talk with Curt? But not now. He's dealing with some hard things. Let's continue to give him the space he needs to do the things he's working on to get his life in order."

"Yes. I understand."

"Thank you." Nora's spirit lifted. "I love you."

Eve leaned into a hug with Nora. When she pulled away, Nora smiled at her niece. "Now, tell me the news from school. And I was wondering, is there a dance coming up?"

Eve jerked her hands to her cheeks. "How did you know?"

Nora's laughter filled the cozy den. "I didn't, but I do now."

Eve tucked her chin toward her chest. "There's this guy." A blush climbed her cheeks.

"Is he in some of your classes?"

"He is. And he's the quarterback on the football team. His name is Ben Milton."

"Have you been talking or texting?"

"A little. The winter dance is coming up, and I was sorta hoping he'd ask me to go. But there's this cheerleader who likes him."

"Seems to me it's up to Ben who he asks to the dance. Do some of the kids go as groups and not take dates?"

"Some. Olivia, Ashley, and I have been talking about all just going." Eve pulled her hair over her shoulder. "I need a new dress if I go."

"Of course. Let's get you one. Sounds like if this Ben doesn't come to his senses and ask the prettiest girl, you're going anyway and will want to look your best."

Eve sat up, the blush faded, and her smile grew. "That'd be great. Thanks."

"When is the dance?"

"December fifteenth." Eve's eyes widened and she drew her hand to her mouth. "That's the night of the theater reopening." She blew out a breath and closed her eyes.

Nora's brow creased. "So, you don't have to go to the opening. Go to the dance. Have fun with your friends."

"Really? That'd be okay?"

Nora smiled. "Of course."

CHAPTER THIRTY-NINE

Thanksgiving morning, Nora cooked breakfast in silence. The invitation to Jim's parents' home would help them get through this first holiday without Liz. Eve came down to breakfast, her eyes red and watery. Nora gave her a hug. No words were needed.

After they ate and put their dishes in the dishwasher, Nora reached for Eve's hand. Through moist eyes, she looked at her niece. "It's hard to think of Thanksgiving without your mom."

Eve wrapped herself around Nora. The two stood in the middle of the kitchen together, crying. Eve pulled away first and snagged a napkin to wipe her nose. "Okay, let's do our thing. One thing we miss and one thing we'll do to remember her. You go first."

Nora grinned. "I'll miss her mashed potatoes today. She made the creamiest mashed potatoes with butter and salt." She pointed to Eve.

"We should find the recipe and make them sometime."

"Sounds yummy. Now you go."

"I miss her French braiding my hair. Whenever we were going someplace special or if I had a new outfit and wanted my hair braided, she'd do it for me."

"We are going someplace special today." Nora noticed the time. "Your grandmother will be here in thirty minutes. Is your room ready for her?"

"It is, and I put clean towels in the bathroom."

"Thank you. I put sheets and a blanket on the sofa for you. We'll pull out the bed when we get back."

"Aunt Nora, I didn't finish what I'd like to do to remember Mom."

Nora stopped wiping the counter. "I'm sorry. I interrupted you. What would you like to do to remember your mom?"

Eve looked at the floor and then back at her aunt. "Would you braid my hair today? I want to look good for our Thanksgiving with Jim's family."

"I'd love to." She wiped the tears that had escaped. "I'll finish the kitchen and will be right up. Shouldn't take me long."

Nora, her mother, and Eve pulled into the long driveway that led to Jim's parents' home. Her mother's jaw went slack.

"Have mercy, Nora. This is a far cry from our two-story in Simpson."

"Mom, we're not comparing. You know Jim isn't pretentious. Neither is his family. They just happen to be wealthy." Nora reached over and squeezed her mother's hand. "You and Daddy gave us a wonderful life."

Her mother swiped her hands across her wool slacks. "We did our best."

"You did great." As Nora pulled in behind Jim's brother's Bronco in the curved drive, Jim walked down the porch steps and opened her mother's car door.

"Mrs. Samuels, welcome." He gave her a kiss on the cheek.

Eve and Nora came around the car. Nora wore a long brown knit dress with knee-high brown leather boots. She accented the monochromatic look with an artisan necklace that featured maroon and orange stones. After she'd braided Eve's hair, she pulled her own back in a ponytail, leaving loose fringe pieces of hair around her face.

Jim gave Eve a side hug and then reached for Nora's hand. "You look beautiful." Jim led them inside.

As Jim took their coats. Nora's mom looked up at the two-story entry and the curved staircase. Jim's mother walked up the hall from the kitchen door beyond the staircase. Like Nora's mother, she was dressed in wool slacks and a sweater. Nora noticed her mother take a relaxed breath. Mrs. Preston dried her hands on her apron and introduced herself.

"I'm Maribel." She reached out and hugged Nora's mom. Jim's dad joined them from the living room.

"I'm James. Glad you could join us." Dr. Preston's six-foot-three-inch height towered over Mrs. Samuels' five-foot-four inches. He, too, was wearing slacks with a shirt and sweater vest.

"Thank you for having me. I'm Vivian Samuels."

Mrs. Preston peeked into the living room. "Not sure where Jim's brothers have gotten to, but you'll meet them shortly." She looked at Eve. "Good to see you again, dear."

"Thank you."

"Come in and make yourself comfortable. James, would you take care of refreshments? I was about to take the turkey from the oven."

Nora, her mother, and Eve followed Jim and his dad into the living room. Jim's dad offered them something to drink and then disappeared into the kitchen to pour them.

Jim bid them have a seat and the four sat in awkward silence. Mrs. Samuels adjusted her sweater and looked around the large living room, which had two sitting areas. One area featured a sofa and two chairs, while the other, which led to the three-season room, had three armchairs and a small coffee table. Jim cleared his throat.

"Did Nora tell you, Mrs. Samuels, that this is the room she redesigned for Mom and Dad?"

Mrs. Samuels perked up and gave her daughter a look. "No, she didn't. It's beautiful. I can't imagine any room in this house not being beautiful."

Dr. Preston returned with their drinks. "Looks like dinner will be ready in about five minutes. Jim, go tell your brothers. They're downstairs playing pool."

"Can I come too?" Eve stood and followed Jim.

James sat across from Vivian. "I understand you're from Simpson. You know, I grew up not far outside Simpson. I moved here when I went to medical school at Oakdale University, and I guess the Lord saw fit for me to stay in the area."

"My late husband and I thought about moving over here early in our marriage, but like you said, sometimes the Lord has other plans. In the early days, we'd come to Oakdale to see a show or celebrate our anniversary. Something special." She took a sip of her sweet tea.

This time, Nora took a deep, relaxing breath. The conversation seemed to flow easily. Her mother patted Nora on the leg. "Honey, shouldn't we offer to help?"

James chuckled. "I wouldn't go in there. On a holiday, the kitchen is Maribel's world. She loves cooking for the holidays."

Eve, Jim, and his brothers came in talking about pool. Jim put his hand on John's shoulder. "Mrs. Samuels, this is my brother John, and my other brother Paul."

"Good to meet you both." Mrs. Samuels put a finger on her chin. "Let me see if I remember from Nora quizzing me earlier. John, you are the youngest and an attorney."

John smiled and nodded. "Guilty."

"And Paul, you are the middle child and followed in your father's footsteps to become a physician."

Paul tipped his head. "Yes, ma'am. Good to meet you."

Mrs. Preston called from the dining room. "Dinner."

Paul walked over to where Mrs. Samuels was seated and offered his arm to escort her into dinner.

"Well, aren't you polite. Thank you." A warm glow grew on Mrs. Samuels's face.

Mrs. Preston directed everyone to their seats. "Vivian, please sit next to me."

From the other end of the table, James looked at his wife. "Honey, you've outdone yourself. Everything looks delicious." He looked around the table. "How wonderful to have you all with us." He took Nora's hand on one side of him, and Eve's on the other. "Grab a hand and I'll offer the blessing." Everyone joined hands, and James offered a blessing for the food and thankfulness for Nora and her family joining them.

As the food was being passed, Jim leaned over to Nora. "Look at our mothers talking. I think they'll be fast friends."

"I'm glad. She was a little nervous, but I knew your mother would make her feel as comfortable as she made me feel the first time we met."

John passed the turkey to Paul. "You know, now would be a good time to tell some stories on our big brother Jim."

Eve turned to John. "Yes, do tell."

Jim raised an eyebrow and grinned. "Careful brother, two can play that game."

"You got me on that one. So, I guess we won't talk about sneaking out or skinny dipping in the principal's pool?"

Jim threw his head back with laughter. "I guess we won't. And we won't mention Paul's shenanigans at prom with the goldfish in the punch bowl."

Paul lifted his hands in surrender. "How'd I get dragged into this? I'm eating and minding my own business."

Nora enjoyed the brotherly banter. Sisters didn't do that. After years of drama with the brothers and Jim's rift with his father, there was unity. So much so that they felt secure enough to tease each other.

After consuming the feast and homemade pies, both cherry and pumpkin, as tradition held, the men cleared the table and rinsed the plates for the dishwasher. Mrs. Preston had long given up using her mother's china, which had to be hand-washed. Five years ago, James and the boys had gone together to buy her a new set of china that was dishwasher safe.

Maribel stood from the table. "Jim, before you join the boys in clearing, may I talk to you?"

"Sure, Mom."

Maribel looked at Nora, her mother, and Eve. "Watch the boys—they will try and charm you into helping. Don't fall for it." She smiled and winked.

Nora looked at Jim and then to her mother and Eve. James came out of the kitchen with a pitcher of sweet tea and a pot of coffee. "I've got this, Maribel. Ladies, may I serve you coffee or tea?"

Jim's mother led him upstairs to the primary bedroom. She turned on the lamp that was on his father's bedside table. The bedroom furniture was made of dark-stained oak. He was maybe ten and they were living in a three-bedroom house in downtown Oakdale when they bought their bedroom furniture. His dad's practice was getting established, and his mother volunteered at the elementary school, returning home every afternoon when the boys got home from school. It was a small house for a family of five, so the three boys were sent outside to play as often as the weather permitted. It struck Jim as odd they hadn't replaced the bedroom suite when they moved to a larger home.

Jim sat on the bench seat at the end of the bed while his mother disappeared into the walk-in closet. She came out with a small black velvet box.

"Jim, your dad and I made the mistake once of interfering in your choice of who to marry. We're not doing that again. But I see something between you and Nora that I never saw with Mandy. If you feel it as deeply as I can see it, you truly love her, don't you, Son?"

Jim rubbed his hands together. This was getting real. "I do. She is everything to me. And Eve is great." Dinner in his stomach rolled over. The truth was out. He was forever in love with Nora.

"Like I said, I don't want to rush you into anything you don't feel is right. But please take your grandmother's ring. You can have the stones reset or give it to her as is."

His mother opened the box to reveal a deep red ruby solitaire surrounded by small diamonds. The thought of that ring on Nora's hand flashed before Jim. His stomach settled and his heart lifted. "Thank you, Mom. I'd like to have the ring." He stood. "Please don't say anything to anyone. I'm still praying about this, and when I propose, I want it to be a surprise." Jim tugged the ring from the box and slid it onto the top of his finger, where he twirled it to admire its beauty from different angles.

"I respect that. Nora's a special one. Your dad and I love her and Eve." She opened the door. "Vivian and I had a delightful conversation at dinner. I really like her."

Jim twirled the ring around his finger. "I did talk to Eve a little. It's important that she be comfortable with Nora and me making a commitment. I didn't mention marriage. She seemed to be good with Nora and me growing closer."

"Sounds as though you are being very wise and understanding what's important to Nora." His mother reached up with both hands to pull him toward her so she could kiss him on the forehead. "I love you."

Just like when I was little and Mom had to have a serious talk with me. It always ended with a kiss on the forehead. "Thanks, Mom. I'll be down in a minute."

When his mom left the bedroom, Jim continued to look at the glistening stones and thought about how he would ask the big question.

Before joining everyone in the living room, Jim slipped the small box into his jacket pocket. A wave of excitement rushed over him. He turned the corner to the living room to find Nora in complete animation, trying to get her team— that included Jim's brothers—to guess what she'd drawn in Pictionary. Eve was on a team with Dr. and Mrs. Preston, and her grandmother. She was giggling at Jim's brothers' goofy guesses.

James waved Jim over. "Please come help your brothers. They need your creative mind."

Jim loved seeing Nora, his graceful, always-put-together girlfriend, being silly. Even in that moment, she was the most beautiful woman he'd known. "I'm in."

CHAPTER FORTY

Nora was wrapping up holiday design plans for two clients, one of whom was Mrs. Preston. With their approval of the design, the crew was scheduled to begin this week. As she slid her laptop into her leather messenger bag, her phone buzzed. Curt. The text was to both her and Phillip.

CURT: Can I meet with you two?

Nora's heart raced. Life was much easier without him. Now he wanted to talk. Forgiveness niggled through her mind. She looked at her phone, hoping Phillip would answer first. Instead, her phone rang.

"What do you think he wants?" Phillip didn't wait for Nora's hello.

"No idea." Nora took a deep breath and sat at her desk. "But we should meet with him. He's around Eve at the theater. If we upset him, he's liable to say something to her. Right now, we've agreed that he'll stay away from her."

"Yes. Ever since you told me he was working and seemingly trying to get his life together, I've had this nagging feeling that I need to forgive him. It's not an easy thought."

Nora's lips tightened. "I agree. For what it's worth, I've had the same nudging. Maybe he's looking for redemption."

"You're right. Let's meet with him."

Curt pulled into the sandwich shop parking lot ten minutes before meeting Phillip and Nora. He had told his support group leader last night how nerve-wracking the conversation would be. Apologizing for the horrific hurt he'd caused. It was the right thing to do, but it didn't make the craving for a shot and a beer go away.

He checked his hair in the mirror. He'd grown to like having short hair and a clean-shaven face. After he exited the only truck he could afford, complete with more Bondo dent filler than black paint, he looked down at his shirt and wiped over the one resistant wrinkle. He'd lost about thirty pounds since he'd started the construction job.

Curt chose a table in the back corner and sat in the chair facing the door. When Nora and Phillip came in, he gave a nervous wave. The two people who sat across from him represented his biggest failures. He felt sweat begin to bead on his forehead. *Deep breath, Curt. You need to do this. You want to move forward.*

"What's this about, Curt?" Phillip's look pierced Curt's nervousness.

Curt fiddled with his fork. "Well, uh ..."

The waitress arrived and took their drink order. Curt shifted in his chair.

"You see, it's like this." He looked at Nora. Her eyes offered more compassion than he expected. "Nora, you may have told Phillip about our conversation a couple of months ago."

"I did."

"So, I … uh … okay, here's my story. Hard as it is, I want you to know what's happened, and yes, I want to talk about Eve."

"Not so fast about Eve." Phillip leaned forward.

Nora touched Phillip's arm. "Go ahead, Curt. What's on your mind?"

"I was messed up at Liz's funeral. I apologize for showing up drunk and for any hurt I caused. And Nora, I'm sorry for the night a couple of months ago I showed up at your house. I am sorry. If you both would let me tell you the full story. It's not an excuse, it's simply the result of a lot of bad behavior and choices. I was involved with some very rough people who had me backed into a corner. They had me running drugs to Florida. The last trip I made, I got pulled over on my way through Oakdale." Curt looked around the restaurant as the waitress brought their drinks.

"Are you ready to order?"

Phillip answered. "Could you give us a few minutes?"

Curt looked at Phillip. "Thank you. So, I was on my way back from what I'd hoped was my last run. I'd been drinking, and after I failed the field sobriety test, they arrested me. I sat in jail with no one to call. No one in my corner, and the district attorney offered me a plea deal. Names for parole and community service." He shook his head. "That was a long night trying to decide. The people I was about to turn on would just as soon see me dead. A preacher came to visit me. He made me think about a lot of things, like the choices I'd made leading up to that point. We talked for a while, and he prayed for God's protection over me. When he was gone, I had this weird feeling of peace. Never felt that before.

"I decided to give them the names. I was given parole with stipulations that I stay involved in a recovery group and stay clean. The pastor introduced me to Greg, who runs the halfway house I live in. One of the many rules is going to church on Sunday. Pastor Sparks has mentored and supported me through the program. One of the support groups meets at George Mason's church. That's where I met him." Curt looked at Nora. "He gave me a job, a decent wage, and warned me he had a zero tolerance policy. One strike and I was out. But he also encouraged and supported me in continuing my journey to straighten up my life." Curt nodded and took a long drink of his sweet tea.

When Nora reached across the table to squeeze Curt's arm, Curt sat up straighter. Telling his story felt like picking up a burden again.

"Curt, that couldn't have been easy at all. I'm thankful George and Pastor Paul have come alongside you," Nora told him.

"Thank you, Nora." He wrapped his hands around the clear, half-empty cup. "I'm trying. I've also gotten involved in a men's Bible study with some other guys on the crew. It started out as a way to keep ourselves out of the bar, but then we started digging deeper." He looked down and then squarely at Nora and Phillip. "I gave my life to Christ. I don't want to run anymore. I am so sorry ..." Curt's eyes reddened and voice cracked. "Phillip, Nora, I am so sorry for everything. I hurt Liz, Eve, and your family. Can you ever forgive me?"

Curt hadn't asked for money, he didn't mention Eve or try to cheat them out of anything. He wanted their forgiveness. Nora looked at Phillip. This was the moment God had been nudging her toward for weeks. The waitress approached the table and refilled their teas.

"I know I don't deserve it. I don't even deserve the grace God, Pastor Paul, and George have shown me. If you can find it in yourselves …" Curt sat back in his chair.

Phillip touched Nora's arm and looked at the broken man. "Curt, you certainly have cleaned up your look. Only God knows your heart." He looked away and drew in a deep breath. "Yes, you hurt my family. It's tough to let go of anger and resentment, but if held onto, it will eat a man's soul. I've wrestled with this moment. I do forgive you. But understand that it's going to take a long time for me to trust you."

The knot in Nora's stomach subsided as she began to speak. "Curt, this is a hard request, one that God has nudged me on as well." She smiled. "Sounds like God has been busy working on all three of us. I forgive you."

Curt bowed his head. "Thank you both." He looked up with a thankful grin. "Thank you. Also, the job at the theater is finishing up, so you don't have to worry about me running into Eve."

Phillip shot Curt a look. "Where will you be working?"

"George has another project downtown starting next week. He's sending several of us there. I want to see Eve, but I need to take care of a few more things. I'm still living in a halfway house on the west end. In the next month, I should be able to move someplace better."

"Here in Oakdale?" Thoughts of Curt in the same town as Eve rolled around Nora's thoughts.

"Yes, because I would like for us to figure out the best way for me to connect with Eve. She is better off living with you, Nora. But I'd like the opportunity to build a relationship with her."

Phillip looked at Curt. "When the time is right, we'll work something out."

Curt smiled. "Thank you both for your time." He checked his phone. "I need to be somewhere." He pulled out his wallet and pulled out fifteen dollars. "It's on me. Leave what's over the ticket for the waitress." He stood and tucked his wallet into his back pocket. "Thank you again for hearing me out ... and for your forgiveness. There is one other thing." Curt reached in the side pocket of his corduroy jacket and pulled out a gold necklace with a locket that hung from it. "By some miracle, I still have this locket I bought for Liz after one of the times I left." He held the necklace up and the heart locket dangled. "I was going to give it to her when I went back. But ... well ...." He fingered the heart-shaped charm. "I'd like to give it to Eve."

Nora reached for the necklace. "Curt, this is beautiful." She opened the locket to see a small picture of her sister from fifteen years before.

"I had both our photos in it, but I took my picture out. This is about remembering Liz."

Nora handed it back to Curt. "I think Eve would like it. We'll talk about when you can give it to her."

"Thank you, Nora." Curt smiled.

Phillip and Nora stood. Phillip put his hand out to shake Curt's hand. The tension had surrendered to the renewal that forgiveness brought. Nora squeezed Curt's arm as he passed her to leave.

CHAPTER FORTY-ONE

The aroma of cookies wafted through Nora's kitchen. Christmas music floated throughout the house. As the first batch of her grandmother's cranberry orange cookies came out of the oven, Eve and Jim came in from the garage with boxes overflowing with garlands and ornaments. With the boxes deposited in the den next to the tree, it was time for cookie sampling. Jim reached around Nora to snatch one off the baking sheet.

Nora swatted him away with a chuckle. "Not yet, they need to cool."

"They smell great." Eve peeked over Nora's other shoulder.

"You two can wait."

"I'll go start putting the lights on the tree." Jim tried again, unsuccessfully, to snag a cookie.

Nora laughed. While she slid the cookies onto the cooling rack, Eve pulled the hot chocolate mix out of the cabinet.

"Aunt Nora, I think Olivia, Ashley, and I are going to the dance as a group."

Nora nodded. *Is this going to be a disappointment?* "No word from Ben?"

"We talk all the time, but he hasn't asked me. It's kinda strange—he seems to need a friend more than a girlfriend right now. You know?"

"I'd rather you be friends and not rush into dating and all the pressure that comes with it." Nora gave Eve a light poke on her nose. "You said he seems like a mature person. Maybe he doesn't think he's ready to date."

Eve reached in the batter bowl and swiped a small bite of the sweet batter. "Maybe. But what I wanted to ask is if you would let Ashley drive me to the dance." Eve waved her hands. "I promise we will go straight there and straight home. I thought maybe she and Olivia could spend the night here afterwards."

Nora had a feeling that plans for the dance would lead to wanting to ride with her friends. Since that one misstep early in the school year, Eve, Olivia, and Ashley had kept themselves out of trouble. "Well, I think we can make that work."

Eve squealed and danced around the kitchen. "Thank you, thank you, thank you!"

Jim turned the corner into the kitchen. "My goodness, what is all this about?"

Eve grabbed Jim's arm. "Aunt Nora is letting me ride with Ashley and Olivia to the dance."

Jim chuckled. "That's great. Guess that means the boneheaded football player will miss out on escorting the prettiest girl in the school."

Eve stilled and her jaw dropped. "How did you know about Ben?" She looked at Nora, who put her hands up and shook her head.

"Wasn't me."

Jim pulled on a sly grin. "I know things."

Eve stood with her hands on her hips. "How did you know about Ben?"

"Let's just say, voices carry at the theater. You and Sara were stuffing the invitations to the opening and having a lovely chat about a certain quarterback. I've seen his name in the sports section of the newspaper. Good athlete. Sounds like a stand-up guy."

Eve shook her head. "He is. We're friends, and I heard he wasn't taking anyone to the dance. Which of course infuriated the head cheerleader."

"Sounds like it's worth going to me." Nora put three cookies on a plate and offered them to Jim and Eve. "Now, let's decorate the tree. Tomorrow, we shop for a new dress."

Jim arrived at the theater early. The construction was complete. It was moving day. With the office reconfiguration and the lobby remodel, the desks from the trailer and storage needed to be moved in and offices set up again. Jim took advantage of the quiet to walk through every space, including the new auditorium and stage. As he stood on the balcony, he drew a breath, closed his eyes, and whispered a prayer of gratitude. Insurance had paid for the rebuild, and grant funding had come through to cover upgrades in lighting and a revision of the costume room, allowing for better organization and working space. They had salvaged the original hardware on the doors and the windows that had been destroyed. He leaned over the brass railing to see the new seating and how well Nora had matched the original upholstery. Nora. Amid her own challenges, she had been his champion throughout the highs and lows of stretching the funding as far as possible.

The door to the auditorium opened below where Jim was standing. "Who's there?"

Nora appeared from under the balcony. "It's me. I dropped Eve at school early and thought I'd bring you coffee."

"You know me too well." Jim looked down at the woman he'd fallen deeply in love with.

Nora looked up at him. "Shouldn't this be the other way around?"

Jim cocked his head. "What do you mean?"

Nora giggled. "Wasn't Juliet on the balcony, and Romeo on the ground?"

Jim let out a deep laugh. "You're right. I'll be right down."

Nora met Jim at the bottom of the steps and handed him his coffee.

"Thank you." He gave her a welcoming kiss. "I was walking around looking at the rebuilt and remodeled version of this old theater."

They walked down the aisle. Nora linked her hand in his. "The ole girl survived, didn't she? And you've made her better than before."

Jim stopped to face Nora. "We couldn't have done all this without you."

"What'd I do? A few discounts here and there on fabric and free design consulting."

"Nora, you did so much more. You saved us thousands of dollars on the stage curtains and upholstery." He ran his finger along her jawline. "You were the calm in the storm so many times. Our time away from here, having fun or a quiet dinner, restored me, so I could get back into the thick of contractors, staff, and keeping things going here." He leaned in to let their foreheads touch and whispered, "Thank you so much. I love you."

Jim's words draped Nora with warmth. "I love you too. I didn't realize I was doing so much for you. I thought I was being selfish, because all those times with you were fun and sweet and renewing to my soul."

The two stood in silence. It didn't bother Nora to be still and silent with Jim. Being with him was enough sometimes.

A loud beeping squelched the quiet.

"What's that?" Nora jerked her look at the doors.

"It's the moving truck backing into the delivery docks. That will be our furniture we had cleaned and restored." Jim hustled up the aisle with Nora on his heels. He stopped before leaving the auditorium and turned back to Nora. "Before things get crazy with movers, thank you for stopping by. You've made this a great start to the day."

"You're welcome. Is there anything you need me to do for the opening on Friday?"

"No, Maggie and Sara have those details under control."

Nora reached out to put her arms around Jim. In the dim, quiet auditorium, he gave her a full kiss that spoke volumes of the extent of his love.

"That was quite a kiss. I hope the move goes well. Have fun setting up your theater again." Nora gave Jim a nudge.

As she drove to work, Nora's lips were still warm from Jim's kiss. Six years ago, she couldn't imagine such love. She didn't want to. But the Lord knew her heart, and her capacity to love again. His perfect timing had brought Jim to her when she was ready. When Jim was ready too.

Friday morning, Nora and Eve had hair and nail appointments. Eve was excited about the dance that night, and Nora had the theater reopening. Both were formal events. Eve chatted away about her friends and what they were wearing. Olivia and Ashley were coming to the house to get ready, and their parents were coming to take photos. It hadn't seemed to bother Eve that Ben hadn't asked her to the dance. She and her friends were excited about a fun night. Eve was sitting with her fingers under the nail dryer, and Nora was paying for their services when her phone vibrated.

"Hello."

"Nora, it's Curt. I heard tonight there's a dance at the high school. Is Eve going?"

Nora stepped into the lobby to talk. "Yes ... why?" Her words were deliberate.

"Well ... uh ... I was hoping to give Eve this locket so she could wear it ... if she wants ... I'm not pressuring."

Nora heard his carefulness. The same humbleness she saw at the coffee shop. "Curt, I don't know. This is her first dance at Oakdale. She has her friends coming over."

"I'll come before they get there and be gone. Please. I've been told this is a big deal to the kids."

Phillip, Judy, and her mom were coming for the theater event. They'd be there if things went south with Curt. *No, I can't think that way. We're trying to give him the opportunity to show us he's changed.* "Curt, let me talk to Eve about it and call you back. If she says no, then I need you to respect that."

"I will. Thanks, Nora. I'll wait for your call."

"Ask me what?" Eve was standing in the doorway.

Nora turned around. "Can we talk about it in the car?"

Eve hurried to get in the car. She buckled in and twisted toward the driver's seat as Aunt Nora got in. "Aunt Nora, you've got a funny look on your face. Is everything okay?"

Aunt Nora put her keys in the ignition but didn't start the car. "Yes, that was Curt on the phone. He'd like to bring a gift by the house today."

Confusion coiled in Eve's mind. "A gift. Today. The day of the dance. Really? Why today?" The last several weeks of school and preparing for the dance had been fun. Eve didn't want to deal with Curt or the drama he might stir up. "Does he have to?"

"No. It's up to you. If you say yes, I will insist he come long before your friends will be there. I don't want you to feel you have to explain him to Olivia and Ashley."

Eve rested her head into her hands. *My friends. No way do I want to explain this to them.* "Definitely. I don't want to deal with that."

Aunt Nora didn't push. She was silent. It was Eve's choice. Thankfulness poked at Eve's heart. Aunt Nora wanted to protect her while giving Eve some control over whether she saw Curt. *Curt. I can't call him Dad. I don't feel in any way that he's my dad.* A gift. *What could he want to give me today?*

"Does he know about the dance?"

"Yes. That's why he wants to give you the gift today."

Eve scrunched her nose. "What is it?"

"I'm not telling you. But it's thoughtful and a little sentimental."

"Sentimental? Curt?"

"Believe it or not, I was a little surprised too. But we're called to extend grace where we can." Aunt Nora put her purse in the back seat and turned to start the car.

"Wait. Yes, I think I'll see him today. You'll be there, right?"

"Absolutely. Mom, Phillip, and Judy will be there too. They're coming in for the theater opening."

"That's right." Eve let the idea of grace float around her mind for a minute. "Let me think about it on the way home."

They rode home in silence. Nora prayed in her heart for wisdom. She didn't want Curt to mess with Eve's excitement about the dance. For the last several weeks, Eve's spirits had been lighter. There had been more laughter. However, it was Eve's choice.

Eve carried her dress upstairs to hang it and returned. "Aunt Nora, okay, I'll see him today. But it has to be way before my friends get here."

"Okay. Are you sure? I don't want this to put a damper on your fun tonight."

Eve stood up straight. "Yes, I'm sure. Partly because if I don't, I'll think about it all night. I'd rather see what he wants, deal with it, and then go to the dance."

"I'll call him back." Nora texted Phillip to let him know what was going on and see how early he could be there. With his reply, Nora called Curt.

Curt pulled up in front of Nora's home. There were two cars in the driveway. No doubt Phillip would be here too. He checked his teeth in the rearview mirror and swiped his hand across the side of his fresh haircut. He had purchased a new shirt and jeans to ensure he looked as clean as he'd been living for the last five months. He reached for the small gift bag on the passenger floorboard. The truck door gave a tired creak when he opened it. It reminded him of something else on his list he was working to improve. He rubbed his hands together, stood straight, walked to the front door, and rang the bell. No turning back now.

Nora answered the doorbell and opened the storm door. "Curt, come in. Eve's upstairs. Let me get her."

"Thank you." Curt stepped in the door and stood in the small entry.

"Eve, your da ... Curt's here." Nora gave Curt a half smile from the top of the stairs. "Come on into the den. Mom, Judy, and Phillip are here. We're going to the theater reopening tonight. You all did a great job rebuilding it."

It didn't go unnoticed that Nora was trying to be kind. "Thank you. It was a good project. George is a great guy to work for."

As they joined Phillip, Judy, and Mom in the den, Phillip stood and shook Curt's hand. "How's it going?"

Curt nodded. "Pretty good."

He shook Mom's hand carefully. "Ma'am."

Eve joined them in the den. "Hi."

Curt turned to see Eve. Her hair was pulled up in a loose knot like Liz wore her hair on their wedding day. His breath caught as did his words. "Evey." He rubbed his forehead. "You look just like your mom."

Curt noticed Eve's uncomfortable look at Nora. "I'm sorry. I didn't mean to make you feel weird."

"It's all right." Eve looked at her aunts, uncle, and grandmother and nodded.

Nora stood. "Mom, Phillip, Judy, let's give them a minute."

Curt gave Nora a thankful nod. The small gift bag in his hand carried not only the weight of the small necklace, but that of the overdue apology he was about to deliver. Curt stood facing his daughter. Practically a young adult. The site of her was both beautiful and sad as her fifteen years represented his fifteen wasted years. Fifteen lost years. But now he was found, and he wanted, no, hoped for, a fresh start with her. He gestured toward the sofa. "Do you have a minute to sit? I won't keep you long. I hear there's a big dance tonight."

"Yeah." Eve sat and Curt took the chair across from her.

"Eve, you probably know some of the stories about the mess I made with your mom." Curt looked across the room to gather his thoughts. "You may or may not understand it all."

"It's fine, Curt. You don't have to explain." Eve crossed her arms.

"Hang on. Please listen for a minute. I need ... no, I owe you an apology. I walked out on you and your mom when I should have manned up to love and support my family. I was weak and arrogant. Somehow, I thought the world owed me more than I deserved. In the end, the world won, and I lost everything."

Eve uncrossed her arms and leaned forward to listen.

What was this man, her father, saying? Was he confessing to all the hurt he had caused her mom? Eve had struggled all morning to balance her excitement about the dance with her dancing nerves about seeing Curt. Curt ... she had tried but couldn't call him "Dad." The feelings weren't there. Their only connection was in DNA and that he was once married to her mother.

He looked so different from the last time she saw him. She could see his face, which had been masked by a scraggly beard. His eyes were much clearer. Had he changed?

Curt looked down at the small gift bag. What could be in the bag that would mean anything to Eve?

"Eve, I've moved dozens of times and even been homeless a time or two since I left your mom. I sold just about everything I owned when I needed money. But somehow, by God's grace, I'm sure, this is the one item I never lost. And I want you to have it." Curt handed Eve the small gift bag with crumpled tissue in the top.

By God's grace. He's talking about God. Eve accepted the gift. She slowly took the tissue out, pulled a small jewelry box out, and looked at Curt.

"Go ahead and open the box. I bought it when I was trying to win your mom back with gifts and desperate promises."

Eve opened the box to find a gold heart necklace. "Oh, Curt. It's beautiful."

"It's a locket. Open the heart."

Eve opened the heart to find a picture of her mom. "Mom." Eve covered her mouth to try and stifle the tears.

Curt moved to sit next to Eve on the sofa. "I owe you so much more. More than I can ever make up for. You were a gift God gave your mother and me." He rubbed the back of his neck. "A gift I tossed carelessly aside. I am so sorry."

Eve couldn't take her eyes off the photo of her mom from almost twenty years ago. Her bright smile and sparkling eyes. "Curt, thank you. This is beautiful." She put it around her neck and fastened the chain. Without thinking, she reached forward and hugged Curt ... her dad. She pulled away and brushed her hand across the locket she was sure would never leave her neck. The picture of her mother lay on her heart. "Thank you."

"Eve, I'm working hard to build a better life here in Oakdale. And I hope one day we can, at least, have some kind of relationship, maybe spend some time together. But I've got a few things I still need to clean up first."

Eve's brow furrowed. "What kinds of things?"

"Well ..."

Nora, Judy, Phillip and her grandmother rejoined them. Curt stood up. Eve looked up at him. *Wait, he can't leave without finishing the explanation.* Eve stood as well. "Wait. Finish what you were telling me."

Curt looked at Eve. "Well, I still have a debt I'm repaying."

Curt felt five pairs of eyes staring at him intently. He'd done what he came to do. *Give Eve the necklace and apologize.* "Conditions of my parole are to participate in a recovery program, hold a job for at least one year without any gaps, and perform a hundred hours of community service. I'm halfway through." He looked at the five of them. "I'd like to be completely free of my parole and have a year of sobriety before ..."

"Before you and I spend time together ..." Eve finished his sentence.

"Yes. Look, I know you're just getting settled here. I don't want to mess that up. If something comes up and you want to talk to me, your aunt has my number. I hope you understand."

The tension, or perhaps it was an awkward pause, lingered. Nora stepped toward Eve. "What did he bring you?"

Eve turned to show them the locket. Nora's mother touched the photo of her daughter with her aged hand, a hand that had aged a little faster with the loss of Liz. "Sweetheart, that is beautiful." She looked at Curt. "What a generous gift."

"It belongs with Eve. Liz did well raising her in spite of the hardship I left her with."

Mom went to Curt and took his hand. "But you are making amends and humbling yourself now. I'm thankful for that."

"Thank you, ma'am. I appreciate the forgiveness from all of you." Curt looked away and took a deep breath. "Well, I understand you have a dance to get ready for. Have fun."

Eve walked Curt to the door. From the corner of her eye, Nora noticed that Eve gave him a hug as he left. Nora looked and her mom and brother. "That went better than I expected."

Phillip sat in the armchair. "It did. I continue to be shocked at what seems to be a transformed Curt."

"God's transforming grace is what that man is living." Mom shook her head. "Amazing." She looked at her two adult children. "I'm proud of how you've handled him."

Eve returned and plopped down on the sofa, careful not to mess up her hair. "Whew. That wasn't as bad as I thought it'd be." She fingered the heart charm. "I love my necklace. And ... I'm glad he's doing better."

Nora watched her niece, concerned that seeing Curt would stir harder emotions. "You're okay? He didn't upset you?"

"Surprisingly, no, he didn't upset me. Maybe it was seeing him in a different way, cleaned up and trying to live a better life. Maybe my emotions aren't as raw as they were last summer. I don't know." She shifted on the sofa. "I know he's my dad, but I don't feel like he's my dad. It's kinda weird. But seeing him didn't bother me."

"Good. I was worried seeing him would squish your excitement about tonight."

Eve popped up. "Tonight. What time is it? I have to get my dress on, the girls are going to be here soon for pictures."

CHAPTER FORTY-TWO

Phillip drove Judy, Nora, and their mother to the theater grand opening. Nora had chosen a long black dress with a Grecian neckline. Her locks of brown hair were swept up into a twist with an airy fringe at her face. The diamond stud earrings she wore, Seth had given her on their tenth wedding anniversary. But it wasn't Seth she was thinking about tonight. It was Jim. This was his night to celebrate the theater he loved. Nora and her family exited Phillip's car. Judy wore a flowing red gown with chiffon sleeves. Their mother was in an emerald-green gown and wrap that sparkled with tiny, scattered crystals.

The theater was lit with spotlights and a red carpet along the ramp leading to the entrance.

"I feel so fancy." Her mother said as they walked up the red carpet.

"Mom, you look beautiful." Phillip offered her his arm, with Judy on the other. "Nora, you're on your own."

"No, she's not." Jim stepped from the landing at the top of the ramp. He reached for Nora's hand. "You look stunning."

A blush warmed Nora's face in the December chill. She felt the tender touch of his hand and admired him in his tuxedo. "Thank you." With her hand on her hip, she gave Jim a look. "You look quite handsome dressed up. I like this look on you."

With a small, welcoming kiss, Jim held the door open for them. The lobby was lit with the soft glow of candles and the warmth of the scent from the live Christmas tree. Caterers were mingling amongst the guests with hors d'oeuvres. The theater reconstruction expanded the lobby to accommodate receptions and other art events. Tucked in the corner was a string quartet playing Christmas music. Nora looked around in amazement. "Jim, this turned out absolutely lovely."

Still holding her hand, he leaned closer. "I had an outstanding designer."

Nora laughed. "You should greet your guests. Looks like your family and Dr. Crosby from the university have arrived."

Jim didn't want to let go of Nora, but it wouldn't be for long. He crossed the lobby to greet his family and other guests. Dr. Crosby introduced Jim to several university foundation leaders. "Jim, I'm scheduling time for us to get together in early January. Making the internship pivot to give students crisis management experience worked well. We're looking at expanding the program."

"That's great. I look forward to talking with you." Jim thanked them for coming and excused himself.

As he turned to scan the crowd for Nora, his father grabbed his shoulder. "Jim, you've done an outstanding job. You kept the integrity of the original building while updating the entire layout. I'm proud of you."

Proud of me. More so than love, a son wanted his father to be proud of what he'd accomplished, of his contribution to the world. "Thank you. I appreciate everything you've done." Jim was handed two drinks. "It's going to be a big night. If you'll excuse me, I need to find Nora."

"Of course." His father smiled and winked.

Jim found Nora with Maggie, Dan, Jen, and Mark. Dan reached out to shake Jim's hand. "Big night. Congratulations."

"Thanks. We're looking forward to starting on the spring production."

Mark shook Jim's hand. "Let us know if you have any problems with the production software we installed."

"I'm sure it will be fine. But thanks to you both for everything you contributed."

Maggie, Jen, and Nora chatted about Eve's send-off to the dance. Nora gave an animated replay of the girls' arrival and pictures. "They were adorable. Trying to be fancy and sophisticated in one picture and then silly in the next. We had a surprise visitor, though."

"I thought you knew Curt was coming by." Maggie put in.

"Not Curt. The girls were inside getting their things and touching up makeup before leaving when Ben Milton arrived in his uncle's Escalade."

"What?" Jen perked up. "He's a great guy. I met him at the gym last summer. Completely dedicated to his off-season workout, and the politest of all our high-school athletes."

Nora nodded. "That's the feeling I got. When I answered the door, he introduced himself and asked if Eve had left for the dance yet. You should have seen Eve's surprise when she, Ashley, and Olivia came downstairs. He brought her a single pink sweetheart rose."

Maggie and Jen leaned in closer. "What happened?"

"He asked me if he could drive the girls to the dance. I said it was fine. He gave Eve the rose and explained he hadn't asked her earlier because he wasn't sure he'd be able to go. Ben had a part-time job to pay for his insurance and wasn't sure he could afford to rent a tux until earlier this week." Nora put her hand on her heart. "He was so sweet and humble. I texted the other mothers to be sure it was okay with them for the girls to ride with Ben. And we let them all go."

Jim touched Nora's elbow. "Sorry, ladies, I need to steal this lovely lady from you. I'd like to show you something new in the auditorium."

"Sure." Nora easily left her friends to go with Jim. Easy. Their relationship had become an easy connection.

Jim stopped to meet and greet a few of the guests as they made their way through the crowd. He let go of her hand long enough to shake hands and have a brief exchange. They slipped into the auditorium.

"Jim, shouldn't you be mingling with your guests?"

"We'll get back to that. I want to talk to you for a minute." He lightly touched the small of her back as they gradually made their way down the aisle. Jim led the way as they walked up the three steps onto the stage.

The stage was lit enough for them to see the first few rows of seating. Nora and Jim stood shoulder to shoulder, taking in the refreshed soul of the theater. Jim linked his pinky finger with Nora's.

"This theater has meant everything to me. It represents my starting over after feeling lost for a long time. I'm grateful we were able to rebuild." He turned to face Nora.

She turned to face him and reached for his other hand. "You've put your heart into this sweet place."

Jim shook his head. "I have, but it's no longer the most important thing to me."

"What? You love this theater."

"Nora, you've seen me at my worst. And you have forgiven me more times than I deserve. I love this theater. But I love you more. Besides my faith, building a life with you is more important than anything." In a single move, Jim pulled a small box from his tuxedo pocket and got down on one knee. "Nora, will you marry me?"

Nora's breath caught and her heart began to race as Jim went down on one knee. *Is this happening? What did he say?* She saw the man to whom she had opened her heart. The words he spoke swept through her. The ring was a beautiful ruby and diamond ring. *He asked me to marry him.* Without a single doubt she wanted to say yes, but what about Eve?

"I know you're worried about Eve. She's great. I should've seen that from the start. Nora, I'm ready to love and support you for as long as we live. That includes Eve as part of our family. And I may have had a little conversation with her earlier today. I think she's on board with my request." Jim smiled and winked.

He knows my heart and spoke with Eve to be sure she would be okay with a proposal. "Yes. I will marry you."

Jim stood and slipped the ring on her finger. Nora admired the perfect fit of the beautiful ring. She looked up into Jim's eyes. "I love you."

Jim pulled her into a deep kiss. His question and her answer launched Nora's thoughts forward to a renewed life.

ABOUT THE AUTHOR

Karen Richardson has one goal—to make an impact, wherever she is, whatever she's doing. It's people first, progress second. She has deep faith and believes in the importance of working hard. Her writing, while fiction, encourages and empowers the reader to overcome the challenges they encounter. Rediscovery, refreshing, and renewal are the themes of her novels.

Her debut novel, *Curtains for Maggie*, was published in 2023, and was ranked #1 on Kindle within its genre. She has published several articles and hosts a blog, "KK's Candor." As a person who loves to learn, Karen recently completed the coursework to become a master gardener. In addition to gardening, she enjoys pickleball and reading. Karen and her husband, Jay, live in Louisville, Kentucky.

Follow Karen on Facebook, Instagram and X @KHRAuthor

OAKDALE NOVELS BOOKS

Curtains for Maggie
Designs for Nora

Available on Amazon.com
Kindle or Paperback

www.ingramcontent.com/pod-product-compliance
Lightning Source LLC
Chambersburg PA
CBHW071203020726
47502CB00002B/522